TURNABOUT

TURNABOUT

LAUREL GREER

HeartEyes Press

For everyone who really loves tracing their fingertip along a luscious piece of paper.

1

CARTER

Few things are as satisfying as cracking open a box of freshly printed cardstock.

The rip of the seal. The tang of new paper. The thirty-two-point thickness, smooth under my fingertips. Each black letter proving I've earned the corner office I've yet to properly settle into.

Sure, my dad will sneer at the business cards being printed digitally instead of inked by hand with one of his antique letter-presses.

I'm willing to overlook this "flaw."

The lack of bespoke debossing doesn't change the fact CARTER PRESCOTT is emblazoned right above the VP title I've worked my ass off to achieve.

I tap one of the red-seamed edges of the card on my desk and shake my head. I can't hand them out. The double thickness isn't standard OfficeMart corporate branding. These are just for me.

Dickhead posturing through stationery? Certainly, but I've waited years for this. Sue me if I got a little carried away.

And forgive me for wanting to mail one to my dad. With a handwritten note like he prefers.

THANKS FOR THE MOTIVATION. I COULDN'T HAVE DONE IT
WITHOUT YOU TELLING ME I SHOULDN'T DO IT.

The rending of garments when I sold out to Soulless Big Paper
(™ Francis John Prescott) could be heard all the way from his
Vermont artisan shop to Montreal.

I stand and slowly circle my brand-spanking-new office,
puzzling over how to set up my furniture. If I angle my desk
along the far wall, I'll get a view of the spires of the Notre-Dame
Basilica and the green swaths of the parks on L'île Sainte-Hélène.
I'd have set it up to face the Gay Village in the distance, enjoy the
vivid rainbow stripe of the plastic-ball street ceiling that stretched
for a kilometer, but the installation got taken down a couple of
years ago.

When the balls went up for sale, nostalgia demanded I buy a
string of each color and drape them on the balcony of my condo
in a rainbow of my own. It was for charity after all. And I had a
lot of good times during the couple of summers when the strands
turned the street into a magical queer grotto.

Maybe I'll fix a few of each color onto some fake stems and
create a bouquet for the bookshelf running along the doorless wall
of my office. A little *hey, this is who I am* under the guise of local
memorabilia.

My cell buzzes in the pocket of my suit pants. I pull it out.
Imprescott Designs.

Shit. Dad's calling from work? Maybe he's actually going to
congratulate me.

An odd warmth spreads in my chest, and I answer. "Dad,
hey—"

"Carter." He sounds oddly emotional. "Do you have a
minute?"

To hear him acknowledge my success? Always. "Sure,
what's up?"

"Your mom—"

He doesn't finish.

My stomach plummets, and my earlier cockiness dissolves into sludge. "Is she okay?"

"She… She…"

Mom's only fifty-nine, and she's spent her life eating steel-cut oats and kale. I can't imagine her in anything but perfect health. But Dad is choking so hard on his words that I'm running through all the possibilities. Heart attack, stroke, cancer—fuck, maybe a car accident—

"She *left* me," he finally mumbles.

What? It's not a terminal illness or death, but it's still unexpected. I skirt around my desk and ease into my chair. My knees are still shaking from my trip down worst-case-scenario lane.

"Left you? For good? Where are you?"

"I… I don't know." He pauses. "I mean, I don't know if she's gone for good. I know where I am. At work."

Of course. A waste of breath, that question. He's probably in his cluttered office, bewildered and running a hand through flyaway blond hair that's in need of a good comb. I'm also cursed with it. Hence, keeping mine trimmed AF. I polish my glasses more than once a century too. And I purged all my T-shirts sporting the logos of various Burlington annual festivals the minute I got my first real paycheck.

"What did you do?" I ask.

"I…" He clears his throat. "Nothing."

"It can't be nothing. You've been married for almost forty years. People don't just up and leave for no reason." People leave because of good reasons, like being offered a once-in-a-lifetime opportunity to work in a breathtaking, cosmopolitan city.

And when a boyfriend decides he's not willing to move, not willing to take the risk to be together, well, that's on him.

"No." Dad's tone is defeated. "It really was nothing. As in, 'Francis, you've put everything into the letterpresses and nothing into this fucking marriage since before I went through menopause. And I'm done.'"

"That's a shitty kind of nothing, Dad."

3

"She's right, isn't she?"

"I honestly don't know." I'm typically only home for holidays, when everyone's on their best behavior. Granted, "best behavior" usually involves my dad getting too deep into the pot of mulled wine at Christmas and calling me a corporate mouthpiece, but him taking umbrage with my career choice is well established. I've never gotten the impression there was animosity between him and my mom.

I picture the sunny kitchen without Dad puttering around, making molasses-thick coffee, and the garden without Mom lost among her dahlias. A lump fills my throat. I can't fathom them not being together.

Guilt grips me. If I'd managed to sell him on the business plan I crafted from sweat, tears, and hubris during my MBA program, had convinced him to bring the shop into the twenty-first century, would he be going through this?

No point in running presses from the 1900s like they're products of the 2000s, Carter. Respect the history.

Right, this isn't on me. It's one more example of my dad being a stubborn ass.

I was right to walk away from Imprescott Designs.

Heat creeps up my neck, the residual kind from past arguments that lies deep in your belly, just waiting to emerge and snap with ferocity.

"It's not the first time you've let the business come between you and a family member." The accusation tumbles from my lips before I can edit out the obvious bitterness.

"Jesus, Carter. I didn't call for you to unload on me too."

"Then you should have called Jill."

"Your sister's not speaking to me," he admits. "Taking your mother's side. Keeps texting me, asking how I want her to answer Cypress's questions about whether or not Gran loves Pops anymore."

My eyes widen. "I should get ahold of Mom." No way am I

getting between them on this, but I want my mom's side of the story and to see if she needs me to support her.

He sighs. "You can try. But she… she left for Paris last night."

I almost drop my phone. When was the last time my mom had traveled farther than Boston?

"With no warning?" I say.

"Claims she's tired of waiting for me to unchain myself from the Vandercook."

The visual's fairly accurate. My dad spends more time wearing his leather apron and fussing with his cast-iron letterpresses than not. I wouldn't be surprised if he wants to be buried with his beloved machines, let alone be unchained from them while he's still upright and breathing. It's not hard to understand where Mom's coming from.

A corner of my mouth creeps up. I'm proud of her. I can envision her wandering through the Latin Quarter, eclectic skirts and scarves swirling as she nibbles on a *pain au chocolat.* Whenever I'm in Paris on business, she always asks me to eat a new kind of pastry and send her a picture. And if her goal right now is to finally live out all the travel on her vision board, I'm here for that. I'm all about laser-focusing on the future and knocking things off the to-do list.

My gut's still uneasy.

"Dad…"

He sniffles.

"Maybe you *should* unchain yourself from the Vandercook. Take some time off."

"You haven't taken more than three days off since you started working for that sellout of a company," he says. "So maybe you shouldn't point fingers."

It's such a common refrain I'm immune to it.

Almost.

"This isn't about me. I'm not letting anyone down by working." Anymore. "*You* are. And isn't fixing things with Mom worth taking drastic action?"

"Again, that's rich coming from—"

"Again, this is not about *me*. I'm *not* committed to someone. *You* are. So do the fucking work."

The defeated hiss he lets out almost bursts my eardrum. I wince.

"I don't know how," he admits.

I blink long. I'm not used to him being anything but a thousand percent certain his way is right.

"Well, Dad, maybe ask her—"

"Carter!" A head pops into my doorway. Anne-Emmanuelle, one of the directors on my merchandising team, is a little out of breath. Her hair twists bounce like she ran from the conference room. "*Notre* meeting. *Est-ce que tu viens?*"

There's nothing like Montreal franglais, especially when it's delivered in Anne-Emmanuelle's Guadeloupean accent.

Meeting. I jolt, checking my watch. Shit, I'm late. I hold my cell to my chest. "Uh, *j'ai un urgence familiale. Peux-tu faire un excuse pour moi? J'ai besoin de, enh... Cinq? Non, dix minutes.*"

Her dark eyes go saucer-wide, probably at the mention of a family emergency. She nods that she'll pass along my assurance I'll be at the meeting in ten and scoots away from view.

I refocus on my dad. "You need a plan."

"I'm keeping you from work," he says.

It's between the hours of seven a.m. and eight p.m. Of course he's keeping me from work. "Yeah, Friday afternoon merchandising team meeting. I'm still in the process of establishing myself in my new position."

"Your new— Oh right." His voice flattens as if it's a disappointment that his son is one of the youngest VPs ever hired by OfficeMart, one of the most profitable global office-supply companies currently in operation.

What am I saying? For Francis Prescott, it's more than a disappointment. It's a betrayal.

It's no secret he'd be prouder of me if I were back in Vermont, with ink streaked across my old, cow-emblazoned I'VE GOT THE MOOS LIKE JAGGER T-shirt.

I'll admit I didn't throw that one out. It's in a drawer somewhere, probably underneath my collection of pocket squares and the Burlington University water polo hoodie I nicked off a man I pretend to forget.

The thought of the last time I wore it—the last time someone took it off me—sends a flood of something as bittersweet as my dad's coffee through my veins.

Not regrets.

I don't have regrets.

My dad will though, if he doesn't fix things with my mom.

And if I don't offer to help, I might too.

"What can I do, Dad?"

"Figure out a way to duplicate me so I can chase after your mom?" It's clearly meant to be a joke, but the watery tone steals its punch.

And it shouldn't be a joke. He *should* be chasing after my mom.

"Your assistant can't handle a week without you?"

"It's always a zoo... Contracts out the ying-yang. A big one I need to finish up today, for one."

More like an owner who frequently double-books himself and is allergic to using a computer for anything but design work, so the sole employee he can afford spends half his time fighting managerial inefficiencies.

I picture Dad's record-keeping system—a tattered Blundstone box from a pair of boots I owned in high school—and my blood pressure spikes.

"Could... Could you come pitch in?" he says.

I must have misheard him. "I'm sorry. You want me to work for you?"

"I've always wanted you to work for me."

I grit my teeth. That argument got stale around the time Beyoncé was telling the world to put a ring on it.

But he's not asking for a lifetime commitment here. He knows

I have no interest in playing his lackey while he bumbles his way to a marginal profit. "You want me to come home for a few days? Cover for you while you chase after Mom?"

"Would you?"

"Well..." The lump is back. I swallow, trying to make it dissolve. The sliver of shared space in the Venn diagram titled *Carter Prescott vs. Francis Prescott* is about a millimeter wide.

That doesn't mean I want him to be lonely and work himself into a stress-induced grave.

Nor do I want my mom to be unhappy or for my sister to have to explain to her kids why Gran and Pops can't both come to their birthday parties anymore.

"I should be able to swing a bit of time off." As much as Dad likes to go on about my company being soulless and the root of all evil, HR is understanding when it comes to family emergencies. Executives have worked remotely before. I'm new to my position, sure, but with my track record of taking all of one week of vacation a year, they'll know I wouldn't ask if it wasn't necessary. "If I come home, do you promise to grovel like you've never groveled before? Actually try to figure out what's wrong and do something about it?"

"I probably can't fix it."

"There are unfixable problems." Like, say, your boyfriend taking your dad's side when you propose a way to expand the family business. "But there are fixable ones too. Just be prepared to come up with some Patrick-Swayze-pulling-Baby-out-of-the-corner levels of brilliance. I can manage the business, but the relationship work is up to you."

He goes silent for a few seconds. "What about Auden?"

"What about him?"

"Can you work with him?" Dad's tone is doubt-ridden. "He's still—"

"I won't be home long enough for my history with Auden to be an issue. Go to France. Fix things with Mom. I'll step in."

Whether I'll be stepping in knee-deep shit remains to be seen.

2

AUDEN

I'd never claim to have a Saturday-morning routine.

Routines eventually lead to having to explain to an entire village of people why you've started fishing in the loch with your uncle instead of your da.

Habits though, those are unavoidable. On January weekends, if I'm not out for a snowshoe, I probably have a coffee in hand and am poking around the shelves of the bookstore half of Vino and Veritas. Morning coffee, evening wine, pretty books, and paper all sprinkled with a healthy serving of rainbow joy? It's my happy place.

This morning is no different than most. Cradling my large latte with extra foam, I inhale the sweet smells of paper and pastries and mosey over to the low display of stationery near the checkout. Satisfaction fills my belly—my little pet project is still nestled amongst sets of deliciously posh fountain pens and luxe, hand-stitched notebooks. The stack of monogrammed paper-and-envelope sets is squatter than when I last looked on Wednesday afternoon.

I flick through the stack with one hand. *S* and *A* are popular choices. Noted.

Chuffed that even a couple of people liked my work enough to shell out their hard-earned cash for it, I point at the shrunken pile and give a thumbs-up to Briar, the employee working the cash register.

His expression flashes with wariness.

Hmm. "Everything okay?" I call over.

"Uh, sure." His mouth is downturned.

Odd, but Briar is on the reserved side. Less so since he fell in love, but still quiet.

He palms the top of his beanie-covered head. "If you see Mr. Fletcher…"

I wait, but he doesn't elaborate. My stomach wobbles. Maybe the bookstore's owner is unhappy with the sales of my stationery. "Something I should know?"

"It's not really my place."

"Got it." Hmm. Do I want to hunt Harrison down or wait for him to find me?

The latter. Finish my coffee first, make sure I'm well-caffeinated for bad news.

Ignoring my sparking nerves, I make my way over to the thoughtfully curated new arrivals shelf. It's always good to know what's popular and exciting. Gives me something to chat about with the patrons of the wine bar half of the business where I moonlight as a bartender a couple of times a week. Serving up local vintages and inventing custom cocktails is almost as much fun as playing with printing presses, and the extra cash comes in handy whenever my mum needs a financial boost.

I'm checking the shelf for new titles when a blur of Oxford blue scoots in front of me. Harrison Fletcher's a good-looking bloke in his early forties. He's always city polished, even in Vermont. Even after moving to his fiancé's chicken farm, which must take effort.

Vermont has a way of growing on you. I should know. You come here to attend college, to get the hell away from Scotland and the memories that stifle every second of your days. A few years later, you're in love with a local boy and covered in flannel and knitwear like moss on a rock.

Harrison's committed to his button-up shirts though. Right now he's fidgeting with his cuffs and studying me like he doesn't know where to start.

"Problem with the monogram line?" I venture. "It's okay if it's not working out."

I enjoyed coming up with the concept, but if it's not a success, so be it.

Better to have a wee heartbreak early. Saves you a bigger one once rings and houses and children are involved.

I jolt at the echo of my mum's advice post breakup with Carter. Christ. As if that glitch in my romantic history is in any way connected to designing stationery for Harrison's shop.

"Your sales are fine," he says.

"Grand." I take a drink of my coffee.

He leans in a little. "Is everything okay with Francis?"

I cringe. My boss at Imprescott Designs, where I work full time as a designer and letterpress operator, had a hell of a week. "What did you hear?"

"Caro asked for a divorce."

"She did. He's right stunned."

I know Caro has a point about Francis overworking to the detriment of everything else in his life, but the devastation on his face was uncomfortably familiar. My mum wore a similar expression far too often in the years after my da left. I wore it myself for a time. It breaks my heart to see the man I consider a father walking around like the ground's fallen out from under him.

I rub my chest, willing the rising ache to dissipate. I'm not sure what else to say to Harrison. I'm not much for sharing someone else's stories even though I know Harrison asked out of kindness.

"Given Francis and Caro's troubles, I feel like a heel and a half for having to bring this up..." His next words come out in a rush. "I was supposed to get our save-the-date cards in the mail this past week. Francis asked for some grace time—something about

11

a booking glitch—and you guys do the best work, so I don't mind being patient. I really need the first part of our order though."

"Ah, damn," I mutter. Francis promised me he was on top of Harrison and Finn's wedding suite. Save-the-dates, invitations, response cards, directions to the ceremony and reception, an in-lieu-of-gifts card... "I'm so sorry. I'll run over to the studio and check on it for you. If nothing else, you'll have the save-the-dates by this afternoon."

It's Francis's project, but he'll have to accept some interference. Asking a client to be patient and empathetic in the face of an emergency is one thing; downright unprofessionalism is another.

Relief softens Harrison's panicked frown.

I smile, nod my goodbye, and head to the coffee counter to switch my drink from the ceramic mug to a to-go cup. Coffee in hand, I wrap my wool scarf around my neck and head into the winter chill.

At least I won't need to freeze for long. Imprescott Designs is only a block from Vino and Veritas, nestled in a small, ground-floor office space around the corner from Church Street. I approach the store. The blinds are down, blocking the customer and work areas from view. Unusual. Francis likes to let the light in, and damn the consequences on the heating bill.

Our BE BACK SOON clock sign is displayed on the door, pointing to eleven thirty. I unlock the door and scoot inside, discarding my winter layers on one of the leather chairs surrounding the small table we use for design consults.

The usual clutter is cleared off the long counter running parallel to the windows. Bloody annoying, that, because Francis should be working on Harrison and Finn's order, not worrying about tidying.

He's nowhere to be seen. His cast-iron pride and joys sit, currently silent, in the workspace on the other side of the counter. Shelving lines the side and back walls, mostly a discombobulated arrangement of ink pots and angled holders full of antique type.

We have more storage in the back next to Francis's office, which is where he must be hiding.

Pushing through the swinging door attached to the counter, I whistle in disbelief. The front counter might be cleared off, but the main worktable centering the room is a right mess.

The recycling bin catches my eye. It's full of error-riddled paper. Francis has obviously been working on the wedding suite, as promised. Not effectively though. If we're going to get this job done today, and his mind's that scattered, I'll need to step in.

I head to the press in use and check the alignment on the gauge pins we use to hold each sheet of paper in place. There should be three, but the side one is missing. Christ. No wonder there's a raft of misprints.

After getting the pins set properly and freshening the ink, I settle in, finding my usual rhythm with the foot pedal and handle. The repetitive clunk and click of the press soothes away some of the tension in my chest. Ideally, I'll have the whole shebang finished and in Harrison's hands by the time I need to start my Saturday bartending shift.

I'm close to being done with the save-the-dates when footsteps sound from somewhere down the back hall. Not Francis's usual work boots, but if he's off his game enough to forget basic setup shite, who knows what shoes he put on this morning? He's liable to show up in flip-flops or gardening clogs.

Or... dress shoes?

Fancy ones appear in the corner of my vision.

Not Francis's.

My breath catches in my throat, and I narrowly miss pinching a finger in the press. I stop feeding it paper.

"Auden. Hey."

"H-hello."

Carter Prescott hovers in the doorway to the hall. He's a handbreadth shorter than my own six two and slimmer than I am, but somehow he manages to fill the entire studio. He's wearing a crisp white dress shirt and charcoal trousers. The playful smile I loved in my college years is nowhere on his face now. His full lips are pinched, tightening the skin on the angled jaw I used to make a study of kissing. I can't see his eyes; he's wearing a pair of nondescript, but no doubt pricey, mirrored sunglasses.

"Here to support your dad?" I ask.

"Yeah." He nudges the shades to the top of his head, into the dark blond hair the color of beach sand when it runs through your fingers with the tide.

And his brown eyes—they aren't the color of anything but heartbreak.

"Thanks for finishing up for me," he says. "I was in the middle of it."

"*You* were?"

He lifts a shoulder. "Someone had to."

My neck heats. It's not the first time I've seen my ex since we broke up or anything. We've crossed paths now and again when he's come home for holidays and family milestones.

Never at Imprescott Designs. Not since he tossed his MBA project in the garbage and stormed out.

What, does he expect a medal for chipping in on *one* project? I've been an employee for over ten years. The implication he's doing Francis a solid because I wasn't here on my *day off* is a right piss off.

I put my hand on the cold metal of the machine. It might be Francis's baby, but I'm bloody attached to it too. "You forgot the side gauge pin. Could've wrecked the whole order."

His mouth tightens. "One more try and I would have had it perfect."

"One more try would have left us in the lurch while we waited for more paper to arrive. It's a special order." I run a thumb along the stack of smooth, thick stock, eyeballing whether we still have enough sheets to finish the job. "You should have asked your dad for a refresher."

He crosses his arms. A streak of dark cyan ink—Pantone

Stargazer, if a person wants to be precise—runs down the underside of his sleeve from wrist to elbow.

"Bit hard with him being in Paris," he says.

Paris? My jaw hits the floor. "What? Why?"

"Begging my mom to take him back."

I could not be more confused. "Isn't she staying at your sister's place?"

"Nope. France. He left a note for you."

"A note."

His brief chin lift indicates a single sheet of scrap paper on the worktable.

I can read Francis's bold script from two yards away.

Auden~

Had to leave town, prove myself to Caro. It'll only be a few days.

Carter's willing to pitch in. If you can stay on top of things, I'll owe you.

~Francis

I shake my head to clear away the shock. First Caro left Francis, and now the country? She must have been hiding her unhappiness for a considerable time. I feel like a bastard for not noticing. She and Francis seemed so solid. Their relationship has been my touchstone for years, one last fragment of evidence love can last, despite reams of proof it can't.

Uncertainty buzzes in my limbs, and I need to do something with my hands.

"You're telling me you're here to pitch in?" I ask Carter as I start feeding the press again.

"Yes," he says. His tone is sincere, but the flexing of his clean-shaven jaw says otherwise. "I want my parents to fix things."

My hand slips while sliding a sheet in place, and it prints askew. Fix a relationship? That's rich coming from Carter Prescott.

I run the press fast enough that I don't have time to put the misprint to the side. I add it to the stack of good copies in front of me and keep going, not making eye contact with Carter because I can't even glance away if I want to get through the last twenty-five cards without losing a finger.

Nor do I want to see if he's giving me a who-made-a-mistake-now look.

"How much ink did you mix?" I frown, checking the stack for consistency.

"My dad did it before he left this morning. Said there was enough for the whole job."

"Minus the streak on your sleeve."

Carter's too-pretty face carries an edge of warning. "Let's call my contribution a warm-up run."

"Next time you need to practice, use the paper that doesn't require three weeks' notice to order."

He nods, as close to mollified as he's probably capable of being. "Would you rather take the whole shop on alone?"

And risk any permanent damage being my fault? No, thank you. "We're already behind enough."

"We can handle a few days for the sake of my parents' marriage," he tells me.

"As long as you can follow instructions."

His gritted teeth inspire zero confidence.

I take the stack of save-the-dates over to the worktable, remove the misprint, and jog the remaining cards into a precise, square pile. "Pro tip: wear a shirt that doesn't cost the same as my monthly rent when you're working with ink."

"I had one last meeting before I left Montreal this morning."

He's on the other side of the table. It's not enough space between us. Bloody hell, was his shirt that tight five minutes ago?

And you're noticing his pecs why?

"How, exactly, are you intending on helping?"

"Look." He jams a hand into his hair, knocking his sunglasses off. They land on the painted cement floor with a clatter. "Fuck." He snatches them up. "From what I can see, you're not the inefficient one here. I'll focus on what I'm good at. You work on whatever contracts are the top priorities. And hopefully by the time my dad gets home—with my mom, mind you—we can have things running smoother."

Always the one with the plan, Carter.

Though his plans don't usually take anyone but himself into account.

I inhale, slow and silent, forcing myself to bring the irritation down a notch.

"This project is our first priority," I say. "It's not my design, so I don't know the specifics, but from the incomplete look of the layer of blue ink, there's more to it than just the lettering."

"Yeah, there's a chicken motif."

I smile. That's cute and totally on brand for Harrison and Finn. I grab the grooms' client file from where Francis left it on the worktable. Flipping through the sheaves of paper, I find the proof.

"Do me a favor and clean the press?" I point toward a jug of vegetable oil and a rag. "While you're doing that, I'll prep the next color."

Surprisingly, Carter jumps to it, rolling up his sleeves and grabbing the cleaning supplies. He's wearing a watch fancy enough it probably tells time down to the nanosecond. One of those thick metal ones that turns a wrist into the sexiest body part in existence.

Unfh.

"You could keep all those records on an online database, you know," he says. "Access it either on a phone or on a monitor out here. Way more efficient." He rubs one of the rollers way harder than necessary.

"Christ. Ease up. She needs a gentle touch," I say, ignoring his unwanted opinion on how Francis and I could improve our record keeping. I know how to use databases. I choose not to. Life is better on paper.

After putting on my apron over my T-shirt and jeans, I go over to the wall by the sink and snag two plastic pots of ink from the shelf.

Weighed smears of Pantone yellow and process blue… A few passes of the paint knife, and they're no longer their own entities. Never to be separated again.

I thought that was Carter and me, once upon a time.

"Fuck!" He jumps back from the press, arms wide.

The front of his shirt now matches his sleeve.

I snort.

He plucks the shirt away from his chest and then groans again. Two greasy fingerprints now mark the fabric. His lips flatten.

Most people would think he's pissed off, given the whole control-freak mood, but they'd be wrong. He's embarrassed.

God, why do I still recognize his facial tics?

He hangs his head for a second. When he lifts it again, he's wearing a plastic, boardroom-winning smile. "I'm going to be more useful in the office."

"Are you?"

Shite. Why did I say that? He's *not* going to be useful there. And yet he's doubly a problem out here. With him in the studio, my productivity is dangerously close to tanking. His gaze is like a burr under my collar, prickly and itchy.

I swallow, making sure my voice isn't rough. "I mean, things are running just fine."

"Doubtful."

Wow, the disdain. Don't need almost three years of screwing every night to decode that one.

"Your dad didn't ask you here to change anything."

"Oh, I'm well aware," he says quietly.

I straighten. "And he's right about that."

His eyebrows lift. "Really? You like working in a place where deadlines are missed, the filing system is from the 1960s, and your boss hasn't checked the company email in a week?"

"Better than replacing the letterpresses with digital printers and selling off Imprescott franchise licenses."

The callback to his long-dead proposal hangs in the air between us.

"I'm not... I mean, I'm not planning to..." His too-fast breath is the only sound in the shop.

I've gotten used to his jaded facade, his go-to expression in the years since he left. Today though, there's something different about it, a yearning in his dark brown eyes. I haven't seen it since the day he presented that catastrophe of a plan. Since he asked me to trust him and then proved I was right to refuse.

I hope he doesn't waste his breath with some such shite today.

"You've already been poking around the records?" I'm feeling defensive of Francis. Yeah, he's disorganized, but he—we—put out gorgeous work. And we manage to keep the lights on, and both have food on the table, so what's the need in wanting more?

"Just following directions. 'Keep up-to-date on voice mails and the books, Carter. And pitch in when Auden needs you.'" He grips the handle of the Chandler and Price as if it's the only thing keeping him from bolting.

Fair enough. If he left it up to his legs, they'd probably revert to muscle memory and walk him straight out the door, never to return.

The tension in his biceps, hard under the fine cotton, broadcasts his determination to stay.

Why? To mess around with Francis's business model and force his dad to change? To take risks his dad isn't willing to take?

In my experience, reaching too high means falling on your arse, but Carter never got that memo.

Once I've done the job for Harrison, I'll see if I can figure out what my ex-boyfriend's up to. I'll have to make sure he doesn't do anything irreversible in his father's absence.

At least I know he won't make me care about him again.

3

CARTER

I glance at the irreparable damage to my shirt and the useless paper in the recycling bin. I can't remember the last time I made such rookie mistakes. Frustration builds in my chest. Goddammit, this place is my Achilles' heel.

I go over to the sink, strip down to my undershirt, and work at the paint, but it's a futile exercise.

"Wear an apron next time," Auden mumbles from behind me, his burr more pronounced than I remember it being. "Or roll up your sleeves from the get-go."

R-r-roll.

That sound has gotten no less hot.

I live in Montreal, for Christ's sake. I should be used to men with sexy accents.

Doesn't erase how Auden Macarthur's is enough to keep a man up at night.

"Noted," I say, scrubbing harder. I don't know why I'm bothering—no fucking way am I getting oil-based paint out of fabric. I guess it's easier to take out my irritation over the error on the shirt than on myself.

I used to be half-decent at running a press. Auden and I both worked part-time for my dad while we were Burlington U students.

The man currently making artistic magic with the Chandler and Price is obviously the same person I met in my junior year of undergrad, though he barely looks it. We were just kids, really. Pushed together by a few straight friends who wanted to set up the only queer guys they knew. He was a little softer then. There's an edge about him now I didn't notice the past few times I ran into him. I'm not sure it suits him.

Physical maturity does though. Auden lost his baby face around the time he lost his virginity. (To me.) And he's filled out over the years. Broad and burly, with a beard worthy of any of the hipster establishments lining the marketplace.

I stiffen. I am not here to make a fool of myself by botching print runs and musing over my ex-boyfriend's facial hair. I'm a fucking executive for a global corporation and need to take the advice I always give my team—identify your skills, use them well.

My skills—and my sanity—are both in the office. Away from Auden.

I toss the shirt in the garbage. "My dad asked for me to keep an eye on the books. I'm going to do that. See if I can make sense of his chicken scratch."

I stride away. With any luck, I look like I'm purposefully moving toward a goal, rather than fleeing the studio and Auden's competent hands and the thoughtful furrow between his dark brown eyebrows.

It's a chilly jaunt out back to the loading area where I parked my car. Ruining one dress shirt is enough for the day, so I grab one of the sweaters I packed. Cashmere isn't much more practical, but at least it's warm enough for the drafty office at the rear of the shop.

My dad's domain is small, with the wall opposite the door taken up by an antique behemoth of a desk. Shelves line either side, full of magazine holders stuffed with paperwork. In a logical organization system, all that shit would be stored in filing cabinets. Or, for anyone living in the twenty-first century, on a computer. There's a waist-high stack of files piled on the desk that I'll have to sort through before I can even get at the keyboard.

This feels like too much, and I'm starting to label my father with some really unkind words like *inept* and *amateurish,* and Jesus, *I'm* going to need a trip to Paris after this to decompress from all the disorder.

I promised him I wouldn't warn my mom he was coming. I *didn't* commit to not talking to her at all, and for whatever reason, I need to hear her voice.

I call her cell from mine, not wanting to clue her in to where I am by using the business's landline. If I could even find that phone. The thick, overflowing manila folder next to the computer monitor is probably hiding the handset. Or, if I'm super lucky, I'll unearth a collection of half-filled coffee mugs serving as mold colonies.

Ring. Ring. I honestly expected her to have it turned off because of the roaming charges. *Ring—*

"Carter?" A question, not a greeting. Maybe she thinks I'm taking Dad's side.

"Mom. I'm glad you picked up."

"Oh, Carter, sweetie. I debated calling you but was worried you wouldn't want to talk to me." Street noise echoes in the background. Hopefully she's enjoying a glass of rosé and a platter of super barnyard-y French cheese at a sidewalk café that reeks of Parisian superiority.

I'm not going to bother with something obvious, like, "Why wouldn't I want to talk to you?" because I know exactly why she'd think that. And quite frankly, it hurts. "Why do you think I wouldn't see where you're coming from?"

"Women in my generation who leave relationships don't tend to be looked on kindly, Carter."

"By me though?"

"I don't know. Life's been so different since I retired. We didn't

22

retire together because everyone says it's a terrible idea, but I don't see how it could be worse than this."

"Oh, Mom." And she'd been so ready to hang up her work boots from the gardening store she used to manage. "I fully understand you cutting your losses over how he runs the shop. You're not the only one who's walked away from a relationship because of the business."

"Oh, honey. You were all of twenty-four."

I was, but the day I left Auden is still a sharp memory, as if the Chandler and Price debossed the image of his heartsick expression on my brain. My dad looked similarly wrecked this morning when he left for the airport.

And in both cases, the person initiating the breakup had a damn good reason for doing so.

"I didn't call to talk about me," I say.

She lets out a long breath. "Right."

"How's Paris?"

"It's not Vermont."

She sounds happy about that.

I understand why. The craving to be somewhere, anywhere, different. Of having a dream yanked away from you and knowing your only way to find a better one is to leave. Moving to Montreal let me forget, reshape myself into the person I needed to be to get where I wanted to go.

"Make sure to wander down Rue Mouffetard one afternoon," I say. "Nothing like getting lost among the fromageries and wine shops. And it's your turn to send me a selfie with a pastry every day."

If Mom's all the way in Paris, she might as well enjoy it.

I'm sure as hell not. Ten minutes in Dad's hovel and I'm itchy for my spacious corner office.

"I don't like how unhappy you've been for so long, Mom."

"Thank you for seeing that," she says.

"Could you be happy? With Dad? If he makes some changes?"

"Maybe? Depends on the changes."

Going off this office, yeah. It's the nucleus of his problems.

A rhythmic clunking sound comes down the hall. Auden's starting up the press again. I can't even swing the door shut—there are stacks of supply catalogs and boxes of ink in the way.

"What's that noise?" Mom asks.

"Uh, machinery."

"It sounds like one of the presses. Are you *with* your father?"

"Nope. Remember, we have stationery presses in the warehouse at work too." Both true statements but entirely lying to my mother, which I hate doing. "I'd better go, Mom. I have a ton of administrative shit to get through today."

"You'd better be telling the truth, Carter. Do not let your father suck you into his mess."

"I'm not," I assure her. I'll explain more once Dad's arrived in Paris and starts groveling. "Have a wonderful trip, Mom."

"Carter, if you're—"

"Gotta go. Love you."

I hang up. Okay. Time to stop stalling and at least unearth the computer.

Moving the first stack, I groan.

Column B: moldy mug farm. Gross.

It takes me a full hour to clean away enough detritus to even get started on bank statements and the physical ledgers and calendars. The rhythmic on-and-off of the press reminds me Auden's only a few yards away, keeping my stomach in a constant state of tension.

After three hours of crunching numbers and cross-referencing to make sure there aren't any other contracts Dad's forgotten about, the knot has solidified to concrete.

Partly because I'm starving.

Mostly because my father has mismanaged himself into a tenuous financial position. And I know from a zillion arguments that my dad hates the obvious choice—bolster fluctuating local contracts with online orders.

Maybe I can come up with something else.

Needing a walk and a meal—yeah, yeah, I'm no different from a fussy French bulldog sometimes—I get bundled up and head for the front door.

Auden's still working away, steady and sexy in that apron he put on.

"I'm headed to get something to eat. Want anything?" I offer.

"No, thanks," he says, not looking up from the paper cutter. "Sandwiches are good at Petunia."

He's still so fucking decent. And *calm*. Unaffected. How? I've been in a fucking state since he walked in this morning.

Maybe because he doesn't give a shit about you anymore.

My gut turns another degree as I escape outside and head for the pedestrian-only outdoor mall. The cold AF weather is keeping foot traffic to a dull roar, but it's still picturesque. Snug, brick-fronted shops full of delicious food and pretty treasures, contrasting with the towering steeple of the church off in the distance. It's no Sainte-Catherine Street, but it's among the more tolerable places to be in fucking Vermont.

And anywhere is better than Imprescott Designs.

The last time I walked out that door, it was on the heels of a hell of an argument with my dad. And Auden. He might be decent, but he still has opinions, and when it comes to the studio, they've always been the opposite of mine.

Jesus, I was naive back then, thinking we'd ever be able to run the place together. My vision was a goddamn solar system away from what he and my dad were comfortable with. For the middling, safe status quo they asked me to settle for.

I've never been happy with anything less than a wildly successful career. Even now, *having* said career, I still want to push higher. CEO sounds mighty appealing.

And Imprescott is a persistent reminder that neither my dad nor the man I loved trusted me enough to build the business into something capable of bringing us industry accolades *and* financial security.

Must be why I'm all pretzel-twisted today. It's the shop, not latent feelings for my ex-boyfriend.

I inhale the crisp winter air and try to unwind, one pinching breath at a time.

I'll give my dad one thing—the storefront around the corner from Church Street is the perfect location for the studio. The hand-tooled Imprescott Designs sign is eye-catching enough for all the foot traffic passing by on the main thoroughfare. He should try some in-studio sales beyond the single rack of greeting cards and bookmarks on the counter.

I'm tempted to run back to the office for my laptop to start mapping out possibilities, but my stomach is ready to eat itself. Figuring Auden wasn't being spiteful by purposefully recommending a crap restaurant to wreck my late lunch, I duck into Petunia.

The soup-and-sandwich restaurant has white walls, curvy chalk script on the board hanging behind the register, and nary an empty table in sight. I order what turns out to be one of the best sandwiches I've ever put in my mouth: tender, sliced chicken and rustic bread that was guaranteed made with a ninety-year-old sourdough starter by someone wearing flannel. The sour cherry jam makes my mouth pucker and water all at the same time—it's like giving a goddamn blow job.

Great. Now I'm going to have to thank Auden for pointing me in the direction of heavenly blow job sandwiches. I take my meal over to the stand-up bar by the window because the wind off the lake is enough to freeze my pants to my legs. It gives me time to scan the nearby businesses. See if there's a way to use the location to Imprescott's advantage.

Possibilities percolate in my addicted-to-merchandising lobe. I'm finishing my last precious bites of sandwich when a flash of a rainbow flag in a window catches my eye. Is that... Holy shit, there's a queer-friendly bar in Burlington now? I mean, it's as progressive a community as you can get in as progressive a state as you'll find, but I didn't think it had the population to justify it.

I need to see this.

Once I make my way to the front door of what turns out to be a wine bar, I'm even more surprised. There's a bookstore attached too. Seems like an excellent place to scope out what paper products are selling in Vermont these days, so I enter and hang a right into the bookstore.

Mmm, wood floors and shelves of colorful spines. A hint of quality coffee floats on the air, as well as a mix of botanical scents from a high-end line of candles for sale, dotted among the best sellers displayed on the front islander. Not much of an action alley, only two tables, but the sight lines are good—it'd be easy to find what you were looking for. There are also enough points of interest along the way to convince you to buy something you didn't know you needed.

I know exactly where to go for what *I'm* looking for today. The shelf of stationery is almost in front of my face. As is the low table scattered with what looks like the premium goods. A pen brand I'd sell my soul to be able to carry at OfficeMart. There's one on display in an open box, and I stroke it lovingly.

It's way too easy to carry on the tactile experience, circling my fingertips along a thick leather diary cover. And the paper sets right next to the journals—wow. They're as personalized as you can get without using someone's actual name. Monogrammed letters and botanical designs create beautiful headings on thick loose-leaf. It looks almost handcrafted.

I narrow my eyes and run a finger over the relief of the design. Wait. It *is* handcrafted.

And that little logo—an *A* overlaying an *M* with stylistic serifs —something tells me it stands for Auden Macarthur.

What the hell? Why isn't my dad standing outside the shop with a bullhorn, selling this to every person who walks by? And when everyone and their dog in Burlington has bought a set with their initials, convince them all to give them as gifts? And the internet, or getting the product placed in other stores—

I'm getting ahead of myself. For all I know, Dad has a list in some pile somewhere of all the places carrying Auden's handiwork.

"That's made by a local artist," a voice interjects.

A handsome, nattily dressed guy, a few years older than me, probably, stands to my left. Must have sidled up while I was goggling.

He smiles. "Makes a wonderful gift. It's been flying off the shelf since we put it out a couple of weeks ago."

Ah, it's a new project. Could be why it isn't marketed far and wide yet. I nod at the man. "Is it sold anywhere else, do you know?"

"Not that I'm aware of." His brows furrow, guarded. Like he's used to the occasional person missing the blatant signs of queer joy decorating the front of the shop and then ending up confused as to why they're standing in a place with a feature shelf of trans authors and a calendar on the wall full of upcoming, inclusive events.

"Sorry," I say, holding up both hands. "I didn't mean that in an I'll-shop-anywhere-but-your-goddamn-rainbow-store way. This place is scratching every queer lit itch I've ever had. And those pens… I'll probably give in and buy one in every color. I just— I know Auden. I didn't realize he had a stationery line."

And I hadn't fathomed he held a potential solution to Imprescott's bottom-line crisis. Not in this way anyway.

The bookseller studies me. "He's very talented."

"I know, I—"

Startled for a second, he peers past me. "Speaking of! Were your ears burning?" He puts his hands together as if in prayer. "Is that my order? If so, you're a miracle worker."

"I did my best," Auden drawls.

I glance over my shoulder, taking in my ex-boyfriend and those shoulders that go on for miles. The knit scarf and hat, the thick, flannel-and-down jacket… Everything about him is cozy.

You don't get anywhere in life by being comfortable.

Right.

"I couldn't be sorrier this is late, Harrison," Auden says, passing a craft-paper-wrapped box to the other man with an apologetic smile. "I'll make sure you get a discount."

I cringe at the idea of losing profit, but Auden's right. A percentage off is in order.

Harrison tucks the box in his arm and grins at Auden. "I can't wait to open them. And I think you've got a buyer in this one if you play your cards right." He indicates me with a hand, then nods a goodbye and disappears behind one of the shelves of books.

"A buyer?" Auden cocks a brow. He almost smiles at me. I almost want him to.

Fine, the thought of his smile is damn irresistible.

It's not a connection thing or anything. I just happen to like looking at men with friendly grins and sexy beards.

My days of relationships being anything more than physical attraction are long gone. At least until I'm where I want to be in my career. There's no time for both.

Really, there's no time for me to be in Vermont either. I should be sitting in my new office, troubleshooting OfficeMart's upcoming national merchandising overhaul, not browsing through a Burlington bookstore, brainstorming ways to fix Imprescott's bottom line.

Except it's about more than the health of the business. If Dad doesn't figure out a way to spend fewer hours at work, he's not going to be able to mend things with Mom, no matter how much he wants to.

The more I stare at the intricate design work on Auden's stationery, the more I see his talent being the key to my dad's problems.

"I was admiring your work," I say to Auden, gesturing to the paper-and-envelope sets. "They're gorgeous. And really fucking marketable. With the location of the shop, you could increase the product sold out of the front. Not to mention expanding the website and selling product online—"

"No." It's not an angry refusal. It's placid. Firm. A thousand percent believable.

"No?" I ask.

"It's just a pet project, Carter. Nothing serious."

Oh sure. Try to distract me from the task at hand by rolling the *R*s in my name. He always knew he could turn me on with that.

I don't think he's doing it on purpose now though. He's not interested in flipping my switch any more than I'm interested in having my switch flipped.

"Why wouldn't you want to see if you could grow it?" I ask.

He puts his chin to his chest for a second, but with the extra inches he has on me, I can see his grimace. "Because it's *nothing serious*."

"It could be. There's no reason you should accept mediocrity."

Staring at me as if I've lost my mind, he shakes his head and backs up a step. "I see you haven't learned to listen since you moved away."

"Hey, I—" I'm not going to have this argument in the middle of a bookstore. The Vino and Veritas owner has enough reason to be irritated with anyone with the last name Prescott as it is.

I lower my voice. "Any chance you'd be able to work overtime tomorrow? If we dug in, we could probably deal with part of the backlog."

His gaze shifts around as if he's checking to see if people are listening. "Your dad can't afford any overtime, Carter. It's why I bartend here."

I frown. "He isn't paying you enough?"

"No, my wage is fair. The extra isn't for me, it's—" His cheeks redden above his beard. "Never mind."

He turns on a boot heel and strides out of the store.

My stomach sinks. I'd better start practicing with some of the scrap paper Auden insisted I use. Because if I'm going to get caught up on the rest of my dad's outstanding-project list, it's not going to wait until Monday.

4

AUDEN

Halfway through my Vino and Veritas shift, I serve up a flight of Finger Lakes reds, trying to stretch out a kink in my neck without being too obvious about it. I usually don't work the press at fiend-speed like I did this afternoon—leads to too many mistakes—so when I do a rush job, I feel it in my arms and back.

My awkward motions earn me side-eye from the other bartender. Rainn's down at the opposite end of the wood-topped bar, taking on more than his fair share of the flirting-with-the-customers load. Not that any of the customers mind—he has these blue eyes you feel like you could fall into. He's also madly in love with someone else, so he isn't someone I've considered beyond objective appreciation.

The place is busy as it always is on Saturday night, lit low and intimate. The voices of the crowd packed into leather-seated booths and high bar tables compete with the chill jazz on the speakers.

"Need help with that frown, cutie?"

I smile at my new but exceedingly familiar arrival. "What frown, Brenda, love?"

She lifts her eyebrows as she takes one of the open stools. Her bobbed hair is a dark, rich red, matching her boldly painted lips. "I thought bartenders doled out advice, but it looks like you're in need of some tonight. I hear my errant nephew's returned to town."

She might be one of my best friends, but she's also Carter's aunt, and I don't want her to feel caught in the middle between our friendship and her "errant nephew." She can allude to my past with Carter all she wants, but I'm not biting.

"The usual, Bee?"

"A half liter please. Gracie will be here in a couple of minutes."

I pour two-thirds of a bottle of merlot (gotta appreciate someone who picks their drink because it matches their hair) into a small carafe and set her up with glasses for her and her wife. My left shoulder pinches, and I roll it.

"Hot yoga tomorrow? Class is at ten. Helps with stiffness." Bee seems to exercise out of actual enjoyment more than needing to compensate for aging and a love of fermented grapes.

"Who says I'm stiff?"

She smirks. "Carter would probably make some sort of 'stiff' innuendo right now, but I'm not him and I don't like dick, so…"

"He might have back in college. I don't think he's that guy anymore."

She takes a sip, gaze concerned over the rim of the glass. "I love him to pieces, but he's had his head up his ass since he moved away."

Carter's arse. Thanks, brain, for latching on to the exact wrong part of Bee's comment. It takes every ounce of willpower I have left not to think of all the things I used to do to that perfect body part back when we were young and stupid and so far in love I expected it would last forever.

I was such a naive git.

I grab a new order slip off the printer in desperation. I have never needed to make a vodka gimlet more than I do in this exact moment. "This isn't the place."

Bee looks around. "For musing over love lost and life crises? I'd say this is exactly the place."

"For me to dole out advice, not ask for it," I protest.

"Then come over for dinner this week. Monday. I'll make ribs. You can talk unimpeded."

Total honesty? No way, no matter the location. But I'll never turn down Bee's food. She's a bloody genius in the kitchen. "What can I bring?"

"A few bottles of that really good shiraz you have hiding in your wine fridge. You can crash on the couch."

"Oh, a *few* bottles. Better be some dinner," I say with a wink.

For the rest of my shift, I'm too busy serving the bustling Saturday crowd to worry much about Carter.

And I stay busy enough on Sunday too that I only end up thinking about him about every third second. Counts as a win, right?

Sadly, some of those every-third-seconds come while I'd ideally be asleep, so when I get to work on Monday morning, I'm yawning.

I enter through the rear door. The usually dim, short corridor is bright. I rub my gloved hands down my face, waiting for my eyes to adjust.

"Good morning!"

I start. Carter somehow materialized in the hall, and I'm not awake enough to figure out how he moved that fast and that quietly. His voice is in my ears, and a hint of his cologne is wafting over me, and his face is too effing beautiful.

"Where did you come from?" I mumble.

He chuckles. "I have something to show you."

"Surely I can take my coat off first?"

"I've been here for hours. Four coffees in. Please don't make me wait any longer." He grabs my wrist and pulls me toward the studio's worktable.

Uh, what? Maybe it's whatever he has to show me, maybe it's the caffeine, but somehow he's gone from being stiff and distant to actually touching me.

I'm not sure what to do with the shift. His long fingers circle my wrist easily, not something everyone can do, given I've never been described as dainty. Those hands... They always felt so right in mine. Or on my body... On my—

"I came up with this," he says, interrupting my thoughts right before they veered into filthy territory. He lets go of me and sweeps a hand at a collection of sketches on eleven-by-seventeen-inch graphing paper. He's almost giddy.

I wince. It's offensively early for vocal jazz-handsing. Still feeling his touch on my skin, I rub my wrist and try to focus on whatever's got him wound up and crossing boundaries I hadn't anticipated him crossing.

His gaze fixes on my wrist. His face whitens a little. "Did I hurt you?"

"Not today," I mutter.

Neither of us says anything. Me, because I'm drowning in regret for letting that admission slip. Him, because he's feeling whatever he's feeling that's making his lips thin and his eyes darken behind his clear plastic-framed glasses. His giddiness disappears, and the poised executive is back in full force. An executive who's dressed for casual Friday, mind you, in a pale blue dress shirt open at the collar, tucked into a pair of casual trousers. Not the bottom half of a suit like the ones he was wearing on Saturday.

He's still ridiculously overdressed for being in a bloody Vermont print shop. I barely own two dress shirts, and the only thing I have approaching a suit is a jacket, vest, and matching kilt I wore as my cousin's groomsman a few years ago.

At least Carter lost the tie.

And unbuttoned that button...

I focus on the sketches. Anything to avoid musing over whether the exposed notch of his throat still tastes like salt and secret promises.

"Not today?" he echoes quietly.

It was absurd of me to allude to him hurting me in the past. Is he being purposefully obtuse by not letting it slide? He can't *want* to go there.

"Forget I said that." The request is like marbles in my mouth. The tips of my ears burn, and I stare at the skilled renderings of the front of the studio.

The front of the studio but set up as a retail storefront.

With my stationery line placed front and center.

I grip the edge of the table and glare at the drawings. He wasn't listening at all yesterday, was he?

I point at the papers. "What is this?"

"You always did better with visuals. So I figured rather than trying to persuade you verbally, I'd speak to how you think."

I stare at him. "Are you being serious?"

He stares back, slick and polished, so damn confident in his ideas and in whatever misconceptions he has about my priorities.

Mainly, that I'd be happy to risk the financial future of the studio on a stationery design whim I had at two in the morning.

"Of course I'm serious," he says.

"Pretty irrelevant *how* I think when I told you *what* I think yesterday," I say. "I was right clear about it."

"Sure. But sometimes ideas seem more reasonable when they're presented more elegantly than two opinions thrown around next to a candle display in a bookstore." The corner of his mouth twitches up a fraction. "Your letterhead might be a pet project, but it's also exceedingly marketable."

Pet project. Okay, so he might have listened. He just refused to accept it. Or did accept it but pushed forward and did whatever the hell he wanted anyway.

Aye, that's Carter, all right.

And the art in front of me bears the marks of him everywhere. Bold strokes, delicate details, block print precise enough it could have been typeset... His vision for product placement and whatever merchandising sorcery he deals with on an hourly basis in his usual life. The sketches catch my eye and refuse to let go.

"You still know your way around a pen," I admit.

"I'm as rusty as I was with the press."

"Was?"

"I couldn't wait for you to get started on the backlog. I practiced"—he holds up a hand—"on scrap paper."

I snort. At least something I said sank in. "Yeah? Manage to finish anything?"

He nods and carelessly indicates stacks of cotton rag on the end of the table.

Two, four, six… "*Seven* orders?"

"It's a start."

"Plus all this here?"

Because his sketches aren't anywhere near a quick draft. The colors and angles and layout would fit perfectly with the marketplace vibe, and the products he's envisioned are differentiated enough from what Vino and Veritas sells.

I trace my finger along the line of the counter where he's imagined what looks like racks of hand-pressed invitations. The fill-in-the-blank sort, for use by anyone, but not generic. Farther down, an expansion of the cards Francis knocks off whenever he goes off on a rabbit trail. On the side, a wall of letterhead and envelope sets.

Christ, I forgot how quick Carter's mind works. In college, he sucked me in with a smile that held wicked secrets, charming me into loving someone, into risking my heart. "You came up with this in a day?"

"It's what I do." He rubs the back of his neck. "It's unfinished. I haven't gotten into the website and the possibility of expanding sales to other—"

"Don't bother."

He bristles. "What?"

"Seriously." I flatten my palms on the table and take on the full impact of his impatient gaze.

Okay, fine. Those deep brown eyes sucked me in too with all their depth and intensity.

I can hold up to them though. I did it once, and I'll do it again.

I owe Francis. He's invested in me for as long as Carter's invested in his flipping corporate ordainment. Helped me get my green card and to establish myself in a new country. I'm not going to repay him with disloyalty. "Don't waste your time. Your dad doesn't want to expand."

"No, my dad didn't want to go digital or sell franchises. And I wouldn't suggest those options again. I'll come up with something fresh."

"What, us working more?"

"No," he says. "Working smarter."

I roll my eyes. "Save me the corporate-speak, Carter."

"I tried. With this." He indicates his sketches.

"They're pretty, but they completely disregard the point of Imprescott Designs."

"Which is?"

"Honor the craft," I say. "Keep the heat on."

"Don't you—" He puts a hand on my biceps.

The warmth of his touch soaks through my flannel shirt. I'll try to scrub away the weight of his hand later, but it'll probably stick, staining my sense memory like permanent ink.

He clears his throat. "Don't you want more than that? You're talented, Auden. You could make a name for yourself."

Christ. Is there an artist on the planet who hasn't considered the possibility of their work going viral? It's an intoxicating possibility.

And dangerous.

I shift my arm out of his grasp. "I'm good with my name as is. And no, I don't want more. I have enough."

Want too much, and you'll lose everything.

Mum's warning.

I know she's ultracautious, but I also lived through the loss of the dairy and Da leaving, so I see her point.

Aim any higher and I'll get knocked on my ass all over again, like the last time I let Carter Prescott share in my life.

The business practices he's criticizing so heavily are the ones that have let me build my own security and contribute to my mum's without fearing it'll be yanked away.

"I know the shop isn't efficient enough to impress your MBA sensibilities. I also know unnecessary changes could result in losses. Losses that *wouldn't* allow us to keep the lights on."

I swear I hear his teeth grind.

"I'm going to prove this to you," he insists. "This place is a disaster, and your fucking ostrich routine isn't doing anyone any favors."

That's borderline insulting, and I got enough of name calling in high school when my rugby teammates figured out I was queer. I was confused as anything about life back then, knowing I wasn't straight but wasn't gay either. I figured I was bi for a while until I got to college and realized pan was more accurate. Of course, in college I only had eyes for one particular sharp-minded, opinionated business major.

I'm not going to take the brunt of his frustration, not even mild comparisons to flightless birds. Pointing at the LESS SWEARING, MORE SHARING poster on the wall above Francis's prized wooden type, I go to grab the rose-tinted paper I need for the birthday invitations at the top of my must-dos for the day.

"Are you shitting me?" he says.

"Yes, and no. Maybe you need to unload. I mean—you haven't cared about this place in over a decade. Why now?"

His mouth hangs open a little, and he rubs his clean-shaven jaw. "I don't need to unload."

He stomps off to the office.

He's such a liar.

On the other hand, I don't know if I want to be the recipient when whatever he's suppressing finally spills over.

5

CARTER

Right after I hear Auden leave for the evening, I get a text from my aunt Bee ordering me to (a) stop working, and (b) get my ass in her car so she can take me home for dinner. I have a ton of emails to deal with for OfficeMart on the heels of an online meeting I attended this afternoon. First—food. I'm starving, and Bee's cooking will be a hell of a lot better than takeout or fumbling in my parents' pantry for something edible. I'll eat, have a quick visit, and then put in a few more hours at my actual job before I go to bed.

Stomach grumbling for the rib dinner she promised, I make my way out to the loading area behind the building and climb into her Subaru.

"You've been avoiding me," she announces, pressing my cheeks between her hands and kissing my forehead with relish.

She's not the only one annoyed with me for that. My sister Jill's been texting me since I got here. Why they think I have the time to be Mr. Social between Imprescott work and keeping on top of my team in Montreal, I have no idea. The OfficeMart merchandising strategy unveiling is coming up in two weeks, and I've been fielding emails all day about where I am. Given it's the project that earned me my new title, I can't ignore it, even while technically being on family leave.

"I've been here for all of two and a half days," I grumble.

"No excuses. I'm going to stuff you full of ribs, and you're going to tell me all your secrets."

"I don't have any secrets. And how the hell did you know I was still at the office?"

She shrugs and points the car in the direction of her lakeside house. She and Grace have been renovating it with what they say is the intent to flip, but given I had braces and acne and a penchant for emo music when they started working on it, no one believes them anymore.

"How long are you going to stay?" she asks.

"I've arranged to be gone from work until the weekend. If Mom and Dad are away longer, Auden will have to manage on his own."

If I even remotely know what I'm doing (I do), I'll convince Auden to buy into my plan between now and Sunday.

"It's sweet of you to want to help, hon, but you're not obligated to add your father's mistakes to your emotional load."

Bee is a psych professor at Burlington University, so it's a rare conversation that doesn't veer into her love of feelings. It's great she loves to listen. It's also a pain in the ass because you'll say something you think is innocuous, and all of a sudden, she has you starting a journal to monitor your cognitive distortions.

I must have waited too long to reply, because she adds, "You can't force change on someone who doesn't want it."

"I'm not. I just want Mom and him to have a chance. And if I can organize things to the point where he sees my ideas—*new* ideas—have merit, it could help him in the long run."

"Everything about you has merit, honey." She squeezes my forearm. "Promise."

"Tell that to Dad," I mumble.

Her gaze homes in on me like she's holding a magnifying glass up to my thoughts. Shit. Here comes the dismissive-avoidant attachment diagnosis.

"Doesn't matter what he thinks, as long as you believe it," she says.

"Of course I believe it." I scoff as she turns into her driveway. "Oh! I'll have to give you one of my new business cards. I splurged on some I can't use at work. Silly, I know, but being a VP seemed worth the expense of fancy paper."

Turning off her car, she pats my leg. "We'll put one on the fridge."

There are two vehicles in the gravel driveway already: a navy SUV and an older model pickup. "You and Gracie got a third vehicle?" I ask.

"Mmm."

She leads me through the carport door into a mudroom.

A big pair of steel-toe Timberlands sits on a rag throw rug next to the rack of Bee's and Gracie's muck boots and work heels.

I stare at the boots, then my aunt. I'd accuse her of being a traitor, luring me out here with the promise of food, only to force me to be at a table with my ex with no vehicle of my own to provide me an escape. Of course, then she'd know how unsettled things are between Auden and me.

I fix a smile in place. "Can I help with dinner?"

"After a tour." She pats my cheek and proceeds to drag me upstairs to show off her new claw-foot tub and the tiling she and Grace mastered after watching a zillion YouTube videos.

"Almost led to us getting a divorce—" She trails off and frowns.

"For real?"

"No. Gracie and I are great. One family crisis is enough at a time, don't you think?"

"Sure. Do I, uh, get to say hello to her at any point on the tour?" *And to my ex-lover, whom I was really counting on* not *having to see until tomorrow morning…*

"She's the grand finale."

We examine new paint in one of the guest rooms. From the second-floor vantage point, she shows off a new firepit and terraced seating area on the path down to the lake. The moon is bright enough to give me a general idea, though the yard's mostly covered in snow.

The smell of ribs is floating up from the main level, and my heart is thumping in anticipation of the company awaiting us. Still, I don't want to let on that a couple of days around Auden has me twisted up like the mangled chicken wire fence sitting in a heap by her backyard shed.

"I feel I'm being rude, avoiding Aunt Gracie."

"Or you want to see who those beat-up old boots belong to," she says, trotting down the creaking stairs.

I follow, groaning at the hope in her voice. She's playing matchmaker, for Christ's sake.

She leads me into the kitchen.

Like the rest of the house, it's a warmly decorated space with lots of plants and natural materials. Similar to my parents' place but with a tenth of the clutter.

"I know who those boots belong to," I say.

"How?"

"Auden wore them to work today."

She grins, then peeks into the oven. "You noticed."

I cross my arms. Yeah, I did. I noticed his ass and thick thighs in his worn jeans too, and the stretch of flannel across his deliciously brawny shoulders.

Nor could I miss the derision on his face when I shared my sketches.

I shouldn't have been surprised or disappointed by his reaction. I get I lost his trust when I proposed a massive expansion all those years ago, and it's going to take some work to prove I'm not suggesting anything drastic this time around. A little credit might be nice though.

Twenty-four-year-old me had loved a big, snuggly, risk-averse man. Thirty-six-year-old me, not so much.

The risk-averse part, that is. Big and snuggly and manly more than works.

And my aunt can't know that, or she'll never let it go.

"What, exactly, did I notice?" I ask.

She stirs a pot of beans. "How Auden is still a hottie."

I cough. She's stirring a hell of a lot more than dinner. "I don't see how that's relevant to anything."

"Neither do I," a low, sex-on-a-flannel-stick voice agrees from behind me. The soft-spoken burr that used to kill me when it rumbled in my ear.

"Bee, you promised you wouldn't push them," a breathy alto adds.

I turn to face Auden and Grace. They're each carrying a basketful of what must be greenhouse-grown winter veggies.

"Aunt Gracie, hi."

Before I know it, I'm wrapped in her soft arms. She clucks over me like she's one of the prize egg-layers in their yard. She's had her curly brown cropped short since Christmas when I was home last. It suits her.

"Who's pushing?" Bee protests.

Auden lifts a brow and sends her a meaningful look.

What meaning, I have no idea. I might recognize Auden's shoes, but I no longer know how to open the window into his mind.

Maybe I never did.

"No one's pushing anyone," Bee says.

"Untrue. This guy is." Gracie plants a finger in the center of my chest. "Lay off Auden at work, okay? Not everything needs to be tainted by capitalistic ambition."

I could do without being reminded Auden fits into my family better than I do, but her teasing smile assures me that, unlike Dad's similar jibes, she's mostly joking. My aunts love me unconditionally.

She gives me another hug. "Welcome home, sweetie pie."

"I missed you," I say. A hundred percent true. I love the big

43

city, and I sure don't miss the shop when I'm gone, but I do miss my aunts. "You need to come visit me soon."

Unlike my dad, Bee and Gracie love a trip up to Quebec.

"So long as you stop giving Auden headaches, it's a deal," Grace says.

I make eye contact with Auden over her head.

He stares at me, expression tinged with apology. "Carter wasn't causing *me* problems."

"I wasn't?" News to me.

"It's not my business," he says quietly. "So, the bottom line isn't my headache. And you've been helpful with getting some of the backlog cleared out."

"How can you be so blasé about it?" Warmth tinges my neck. "Your name isn't on the marquee, but it's your job."

"I do my job just fine," he says.

"Not if the business goes under."

My aunts inhale sharply.

Auden pales. "Is it really that bad?"

"It could be if nothing changes. I've come up with some solid ideas—"

Aunt Bee grips my arm before I can continue. "You're here for ribs, not a business presentation."

I take a deep breath. "I'm here to see you and Gracie," I say. "The ribs are a bonus."

Bee nudges me with an elbow. "As is Auden."

He and I lock gazes. Hurt flickers on his face.

"Yeah," I agree. No need to be flat-out rude.

Bonus isn't the right word. Auden was never an add-on.

He's quiet during dinner. Not unusually so. He's always put a lot of thought into the words he says. Efficient in his speech. It's a good boardroom technique, really. I've used it many a time.

Gracie and Bee are sitting next to each other, forcing Auden and me to do the same. Unfortunately, their kitchen table, a four-seater with spindle legs that looks like it's seen better days, isn't built for two tall guys to be side by side while eating finger food. We rub elbows constantly.

I'm sitting on his right, so he's eating the ribs one-handed with his left hand, and his right arm is plastered against his side, hand splayed on his big thigh.

I would give anything to have him shift it over to my leg, a little finger flirting under the table. We used to be champions at feeling each other up without anyone noticing.

Jesus, distracted from your task, much? I'm not here to fall into college-age fantasies about flirting and fucking and forever.

Maybe I need to take a different tack with Auden. Focus more on *his* job, rather than on the business itself. Work up into the idea of growth strategies.

"Sounds like Mom would be happier if Dad cut back at work," I say lazily. It takes effort—I sped up my speech to fit in with the locals the minute I moved to Montreal—but I want Auden to stay relaxed. *Sell to the client, Prescott.*

"She wants a husband who worries less about how much his antique type is wearing from kissing paper and more about *them* kissing," Bee says.

I sigh at the printing reference. "Nice, Aunt Bee. Are those Mom's words, or did you come up with that gem?"

"Heard your mom yell it at your dad once."

I frown. "Since when do my parents yell at each other?"

"Since always," Gracie murmurs.

"News to me." Have my parents been sheltering me?

Something else to look into.

I glance at Auden, who's focused on his food. "Well, maybe it's time for Dad to step back. You've been there for what, fifteen years now, Auden? Might be time for the assistant to become the boss."

The rib he's holding hits his plate with a clatter. His hard arm brushes against mine as it slackens. "What?"

It takes everything in me not to lean closer and savor the solidity of that arm.

"You, as head printer. It's logical," I say.

"It's a thought," Gracie says to Auden, brows knitted.

"Caro's taken issue with Francis's hours for years." Bee's voice is low, as if she's about to say something scandalous. "And my brother's a lot of things, but efficient isn't one of them."

Not scandalous. Fucking obvious.

"Neither am I." Auden straightens, picking up his rib and reestablishing the inch of distance between us.

I swallow a grumble of complaint. It shouldn't feel so good to have his body touching mine, to absorb the warmth of his skin through our shirts, to recognize the strength in his corded muscles.

(It does.)

I sigh. I guess there's no harm in admitting—just to myself—that my ex-boyfriend has biceps a weightlifter would envy.

"You're sharper than my dad," I say.

He blinks in surprise. "Bit disrespectful."

"The state of books doesn't allow for egos."

"Advice you should take yourself," he spits out. "Excuse me for a minute."

He stalks into the living room and out of sight, no doubt headed for the bathroom. Or maybe for the front door. Nah, he wouldn't walk out on my aunts.

"Sorry, I didn't mean to needle your guest," I say.

"Yes, you did," Gracie says.

"To be fair"—Bee takes a drink of her wine—"Auden's needling him too."

"By refusing to see the light?" I say. "Well, yeah. It's irritating—"

"No, by sitting next to you," Bee cuts in.

"Your doing, not his," I say.

She lifts a shoulder. "A little social experiment."

I set my fork down with a clatter. "What happened to getting permission from your subjects?"

"Sweetheart. I changed your diapers. Ethical rules don't apply."

"You were ten when I was born. It wasn't exactly putting you out." Bee was a late-in-life baby for my grandparents. She's almost fifteen years younger than my dad.

"Yeah, it was. I didn't exactly get paid for babysitting. So I get to meddle as much as I damn well please."

"Put that right to good use then. Help me convince Auden to see reason so I can get back to Montreal and my promotion."

"Be patient," Gracie cautions.

"Easy for you to say. My 2IC is incredible, but my team is expecting me to be there for the merchandising announcement."

"Your 2IC?" Bee asks.

"Second-in-command. Anne-Emmanuelle. She's a fucking saint. It's commonplace to have a replacement strategy for anyone at the executive level, so she's covering for me while I'm on leave. It won't be permanent though. I love my job, and even taking a temporary leave feels wrong."

Gracie reaches across the table and puts her hand on mine. "So go home, honey."

I flinch at the word *home*. "Dad asked me to be here."

"Which is unreasonable if it's going to interfere with your new position," she says. "Auden can manage the shop, and your parents can fumble through their problems."

I shake my head. "I can handle my team remotely. And I can also—" How can I word it without sounding like a child desperate for parental approval? "I know more now than I did when I was in my twenties. And I can do more for Dad than pitch in. I can provide him with solutions that respect what *he* wants to do with the shop. All made easier if Auden's willing to…"

Trust me.

Thank God, I hold in those words.

"…to listen," I say. "He can't be happy being in stasis."

Except he can.

I know this. Too well.

When my dad rejected my shoot-for-the-stars proposal for Imprescott, Vermont shrank for me. Suffocated. I learned in six short words—*your plans will never work here*—that I needed to go elsewhere, to create a new dream.

Auden's *I can't rebuild elsewhere—not again* made it clear I'd be heading off alone.

I must be doing a shit job of hiding my thoughts, because my aunts look at me with twin looks of pity.

Fuck, pity is the worst. "I won't suggest they sell the joint. I promise."

"Find the heart," Gracie suggests.

I force a smile. "And the numbers?" Looking for the heart won't cut it. Dad needs his debits and his credits to line up.

Bee winks at me. "One of these days, you'll learn that both matter."

6

AUDEN

I grip the edge of the pedestal sink in Bee and Gracie's downstairs powder room. The porcelain chills my palms, and I stare into the mirror, willing myself to return to the kitchen and sit next to the one man who makes my blood simmer. He's infuriating, with his bossy opinions and ruinous face.

For God's sake, what am I doing? It's just dinner.

Just touching.

Just a little arm-on-arm nudge here and there.

Just.

Funny word, that. It's wholly inaccurate for Carter and me, in all its usages. Because our relationship sure as hell didn't happen a moment ago. Nor is anything about it precise.

After an hour rubbing shoulders with him, now and then blends into something undefinable. All-encompassing.

Something the opposite of fair.

Of *just.*

I know I've been lollygagging too long, but it's easier to stay in the bathroom. Staring in the mirror, pretending that when I go back to the table, no one will know why I left.

Of course they'll know.

My need to escape Carter and his suggestions marks my face.

I work my mouth, trying to relax the tense muscles pulling at my lips. His aunts know me too well. Bee, especially. She's so in tune with thought processes, and mine aren't hard to understand.

Parents lose the farm and Da walks out? Move to the United States and pretend my world isn't falling apart.

Manage to fall in love with a smart-as-anything boy who was willing to lounge on my dorm room bed for hours while I tried to perfect the angle of his jaw with pencil and ink and charcoal? Pretend I don't know from day one that it's too good to be true.

Lord, I pretended. Threw up blinders every time I saw how different we were from each other. Told myself someone as dazzling as Carter could be real too, like the sketches I worked at until I had calluses.

He introduced me to how bloody addictive paper could be. How brilliant it was to spend my days with a pencil behind my ear and ink on my fingers, drinking in the oversight of a mentor who took the time to teach, to assure me it was all good. And it was all good, working with him and his son, whom I loved more than was wise. Ignoring Mum's weekly Eeyore warnings was easy, considering I was running presses in the day and getting my cock sucked at night and I'd already gone through a rug pull as a teenager. No way would it happen again.

Of course it happened again.

There's always a rug pull.

I cannot forget that.

I don't want to manage Imprescott Designs. I'd never forgive myself if I made a mistake, or a series of them, and harmed the Prescotts' business and, in turn, my steady paycheck.

I need to be employed, not in charge.

The expensive American college degree I used as an escape cost my mom what little retirement savings she had left.

A tidbit I learned when I tried to convince her I should move to Montreal to chase Carter.

If things go tits up, I have no way to help you.

Thankfully, I had a reliable job I could use to help her even if it meant letting Carter go.

My throat tightens and my mouth seizes up, erasing all my effort to look unaffected. Shite, at this point, everyone's going to think I took off without warning. I would never be so rude, no matter how annoyed I am at Bee's interference.

She clearly wants the best for both Carter and me. She always has. How can she not see how he and I are in no way the best for each other?

I let go of the sink and straighten, smoothing out the front of my T-shirt. I'm capable of getting through the rest of dinner without making it obvious that the close proximity to Carter is making me want to slide my hands all over his body. It's ridiculous. Just an echo of the past, the nostalgia of first love.

When I get back to the table, Carter's relaxed in his seat, arm draped across the back of my empty chair. The top button of his shirt is undone, and the gap in the expensive fabric exposes a delicious sliver of skin. He jolts to a stiff, upright position.

My stomach dips. Damn, I'd enjoyed seeing him slouch for a second, the glimpse of a mortal human behind the infallible executive posturing.

I sit and plaster on a smile, because I want to touch him so badly my throat aches. "What'd I miss?"

He mumbles a pat answer about his aunts giving him a hard time. The truth, I'm sure.

The truth for me? I've missed *him*.

Carter's stiff and silent through the rest of dinner, and our shifts together at the shop the next two days aren't much better. He's as buttoned up as the shirt and tie he has on for whatever remote meetings he has scheduled. I'm pretty sure he's been burning the midnight oil, staying on top of his actual job as well as filling in for Francis. Other than a daily visit to a nearby gym in place of a lunch break, he's done nothing but work.

Despite him having declared it One-Word-Answer Wednesday without my agreement, when four thirty rolls around, I find I don't want to leave before saying goodbye. I lock the front door, hit the studio lights, and make my way to the office.

"I'm heading out," I say. "Unless you need me for anything else."

He tilts his chin. His eyes darken, a flash of something wicked. I'm going to read it as annoyance I interrupted, not him wanting me for anything after-hours related. Because the latter would be the pinnacle of folly.

He spins in the chair to face me, feet braced wide on the ground. Like a person could straddle those slim hips and get taken on a ride.

"Everything's under control," he says.

"Is it?" My thoughts sure aren't. I'm not sure if my brain's serving up memories or fantasies right now, but whatever they are, the mental glimpses of strong, lean limbs and powerful thrusts dry my mouth out.

"Would be even more so if you'd agree to a promotion," he says.

My gut twists. "No' a wise idea." Good grief. I only drop my *t*'s when I'm drunk or emotional, something I doubt he's forgotten. And he knows I haven't been tossing back shots on the job.

He opens his mouth to reply, but I cut him off before he can.

"I have a shift tonight at V and V, so I should scoot. Come by if you're lonely."

"With all this to keep me company?" He sweeps his arms to the side, indicating the crowded office. Tidier than it was on Saturday, certainly, but five days does not a decade fix.

I shrug, ignoring my disappointment. "See you in the morning then."

Except a few hours later, an irresistibly hot businessman slides onto one of the stools in front of me.

He looks at home surrounded by sleek, dark-stained wood and leather. The intimate lighting glints off his glasses. Carter's uncharacteristically rumpled around the edges. He's been running his hands through his hair, sending the blond strands this way and that. His collar's crooked. And before he sat, I'm fairly sure I caught a glimpse of a rare pair of jeans on his long legs.

"You came." I brace my hands on the bar and smile.

He doesn't return it, gives me a brief once-over before scanning the liquor on display behind me. "I know I'm at a wine bar, but I feel like a Scot. I mean *scotch.*"

He coughs, and despite the low light, I can tell he's blushing.

Hell, so am I, except I've at least got a beard to cover part of my face, compared to his faint five-o'clock shadow. *Feels like a Scot. Damn.*

Keep it professional, Macarthur. "We've a brilliant fifteen-year-old Speyside single malt," I tell him. "Or I could make you a whiskey cocktail." I point at the discreet tent menu that I print a run of any time the ones on display get spilled on. "If you're looking for a *Dirty* Scot."

"Always was a weakness of mine," he mumbles.

"Carter."

No way can we keep flirting. It'll only end up hurting us both.

I choose a rocks glass and pluck the ingredients off the shelf before turning back to him.

"Sorry." He drags a palm down his face. "I just had a rip-roaring argument with my dad."

I check my watch and do some quick math. "Isn't it two a.m. in Paris?"

"My parents called from a sidewalk café. They were two bottles of wine in. They're extending their stay."

"For how long?"

"Who knows?"

Bollocks.

My hands shake, and I almost slop the blended whiskey I'm measuring. I pour it over the overlarge ice cube, then add a splash of cranberry juice. Marmalade simple syrup. House-made vanilla bitters. Layering cocktails is normally soothing, but no way can I be calm knowing my boss has tossed aside his responsibilities to get trollied with his wife on the other side of the Atlantic.

I clench the long spoon before giving the drink a stir. No. That's unfair. Francis is trying to save something far more important than a business.

Even if my livelihood and my mum's ability to get older without descending into poverty depend on the longevity of Imprescott Designs.

Christ. Maybe I *should* be listening to Carter's daft brainstorms.

"Are you headed back to Montreal on the weekend then?" I ask. "I can do what I need to do while we wait for your parents to return." Which means taking fewer contracts and hurting the bottom line—also risky. I twist an orange rind over the concoction and pass the drink into Carter's elegant fingers.

"Thanks," he says. "All my parents had in their house was a shit bottle of bourbon. I could barely make it through half an ounce."

"So, you drove back to town?" His parents live about fifteen minutes outside Burlington.

The corner of his mouth tilts. Some rubbish part of me wants to taste him there, test exactly how shite Francis's stash is.

"Drink up," I say. "It's complex. You'll like it." I hope he does anyway. I invented it.

He follows directions, taking a sniff and a sip. "Mmm. Nice."

Nice. A bland descriptor, but I could not care less—his smile is the real praise. Slow, mischievous, almost hedonistic, as if he's learned something new, something fascinating, from tasting my creation.

Warmth diffuses through my belly.

Shite. I should not be enjoying making him feel pleasure, not even from a silly cocktail.

He takes another drink, taking his time with it.

"Mmph. So good. Needed this," he says.

"Glad I could help," I murmur.

"Really?" Disbelief rides his lips.

I shrug. "You seemed irritated. Whiskey's a reliable balm, in moderation."

His expression hardens. "Dad was being a pain in the ass when it came to committing to a return date."

"They're having fun in Paris," I say softly. "I can't begrudge them that."

"You can a little. They didn't exactly give you any warning."

"I guess," I concede. Though Francis's abrupt vacation doesn't even come close to the last time a workaholic Prescott left me.

Said workaholic Prescott shakes his head and takes a long sip of the drink. "I'll see what I can figure out. I don't want to leave you flying solo."

"Since when?"

"Fuck." He downs the rest of his drink. "Auden…"

Guilt rides the angles of his face. I can't even look at him.

"Excuse me," I say, heading to the middle of the bar to check on the three young women who are nearing the end of their bottle of Pinot Noir grown on a vineyard on an island in Lake Champlain. "Another pinot? Or something different?"

"Whatever he's drinking!" The blonde on my right waves a hand at Carter as her two friends exchange a lovey-dovey gaze. They look seconds away from snogging.

I serve them their drinks, and the woman leans in. She's cute, and I'd normally flirt a little, but I can't tonight. Not with Carter's gaze piercing laser holes into my side.

"Do you know him? The hottie at the end of the bar?" she asks.

Biblically.

"Yes," I answer, before I lose focus and start dreaming about the glory of Carter's cock.

"Any chance he's into women?"

"Afraid not… What's your name, love?"

"Kelly." She sizes me up. "What about you?"

"My name? Auden."

She giggles. "No, are you into women?"

"I'm otherwise engaged," I say, aiming for vague.

"Lucky fiancé."

Wow, not the vague I was going for, but I don't bother correcting her. She sulks a little and gulps her cocktail. I'll have to keep an eye on the group, make sure they don't get overserved. I share the message with Molly, who's behind the bar with me tonight, and then fix up another Dirty Scot for Carter.

I slide the fresh drink in front of him. "Try to make this one last longer than three seconds."

"Uh-huh. Uh, thanks." He's staring at his mobile like the alphabet suddenly switched to Cyrillic and he's having trouble fixing it.

"If you've decided you're open to more than just dick, the curly-haired woman over there would be a thousand percent interested in whatever you have to offer."

He barks out a laugh and looks up from the screen. "Uh, no. All dick, all the time."

"Glad I didn't point her in another direction unnecessarily then."

"Not the first time I've disappointed someone today."

The wounded ex in me wants to smile at his frown, but my bartender instincts won't let me. "How so?"

"When I mentioned returning to Montreal on Sunday, my parents were sad I'm not staying longer. Dad hinted he'd be open to a few changes were I to stick around." He takes off his glasses, those clear-framed ones that make him look like he should be modeling for one of the LGBTQ fashion magazines Harrison carries in the bookshop. He presses his fingertips into his eyes. "Now I don't know what to do."

My jaw drops. My stomach follows. "Just hints? Or a commitment?"

He clenches his hands and rests them on the bar. "He… he actually seemed open to listening to my expertise."

His eyes look a little damp. Might be light off his glasses. Might actually be emotion.

"That's—" My throat catches. I need to make sure my job is secure. But if Carter's right about the state of the books, my employment could be in worse jeopardy if we *don't* make a few changes.

He brushes a thumb over one eye, then the other. His laugh, forced and tinny, runs down my spine. He gestures to my garnish station with one hand. "Didn't know cocktail onions could make your eyes water."

"They don't."

He stares at his ice cube like he's desperate for it to be an oracle.

I cover one of his fists and squeeze.

His head jerks up. "It's been twelve years since my dad's given any of my work-related opinions the time of day."

"And you want to impress him," I reply, drawing a circle on his thumb knuckle with the pad of mine.

He stares at my hand.

I should pull away. So should he.

He doesn't.

I don't either.

Not even when he lays his other hand over mine, sandwiching my fingers under his warm palm.

A flurry of blond hair and grabby fingers falls onto Carter's arm, severing our locked gazes.

"Oh my God, you guys are *so adorable*," the blond pinot drinker gushes. Kelly, if I remember rightly. I could be wrong. It's only been a short time, but *in* that time, my fingers touched Carter's fingers, and his touched mine, and we looked at each other with something that *wasn't* derision. I'm not sure I remember my name, let alone hers.

Carter's brows rise. "Adorable?"

"Yes. I hope you have a *great* wedding."

Wedding? he mouths.

"Can I have another one of those dirty Scottish things?" she says, a few decibels too loudly.

I catch her friends' attention and tilt my head meaningfully.

"Afraid I can't serve you more alcohol tonight, love. I could get you a water though. Or an espresso."

Her face falls and her complexion turns a little green.

"Or perhaps you need fresh air?" I say.

"Yeah, I should go home."

Wedding? Carter repeats his silent inquiry.

Not for us, no matter how much I wanted it back then.

I glare at him and spend a minute helping the tipsy woman's friends collect her up and shuttle her out the door.

Not my favorite part of the job but preferable to her chundering inside V and V.

Also preferable to standing behind the bar and thinking about the ring I'd bought Carter for a graduation present.

I'd hoped to make it an engagement ring.

It's been keeping the three singleton socks jammed at the back of my sock drawer company since the day he moved to Montreal.

When I turn back to him, any sense of closeness we shared is gone.

"You told her we were engaged?" he asks.

"No, she heard what she wanted to hear."

He takes a drink and licks a drop from his lower lip.

I manage to keep my groan inside.

Mostly.

He bites the fleshy part of his lip he just licked.

"Christ almighty," I mutter, because it's better to spew blasphemy in front of the patrons than to lean over the bar and pull his beautiful face toward mine.

My coworker Molly chooses that moment to drop an entire tray of empty glasses on the floor in a shatter probably heard in New Hampshire.

I juggle all the drink orders while she cleans up.

After as well, because she cuts herself on a piece of glass and needs stitches. It's too late in the shift to bother calling someone to cover for her. While our manager, Tanner, drives her to the emergency room, I sling drinks like a man possessed. I order Carter a cheese plate for good measure. If he's going to drink more, he needs to eat something, and the arrangement of local cheeses, artisan jams, and house-made pickles might meet his urban-dweller standards.

I periodically check in on him as he goes through three more Dirty Scots and dutifully cleans off the wooden cheese board while perusing his phone.

Perusing my body too. I can feel it every time he glances my way. He's spent hours eyeing the plain black kilt I'm wearing, cranking my temperature a bit with every glance. I wish my V-neck T-shirt was also black, so I could lose my thin sweater.

Or maybe I'm misreading it, and he's just plotting some scheme about how to turn the studio into an international conglomerate. He can't just be sitting there, whiling away his evening. I doubt Carter's wasted two hours in the past year, let alone a whole night.

When the lights come on, he's still there. The place has emptied out. Only one booth of people still remains, finishing the dregs of their drinks. Tanner's back from playing Molly's EMT. He's buzzing around, efficiently cleaning and putting tables and chairs to rights. Not to mention giving me curious looks every time I'm within five feet of Carter.

I rub the back of my too-hot neck and ignore both my manager's curiosity and the anxiety eating away at my stomach lining.

Is Carter going to stay past the weekend? Two more days would be torture enough, but longer?

"Where did you park?" I ask him. His cheeks are pink, a whiskey glow. He rolled up his sleeves at one point. Because it's warm in here, or because he remembers sexy forearms are my weakness and he wants to torture me? "You shouldn't drive home."

He looks sheepish. "I'm in my dad's reserved spot. I'll leave it overnight and call a rideshare."

"Aye. Or I could drop you off."

"*Aye*," he repeats, a sentimental half smile on his lips. "Not exactly on your way home though."

True. I live within walking distance of V and V, and there's no way I'd pay for parking to avoid the short stroll, even in the winter. But it won't take more than five minutes to retrieve my truck, and it isn't an unmanageable drive to Francis and Caro's acreage. It won't kill me to do him a favor.

Being alone in a truck with him might.

I shake my head. We're adults; we can handle sitting across a bench seat from each other.

I finish cleaning and get the okay to leave from Tanner.

Carter follows me outside. We're walking fast, burrowing into our coats to fend off the post-midnight chill. The kilt might fill the tip jar, but it makes for cold knees on the journey home.

Snow falls lightly, dusting the shoulders of Carter's wool coat. There's enough on the sidewalk to muffle our steps. One of those nights when you feel like you're the only people in the world. In an alternate universe, we're holding hands and chuckling about the woman who hit on us in the bar. Musing about whose turn it is to go grocery shopping the next day and trying to remember when the oil needs to be changed in the car.

Oh, and shagging until the wee hours when we finally get to our bed.

Alternate universe, fantasy... Sometimes they're not that far apart even if engaging in fantasies is an entirely ridiculous hobby.

"Nice toque," he says.

"Toque? Since when did 'beanie' leave your lexicon?"

"Oh, come on, Mr. Aye-Bollocks-Wanker. Of all the people in the world, you should understand how a person takes on the vernacular of the place they're living." He veers closer to me until we're shoulder to shoulder.

I don't move away. "Except that's a weak example. I've kept some of my Scottishisms *despite* moving elsewhere." On purpose. I'm a language geek—perils of one's mother being trained as an English teacher—and will always be fond of my birthplace. It's what made me. I visit Mum in Edinburgh at least once a year, and we talk on the phone weekly.

"The slang and the kilt combined? Probably gets people ordering extra drinks, just so they can look at you longer," he says.

His half smile is back. The one I don't quite know how to interpret.

"Some nights," I admit. "Except for when my ex-boyfriend is sitting at the end of the bar, all grumpy and hot and inexplicably possessive."

He throws an arm in front of my chest and stops walking. "It was that hard to understand?"

I palm the top of my head, rubbing the hat Gracie knit for me against my crown. "Your mood? No. You're torn about whether or not to stay and help. I get that. And that you're hot? It's not news."

"Inexplicably possessive," he repeats, fingering the collar of my ski jacket with a gloved hand. "I know I have no claim on you, Auden. But you want to talk hot? You. Serving drinks. I couldn't stop watching."

His fingers travel up, splaying on the side of my neck and brushing my jaw. Need rushes through my limbs, settling low.

I should shift away. Saying goodbye to this man tore me to pieces once. Playing around with him again could be even more disastrous, given how tied up I am with his family.

If only he didn't smell so bloody incredible—whiskey and citrus from his drink and hints of warm spice from whatever cologne he has on. His hand on my face brands me, even through his glove. I tilt my head to his.

Our mouths fuse, a blur of lips and groans. He fists the front of my jacket. I'm spinning. There's hard brick behind me and hard man in front of me. He's not bulky like me, but damn, he's strong. I let him take control.

I always did.

I slide down the wall a titch. He's between my legs, lined up like we've been doing this since college, with no long, lonely gap.

I grab his arse and pull him to my front. His coat is thick, making it impossible to tell if he's as turned on and aching as I am. Christ, I want his cock against mine…

"This is daft." I groan at the remnants of peat smoke on his tongue. "But if we're going to kiss, it might as well be a good one."

He draws back an inch. Just his face. Not his hips.

Those he presses into mine, and I'm so bloody aroused I'm bound to do something I know is stupid. Perhaps I already have.

Tugging off his gloves, he shoves them in his pockets before running his hands up my cheeks. One of his thumbs brushes over my lower lip.

I nip at it, then lean in for another taste of him. His mouth is addictive. No logical thought can exist when his fingers are toying with my beard and his tongue is caressing mine with a magic I'd forgotten existed.

I've dated, seriously even, since Carter, but no one who can kiss like this.

He grumbles something against my lips, a mixture of need and frustration. He's going to pull away. It's going to suck, and—

I turn my head before he can prove me prescient.

He stays close, his forehead resting against my temple.

I'd feel embarrassed that my breath is creating fast, expansive clouds in the cold air, but Carter's are coming out just as quick and uncontrolled.

"Was that grunt actually words?" I ask.

"No," he says. He steps back, sucking all the goodness in the world with him.

I'm in a bloody void.

"You sure?" I say. "Sounded like something."

"No." The streetlight reflects on his glasses, making it hard to see his eyes.

That *no* could either mean his grumble was just a grumble or that it was something he was now trying to hide, and—

This is ridiculous. I give him a grumble of my own. "Let's get you home."

Our boots crunch in the snow, out of rhythm for half a block but then falling into step.

"Reminds me of when you used to take me for midnight walks to try to cure my insomnia," he says.

"Never did work."

"Your mouth did." It's quiet enough he could deny saying it.

He doesn't.

And for the fifty-three steps it takes to get to the end of the block, all I can think about is sucking Carter's goddamn dick and then having him snuggle in the crook of my arm and fall asleep, lashes dark against his just-been-shagged, flushed cheeks.

Does he still have nights where he can't sleep?

And if he does, could I still take him from ecstasy to utter relaxation with a curl of my tongue and a suck?

Foolish bastard. Why am I letting myself even go there?

Getting to my truck, I unlock and open his door for him.

He sends me a bemused look as he gets in.

"What?" I say once I've brushed the snow from the windows and am sitting behind the wheel. "My truck's too old to have a key fob, and I like to think I have a handful of manners."

"One or two," he says, mouth twitching.

I start driving and glance at him periodically. The radio's set to VPR, and at this time of night it's all BBC programming. He seems content to let the English reporter jabber on about the continuing impact of Brexit as I steer us out of town. His gaze flits around the cab, as if he's trying to glean hints about my life from the worn floor mats and outdated upholstery.

I can't imagine it's telling him anything except I'm on a hell of a budget.

Taking a deep breath, he stretches out. Long, denim-covered legs splay wider, and he slides an arm along the top of the bench seat. His hand is an inch from my shoulder. Argh. I'm letting him take up so much space.

In my truck *and* in my mind.

Will he stay? Will he turn everything upside down at work?

Will we kiss good night?

A shiver goes up my back, as if his hand, close enough to my body that I can sense it, is pulling at me like a magnet.

The cab of my truck smells like damp wool and the loss of my sanity.

And I can't think of a single thing to say that won't take us into forbidden territory.

The streets and highway are near to empty, but I still drive cautiously.

We're almost there when he shifts closer, just enough to trail a finger along the side of my neck.

"Carter…"

His thumb plays along the edge of my beard. "Shh."

"We shouldn't."

"It's too late at night for shouldn'ts."

My throat tenses with lust and regret. I swallow and pull into the Prescotts' driveway. "It was too late for us twelve years ago."

With a click, he unbuckles his seat belt. He turns to me, one knee touching my thigh. "You're right." His hand's at the back of my neck, massaging lightly, driving me mad. "You also still taste so fucking good."

He leans in.

I thread a hand through his soft, short hair and let him take my mouth.

He tastes less of whiskey and more of himself now. Still a hint of spice, but more subtle.

His hands aren't subtle in the least.

Fingers unzip my jacket and delve under my sweater and T-shirt, dancing along my skin. I'm not complaining. They're magic, those fingers. I want them everywhere.

One hand travels to the hem of my kilt and slides up my thigh, an inch away from discovering I break the no-underwear-under-a-kilt rule when I'm at work.

"Why didn't you wear one of these in college?" he says, voice as gravelly as the driveway. "It's fucking convenient."

He's dangerously close to palming my dick.

"Don't know. Should have." Though college sweats did their easy-access job.

In the house we're currently parked next to, in fact. More than once. Had to be sneaky about it with him living with his parents, but whenever they were out, it was game on. Nearly broke his double bed once.

I'm close to hoping he'll invite me inside tonight, bend me over that same bed, finish the job—

Christ, Macarthur. Something wicked this way comes.

I put a hand to his chest and drop my chin so that our foreheads touch, but he can't continue to short-circuit my brain with his mouth on mine. I'm breathing hard.

So is Carter. He cups the nape of my neck, trapping my head against his.

"I know. We need to stop," he says.

I'm glad he's in agreement. I cannot fall arse over tit for this man again. And the more I allow myself to give in to how good it feels to have parts of him touching parts of me—any of them, really, I'm sadly not picky—the less I'll be able to see how we're truly wrong for each other. That's what happened last time. I slid under the spell of his touch, mesmerized by his intelligence and dreams and how much he made me laugh, and forgot love can't be trusted.

"You're a good kisser, Carter, but you're not good for me, and vice versa. It's best we chalk this up to nostalgic folly."

He pulls away. His face is blank. It wasn't a second ago, but he was too close then for me to focus on his expression. Damn, I wish I could decipher his thoughts. It'll be much easier to manage the next few days if I have a handle on what the hell is going on in his brain.

"Thanks for the ride," he says, shifting back. He opens the door. "And for what it's worth, I disagree."

"What the bloody hell does that mean?"

The door shuts, the only response to my question.

7

CARTER

"Your mother says I have five minutes to clear things up with you, and then I'm not allowed to talk about work for the rest of our trip."

"Jesus, Dad." I clench my cell and aim for patience. "You've accumulated more than five minutes' worth of problems here."

"And I'm... thankful"—he coughs—"you're willing to help."

I almost fall out of the chair in his office. This is not the Francis Prescott I know, and it's shaking me. As is the fact I'm still in Vermont at the ass-crack of dawn on a Thursday morning. I lay in bed last night, barely sleeping, mulling over the feasibility of another week's family leave.

That's not what kept you up. It was those kisses. And over your fucking overshare.

Shut up, conscience. Kissing Auden last night was an afterthought. A little letting off steam after a few long workdays and one too many cocktails.

If only I was as good at keeping my mouth shut as he is with blending whiskey and bitters.

Our kissing... Whatever. Physical shit happens.

Me implying I think he's good for me should *not* have happened.

For what it's worth, I disagree.

For what it's worth, Today Carter thoroughly *disagrees* with Last-Night Carter.

"When we spoke last night, you suggested you'd be willing to make changes," I say.

"I don't have another option," Dad admits, breaking into my thoughts. "And your mom is tapping her watch at me."

Jesus fuck. I finally get the chance to show my dad I know how to solve his problems, and he has me on a timer? "I can't run through solutions in the next few minutes, Dad."

"I know."

"So what do you want me to do?"

"I'm not sure," he says.

"Did you read the numbers I emailed you?" After Auden dropped me off last night—fine, after Auden and I felt each other up in the cab of his truck and I completely lost my hold on reality—I stayed up late, working through options for Imprescott Designs.

"Some of them," he says.

I hear a sliding door and then some honking cars from my dad's end. Jealousy flashes through me. At this rate, I'm not going to be able to take a vacation for years, and being in Paris sounds a hell of a lot better than Burlington. Kissing Auden in the Jardin du Luxembourg instead of on a snowy Vermont street? A guy could get used to that idea.

"Did any of the options make sense?" I say. "The numbers on hiring a part-time admin assistant or a full-time designer? The search won't be hard to start—you have a few voluntary expressions of interest in your email and on your desk."

"I like having a small studio. And one day, if Auden wants, he can buy the place—"

"Does he know that's your vision?"

"We haven't had the conversation," he says. "Doesn't mean he wants to expand. I know him better than you."

I clench my teeth. I'm not sure that's true. As much as I disagree with Auden about the direction of the shop, I at least understand why he's afraid to change. It doesn't take a genius to see that his parents' bankruptcy and his dad walking off left deep scars.

There's no similar self-protection going on with my dad's stubbornness. He's just a shitty businessman.

"Either you let me try to turn things around, or you don't. I'll stay. But I won't half-ass it."

"Carter," Dad warns. "I know you. It would start with one employee. And the minute sales picked up, you'd want to hire more people—" There's some muffled, heated talking. He must be arguing with my mom. "Fine, Caro. *Fine*."

"Everything okay?" I ask.

"Not in the least!"

The pitchy, strangled admission catches me in the chest.

"I won't screw this up," I say.

He sighs. "I don't think like you, son. Bottom lines and strategic whatnot. My business has soul. I'm not giving that up."

Fuck, he never fails to turn a conversation about the shop into a conversation about why I suck.

I rub my chest. "Did anything I emailed you this morning look like I was stripping away Imprescott's *soul*?"

"I don't know, but—"

And there goes my last thread of patience. "If you don't hire someone to take part of your workload, you're giving up your marriage."

Some angry Parisian driver lays on the horn, filling the dead air. Eventually my dad coughs and says, "Your mother has hinted at that, yes."

"Hinted, Dad? She flew over a fucking ocean!"

There's a rustle. "Carter?"

"Bonjour, Maman. Est-ce que Paris est amusant?" Might as well test her French, given she's immersed in the language right now.

She's not in the mood to discuss how much fun she's having. *"I* read the numbers. And I liked what I saw. Hire someone new. And do what you need to do to pay them. Please."

I lean back in the chair. "Decisive. I can work with that."

"Your father told me he was willing to compromise, and if you think this is the best strategy, then do it."

Her confidence warms my chest. Finally someone acknowledging I know what the hell I'm talking about. "I need to hear it from Dad too. I can't make a decision and have him come back and tell me he wasn't on board."

She humphs, and there's some muttering I can't decipher.

"For God's sake, enough!" My dad this time. He's shouting loud enough that any pedestrians passing by the holiday rental are probably complaining about obnoxious tourists. "So long as it doesn't involve franchises, digital printing, selling the place, or letting Auden go, do what you need to do."

"Are you serious? I—"

"Time's up, sweetheart." Mom again. "We'll call you on the weekend. Good luck."

I don't need luck. I need a plan.

I say goodbye and hang up.

Plans, I can do. And this one should be straightforward AF. I need to (a) make my dad more money so I can hire him a new employee while (b) not kissing the only employee he currently has.

An hour later, I've spoken to my CEO and arranged to work remotely next week.

I'm now talking over specifics with Anne-Emmanuelle.

In English, which makes me suspicious. When it's just the two of us, she'll often speak French. She saves English for when she's pissed off and wants to make sure her point sinks in with laser accuracy.

So even though she's coming across as amenable, I suspect she's holding back some choice words.

"I'll drive up for the team meeting tomorrow," I promise. "That should set us up for another week of me being out of the office."

"I can make it work," she says.

"Thanks for being understanding, A-E," I say. "I owe you."

"Correct."

My being in Vermont impacts her the most, and I need to make sure I don't damage our working relationship. "I expected you to be ready to kill me."

"Kill, no."

"Maim?"

"Talk to me by the end of next week."

I snort. "If you're going to require a finger or two as recompense, aim for the left hand."

She laughs. "Look." Empathy floods her tone. "This is a pain, no question, but you supported me through my divorce. It's what we do for friends."

"That's..." That's making my throat tighten more than I would have expected.

I say goodbye to Anne-Emmanuelle and sink against Dad's beat-up leather office chair. I work with some awesome people.

Will Auden be half as accepting?

Probably not, given I spent part of my three-in-the-morning work blitz pulling together a short list of three candidates who have administrative and artistic experience. All people who have asked to be considered for a position were one to open.

All people I'm sure he'll be opposed to hiring *if* he's even willing to help me with the interview process.

Unfortunately, it's only nine a.m. He won't be here for a half hour or so—the door doesn't officially open until ten, and the earliest he ever seems to get here is nine thirty.

Okay. I can do this.

Clutching my coffee, I head out to the workspace.

The air circulation system hums. The solitude is peaceful. Full of the tang of metal, ink, and the potential to play with some fucking exquisite paper.

Knowing I'd be working the press today and not having any video calls with my OfficeMart crew, I wore one of my old commerce faculty T-shirts and a pair of jeans. I'm going to have to put some serious effort into the website later, but first I need to experiment with product.

I root out the plates for five pithy birthday card designs. Print two of each, and it would make a cute set of ten.

Time to make friends with the press. Cutting stock, blending ink—it's methodical work. Makes sense why Auden's so calm. The meditative nature of printing probably does wonders for his blood pressure.

After smearing ink on the Chandler and Price's wide metal disk, I carefully pull the handle. With each eighth turn of the disk, the rich purple covers more of the three rollers. The shade isn't exactly what's on the sample card, but I weighed the ink, so it should be right. Maybe it'll look different on the paper instead of on the disk.

Hmm. It doesn't. It's too red. Weird. Nor have I quite got back my knack for loading the paper straight. No point in wasting the ink though, and the stock I chose isn't any of Auden's precious special-order stash, so I keep at it until the back-door sensor alerts.

He strolls in, carrying a travel mug and a beat-up, leather-bound sketchbook. The hazelnut scent of his coffee cuts through the smell of ink. And fuck, he makes Gore-Tex look good. Or maybe Gore-Tex makes his shoulders look wide enough to hold me up when I'm having a hard time staying on my feet.

Could be either.

"Morning," he says. "Last day for you?"

"No."

"So you're staying longer?"

I can't decide if he sounds hopeful or annoyed or nervous or all the above. "Yeah. I got the okay to work remotely for next week."

"Right." He gives both my stack of work and me a once-over. His gaze locks on the logo on my shirt. "Going back in the annals."

I shrug. "Didn't bring enough dress shirts to wreck another one, and I only packed a few days' worth of clothes. I have a meeting in Montreal I can't miss tomorrow afternoon. Figured I'd make the drive, stop by my apartment, and bring some more print-shop appropriate things to wear."

Last-Night Carter wants me to invite him along, offer to take him out for dinner at the cozy bistro around the corner from my apartment.

Last-Night Carter needs to get his head on straight.

"Having fun?" Auden asks, sipping his drink.

"Yes, actually." I shoot him a sheepish look. In my long-standing anger over my dad disliking my management style, I'd forgotten how much I used to love taking raw materials and turning them into something pretty. I wave a hand at my efforts. "Thought I'd test out some card sets."

"Is this what you meant by not making me fly solo?" Auden's chuckle runs up my spine, like the way his hands played piano on my back last night when I pushed him against the outside wall of the market co-op and gave the sleeping neighborhood a show.

He checks the color of my work against the sample and holds up a square rule to the text, frowning a little. "You used blue instead of reflex blue. It mixes differently with the red."

Shit. I glare at the print job I thoroughly fucked up and then at him. "I've called in every favor I had in my arsenal to work remotely and help your ass. Want to give me a break in the ink-blending department?"

He stares at me. At my mouth, to be specific.

It eases the frustration a little, knowing our kiss is on his mind too.

"Like I told you, go ahead and leave," he says. "I'll muddle along until your dad gets home."

It's solid advice. The OfficeMart CEO, though understanding, isn't entirely thrilled his new VP immediately needing to take family leave two weeks before a major project announcement. Hence my in-person merchandising team meeting tomorrow. It's a bitch of a return trip to make in January, but I need to show everyone I haven't deserted them right before an enormous deadline.

Nor am I okay with Auden believing I'm an unreliable asshole.

"I'm not leaving yet. I'm going to start interviewing people to support Dad with the business end and you with the product creation."

His mouth gapes. "With what money?"

I sigh. "My dad has a business line of credit."

"Going into debt though…"

There's real fear in his eyes.

"It's necessary, and we'll make it back. I'll show you. Everything's on the computer in the office."

"After I clean up the press," he says. "We can't let the ink dry."

"It's my mess. I'll do it."

My hands are covered in purple by the time I'm done. "Shit." I stare at the ink under my nails. "If I don't get this off by tomorrow, my team's going to think I've taken up bareknuckle boxing."

His mouth twists in sympathy, and he motions me over to the deep utility sink. "Here. I'm right practiced at getting in the nooks and crannies."

Mischief dances in his eyes, a rich jade sparkle.

"Nooks and crannies," I repeat. My voice is hoarse, but I don't bother to smooth it out.

"An expert," he says, equally growly, Rs rolling like he's raising sheep on a Highland moor instead of running a printing press in fucking Vermont. "Give me your hands."

I hold them out. He takes one and gently works at my nails

with a brush and some sort of magic solution. His callused fingers rasp against my skin.

It hasn't been that many hours since I had his mouth on mine, and my body won't let me forget. Our shoulders brush, and his bowed head is inches from mine. The scent of the cleaning solution is strong, but I can still catch whiffs of the fabric softener on his long-sleeved rugby shirt. He cradles my palm in his, cleaning my skin with immense care. When did I last let someone be gentle with me?

Not recently. Whenever I do, I'm tempted to want more.

I don't have time for temptation. I don't have time for my dick to go half-hard either, but Auden's tender touch turns me on, even more than his rough kisses did last night.

Goddamn it.

He switches to my other hand, which means getting even closer. I grit my teeth and resist leaning in. It's only a minute, but it feels like an hour.

An hour of having Auden close—wouldn't that be a fucking dream?

"There," he says, rubbing his thumb across my now-spotless knuckles. "You no longer look like you got into a back-alley scrap."

"I think it was a back-alley snog," I say, mimicking his UK slang.

He's still holding my hand, and when he locks gazes with mine, lets me see the need simmering in his eyes, my self-control evaporates.

Hey there, hard-on.

"When I dropped you off last night, you told me you disagreed with me," he says. "What did that mean?"

I could BS him. Sell him on some work-related lie.

(I won't.)

"I don't think we were bad for each other."

He drops my fingers, and cold reality rushes over me. There is no way for this conversation to end well.

"You left me," he spits out, backing up a step.

And here's where he and I are always going to diverge. I might have left him. I know I hurt him when I did that. Him staying?

Equally painful.

And as much a choice on his part as leaving was on mine.

I get why he made the decision. I didn't then, when he was telling me he wanted to keep working for my dad instead of discovering new opportunities in Montreal. Finding perspective was impossible while being swamped by the worst pain I've ever felt.

Now I see reality. Life isn't so simple as being able to prioritize love above all. Family matters. Drive matters.

Self-preservation matters.

We're even in the heartbreak department, and I don't want to talk about it anymore. We have things we need to accomplish. Things I need him on board for. A giant argument about who's at fault for what in a breakup that happened when we were barely more than teenagers won't win me his favor.

I reach up and cup his jaw, run my thumb along the bearded edge. "I'm sorry I hurt you."

He looks at the floor but doesn't resist my touch. "You did."

"I know."

"And it's a bloody mess having you here."

A dry laugh escapes me. "No shit."

He clears his throat and looks at me, expression guarded. "You wanted to show me a spreadsheet or something?"

Back to business. Got it.

"Yes. In Dad's office."

Which puts us just as close as we were when he was washing my fucking hands. Because of that, I'm just as turned on as we go through budgets and website-improvement ideas.

Taking a breath and thinking of imbalanced ledgers—the ultimate boner killer—I present my plan as best I can.

"Of course," I say when I'm done, "you're welcome to any of

the managerial responsibilities we'd be passing on to the new hire."

He grips his jean-clad knees. "I don't want them."

"My dad seemed to think you'd want to buy the business from him at some point. He's worried that won't be feasible if we expand."

His stricken expression presses a sympathy button I didn't know I had.

I'm tempted to wrap my arms around him, assure him with a squeeze that everything is okay. God knows I would have happily lived in his arms years ago. His hugs used to be like a life source. Firm but with the perfect amount of give-and-take and warmth.

Stop it.

"Hey." I splay a hand on one of his biceps and stroke, enough to hopefully soothe. "Dad was just going off on a tangent as usual, talking about selling to you. Don't worry about it."

"I'm not. I mean, I had..." He shakes his head. "Forget it."

Not the face of a man who's happy with his options.

"You sure?"

"Yeah. I don't have some secret dream of stealing your dad's business."

"Stealing? Ha! He'd love to pass the place on to you. You're mellow, happy to just be... You're the son he always wanted."

His face darkens. "Nothing's stopping you from taking that spot, you know. You'd be more than capable of running this place."

"Not the way Dad wants it run," I say. "He's right—I wouldn't be satisfied with solely hiring an extra employee and generating some new income streams."

Auden frowns.

"Don't panic. I'm not making any changes without my dad's okay. I *will* need your input on the hiring process. It'd be pointless to bring someone on who you dislike."

"Fine." He nods curtly and stands. "Keep me posted on when you're bringing in any candidates for interviews. I'll help."

8

AUDEN

I'm in the middle of prepping my garnishes for my Saturday night shift when I catch a flash of sexy glasses and blond hair entering the bookstore.

"Mind if I take a minute?" I say to Tanner, wiping my hands on a cloth.

"You know there's staff on that side to sell books to hot ex-boyfriends," he says.

"Who's saying I'm going to the bookstore?"

He scoffs, ignoring my question to make a pyramid of olive-and-onion skewers.

And I don't bother defending myself further because Tanner has a point. There's no need for me to go over to Carter except for the fact I'm drawn to him like a bloody moth to a flame.

And we all know how that usually ends for the moth.

Carter doesn't notice me approaching. He's examining a shelf of picture books, brow crinkled in indecision. Gives me an extra second to soak in how lovely he looks when he's in his studious mode.

"Can't go wrong with *Worm Loves Worm*," I say.

He starts and turns. "Oh hey. You're here."

"Wednesdays and Saturdays."

"Right," he says, tone thoughtful. "You never did fully explain why you need to bartend. I'm worried you're not being honest about whether your Imprescott salary is fair."

I blink, thrown off. How to explain to a man who makes six digits that the rest of us have to get creative with our money? "Like I said, your dad pays me a competitive wage. Still doesn't cover student debt and helping my mum…"

His eyes narrow. "What's wrong with your mom?"

"Nothing. I just want her to be able to retire one of these days, and with having had to restart after losing the farm, she doesn't have much. So I help her out."

How does he not know this? Not remember me having to scrimp and budget? And finding out my mum had emptied her savings for me…

Unless—wait, no. I found out about that *after* Carter and Francis had their big blow out. Carter was a brokenhearted mess on my dorm room floor. I went outside to call my mum, ask how hard she thought it would be to move to Canada.

And when I went back inside and told him it was impossible, that I needed the security of working for his dad, he walked out before I could fully explain.

Bollocks.

Should I fill him in now? Would it change anything?

Realizing he's talking about something and I'm not hearing him, I hold up a hand. "Sorry. Repeat that?"

"What about your own retirement?"

Talking about money never fails to make me feel itchy. "Christ, Carter, I do not want to get into my finances. Why are you here again?"

"It's a… bookstore. And I'm here to… buy books."

His ability to get me on edge with a snap of his fingers—or a pointed question about my financial planning—is right frustrating. I should have ignored the lure of his lost look, stayed behind my bar.

"You looked confused when you first arrived," I say.

"It's my niece's birthday soon. My sister only wants people to give books as gifts this year, and I don't know what Cypress does and doesn't have."

"The store does gift receipts." *Tell him something he doesn't know...*

"*Worm Loves Worm* it is then." He tucks one of the picture books in the crook of his arm. "And maybe this one too." He adds *Unicorn and Horse*. "And... Yup. A third." One with a sly-looking pigeon.

"Good then. I should, uh, get back to it." Tanner has a couple of reds for a new local flight he wants my opinion on before patrons start arriving.

"By all means."

My feet aren't ready to move.

I rake a hand through my hair. Doesn't make sense. Getting closer to him—I'm asking to be left behind again.

But God, it was good before everything went to shite.

The shite though. It hurt. Meaning I should probably resist the impulse to let him in, in any way.

Except I'm greedy. I want another minute of looking at his face, the ever-present wondering if he'll dish up a smile and destroy me.

"How was the drive to Montreal yesterday?"

"Slow but unremarkable," he says.

"And your meeting?"

He frowns. "Awkward. Stressful, to be honest. I don't like feeling I'm not giving my A game."

Yeah, that's probably keeping him up all night. Back in college, I lost track of the number of nights he couldn't fall asleep because he was stressing over papers and finals and his teaching assistant hours.

"Here. Try this." Picking up one of the to-die-for scented

candles V and V carries, I pry the wooden lid off one of the sample jars and hold it up to his nose. It's a crisp scent, a little naughty, a whole lot like being naked on fresh cotton sheets.

He closes his eyes and inhales. "It smells like—"

You.

"Autumn," I offer.

"I was going to say kissing you up against a brick building, but sure. Autumn." He takes one of the candles off the display. "Not a terrible idea, aromatherapy. And I've been known to like some mood lighting."

I'm aware. We were together long enough that we moved past the *ripping each other's clothes off in desperation* phase, into the more tender, thoughtful kind of sex a committed couple has on the regular.

Well, there was still some clothes ripping too.

And now I have the image in my head of lighting a sexy-smelling candle and peeling Carter out of one of his suits, and I'm close to needing to shed my cardigan.

Damn it.

It's too easy when you've been with someone. Too easy to wonder if, had he stayed, he and I would be running the shop together. Him taking on all the numbers so I could focus on the art except for a couple of times a year when he got it into his head that he needed to be creative, but never to sell. Something just for me, a precious, hand-printed message for an anniversary or because it was Sunday, and Sundays were when we could go slow. Wallow in each other, in knowing every inch of our bodies and minds. Still wanting to know more, even though it seemed like there was nothing new.

Easy. Christ. Not a chance. The possibilities of what could have been flow into my head unimpeded, a swelling river of lost potential. The opposite of simple to process.

"Auden?"

I pretend I've been focused on the table of romance novels to my right. "You should grab a bottle of the diffuser oil too. I think your mum has a burner somewhere."

"Let's not get carried away," he jokes.

Yeah. No kidding. We should be reminding ourselves of that every day we're sharing space, sharing glances, suppressing the desire neither of us wants to be experiencing. We passed *carried away* days ago. I'm no longer certain this pull between us, the lingering knowledge of his taste and the press of his fingers, will ever leave.

"I should get back to work," I announce.

"Mind if I follow? I want to get another look at those menu tents."

"I guess. Just go through the register first." I head back to the bar. Tanner shakes his head at me but thankfully stays silent as he disappears down the back hall to the storeroom.

Prepping lime wedges, I nearly cleave my finger off, given I'm watching for Carter to finish paying.

He finally enters, paper bag dangling from his fingers, and strolls toward the bar.

"Do you make these for any other restaurants?" he asks, tracing the happy hour face on the triangular tent.

"No," I say, resisting the urge to pick up a napkin and fan my too-warm face.

I could spend an indeterminate length of time watching him push up his glasses and study my work.

I never claimed not to be a bell-end.

"We should promote menu printing," he says. "Also, I was thinking of ways we could move into gift shops around the state. Coaster sets, maybe, or—"

I shake my head. His mind is always going. Focused on creating more and having more and being more.

There's why the little fantasy I had a few minutes ago could never be reality. We're too different. Our lives don't run on the same bandwidth. He's urban 5G, and I'm spotty, rural-Vermont service.

"We can talk about new products on Monday," I say.

"You draw that hard a line about discussing the business?"

"I do." I have to draw *some* sort of line with him. Because my boundaries are shite, as evidenced by the stiffening dick in my pants.

"We could talk about wine instead."

Confusion fills me. "Or you could go about your afternoon. Do whatever it is you do when you go back to your parents' house."

He takes off his glasses and rubs his eyes with his thumb and pointer finger. "I'm tired of working."

I purposefully drop my knife. "Say it ain't so."

He gives me the finger. "When does happy hour start?"

"Fifteen minutes."

"Then I'll go poke around the bookstore, get some more ideas for where to position Imprescott products in the market."

"And after, are you going to sit at my bar again and get buzzed to the point of wanting to kiss me?"

"I don't need to get drunk to want to kiss you, Auden." His mouth flattens. "You know what, never mind. I don't want to cramp your style and affect your tips."

He's right, but it's still tempting to tell him that no one would look better sitting at the end of my bar than him.

He pulls his phone out of his pocket, and his expression brightens. "Hey! One of the people I emailed about a job interview is interested. He's eager and available Monday. I'll set up a time with him. Make sure you come in early, okay? We need to prep questions."

An interview. It hurts my heart a little. I guess I've been thinking of the place as partly mine more than I'd realized. Such stupidity. The risks I'd need to take to make it entirely mine—they're unfathomable.

"I'm shocked your dad is letting you start the hiring process while he's out of town," I say.

"He gave me carte blanche," Carter says, gaze darting uncomfortably toward a shelf of wine. "Well, carte beige. There were a few restrictions."

"He's okay that this is happening without his input?"

"Hard to get his input when my mom's banned him from talking to me about work," he says defensively.

"We have to run something like that by him."

"Not yet," he says. "Don't talk to him until I've made a decision."

Something slithers in my stomach. "What about *we've made a decision*?"

"That works too." His brown gaze is almost nervous. "Provided my mom lifts the don't-talk-about-work moratorium at some point, I want something definitive to present to him. He can't be worrying about us conducting job interviews when he should be wooing my mom. I talked to her a few hours ago. They were headed out for a late dinner, and she sounded so fucking happy."

"I won't let you hire just anyone. But fine. We'll leave your dad out of it. For now."

The grin he gives me as he waves goodbye keeps me warm for the rest of the night.

I'm just getting home at two a.m. when my cell rings. Mum and I have a routine after my Saturday shift—we chat while I unwind and while she has her Sunday morning coffee, five hours ahead.

"Auden, love, you sound knackered."

I sigh. Why hide it? "I am."

"Long day?"

"Long week." I hang my parka on a hook behind the front door and shuffle into the kitchen to grab some water before continuing through to my small living room. "Having Carter around…"

"What do you mean, *having Carter around*?"

I wince, settling into my favorite couch corner. It's deep and squishy and accepts all manner of rotten moods. "Didn't I mention that?"

"Funny, you didn't."

"Francis is—" I don't want to worry her, so I'd better downplay the Prescotts' marital woes. "He and Caro are on a Parisian adventure. Carter's here to help out."

And he already got me to agree to withhold information from his dad. Did I capitulate too easily? Hard not to when he looked so bloody anxious. Not to mention, I want Francis and Caro to come home and be happy.

"Oh, love. How are you feeling about it?"

Like I wish he'd been waiting in bed for me when I walked in the door tonight.

"He's still the same man he was when he left Vermont. No amount of time will change that."

"You're wise to be cautious," she says. "Those handsome eyes —they were always your weak spot. And we both know people don't change."

"Aye, well aware." I spent too many of my teen years hoping my dad would change his mind, come home to Mum and me. His desertion should have been enough of a lesson.

"Carter's eyes are as lovely as ever, but I'm not about to be ruined by them."

"He hasn't apologized then?"

"He has to some degree," I admit. "Apologized for hurting me."

"That's how they get you—"

"I know." She's liable to go off for a day if she gets wound up, and I'm ready for at least eight hours of sleep. "He hasn't 'gotten me.' Being sorry about something is one thing, but a person also has to take actions to break negative patterns, which he hasn't done."

Have you? *Doesn't it go both ways?*

I shove away the unwelcome thought. It sounds like Carter.

It's not the same. Putting up boundaries and mitigating risk is being smart.

It's not cutting and running like he did.

He'd spent all his MBA devoting his spare hours to the shop, until Francis refused the digital-franchise proposal. Only then had Carter claimed to need something Vermont couldn't provide.

That *I* couldn't provide.

"I'm here if you need to talk about it more," Mum says. She sighs. "I have a favor to ask."

"Oh?"

"Do you have a few hundred quid you could loan me? My alternator's on the fritz, and I hate to ask, but…"

I know she hates to ask. And she's not taking advantage— we've always helped each other out. We've had to. Two against the world.

"I'll transfer it over, Mum. Don't worry about repaying."

"That's grand, Auden. Thank you." She clears her throat. "Are you seeing someone else? Maybe that'll help deter Carter from any passing fancy he might have. I'd never suggest you need a serious partner, but there's no harm in making time for a little fun now and then."

Did my mother just tell me to make sure I'm getting my rocks off on the regular? "Mum! Too much!"

"Pfft. Don't be a prude."

Carter shoved me up against the grocer's and kissed me until I was ten seconds from dropping my kilt.

It would almost serve her right, but I'm not feeling *that* cranky about the question. "Haven't met anyone lately."

A couple of years back, I was seeing a grad student, Renata, for a while, but they decided it was too hard to juggle their studies and a partner. And the fact I wasn't devastated by their decision, nor by them now being with someone else and coming into the bar for a congenial, not-awkward glass of wine now and again, is probably a sign it wasn't meant to be. Since Renata, I haven't dated anyone for more than a few weeks.

"You work in a bar. Surely there's the odd person who comes in who catches your eye."

"I don't want to be the bartender who picks up at work. It's not my style." Though flirting with Carter for the whole night on Wednesday apparently was. "Anyway, Mum, don't worry about me. Carter won't be here for much longer, and things will go back to normal."

It's kind of her not to call me a liar.

9

CARTER

"There's no such thing as a short jaunt to Whitingham, Dad."

Apparently, a connection of Dad's has rooted out a Golding Pearl letterpress for sale. Dad wants Auden and me to take a three-hour-each-goddamn-way drive later in the week to go check it out for him.

Dad's serious enough about it that he traded Mom a night at the opera for five more minutes of work-related talk with me. He caught me right as I was putting my boots on in the mudroom off the kitchen.

"Worth it for a new press," he says.

A new press. For fuck's sake.

Leaning against the washing machine, I tuck a finger under my collar and tie and wiggle. In preparation for the job interview Auden and I are conducting later this morning, I tied a perfect double Windsor. A damn miracle on a wintery Monday in the cramped, drafty upstairs bathroom where Jill and I used to fight over who got to drain the hot water tank. And I'm two seconds away from wrecking my silk masterpiece for the sake of getting air.

"Close up shop a couple of hours early, and you'll be there before dinner," he suggests.

"Ever wondered why your profit margin is narrow? *That's* why," I say. "Not to mention the capital outlay. It can't be a small investment."

"If we have another press, it could increase our productivity," he retorts. "Give a new employee another press to work on."

Oh. That's low.

And a good point. He has two presses, but they perform different functions. With two employees, he'd benefit from having two platen presses. A Golding's pretty similar to the Chandler and Price—

Argh, why am I letting him talk me into this? "It couldn't wait for the roads to improve? Or for when you get home?"

"There's another buyer. It's now or never. And it's in mint condition."

I polish off the end of my coffee and take the mug to the dishwasher. *Patience. Patience. Pa—*

Nope.

"It's a hundred years old," I say. "How can it be in mint condition?"

"Well, relatively."

Hoofing it down to the fucking Mass border is the last thing I need to add to this week, but knowing Dad, he'll fly home to check it out himself, leaving Mom to draft up divorce papers from out front of the Musée d'Orsay.

"The roads are shit," I say.

"You did an up-and-back to Montreal last week. What's the difference?"

"An hour each way and a whole lot of back roads."

"Please, Carter?"

Oh sure. Poking at my dad-begged-politely button. I exhale. "Fine. I'll do it. Not sure if Auden will want to though."

Of course he's all over it.

The light in his eyes when I get to work and tell him about the possibility of another press is bright enough to illuminate the entire studio.

"Is it a 1912?" he asks, almost bouncing as he sets his travel mug on the worktable.

Oh God. His hair's all messy from taking off his hat. I want to get in there and tidy him up. Then kiss him until he moans, mussing him up again. And then tidy. And muss.

Repeat. It could be endless.

"Carter. Yoo-hoo," he says, waving a hand.

Fuck. "Yoo-hoo?"

"Is it a *1912*?" His gaze goes middle distance as if he's visualizing whatever it is about a Golding Pearl that gets him going. "And is the trundle intact?"

He asks this as if I would have the inclination to poke my dad for specifics about foot pedals on a morning where all I want to be doing is getting ready for our interview. "Don't know that either. I heard 'drive for six hours' and was too irritated to ask for details."

"It'll be worth it. Goldings are brilliant. I've had a hankering to own one of those since I got the chance to use one the last time I visited Mum."

"Of course you check out other letterpress shops when you're traveling."

If he smiles any wider, his face is going to break in half. "Wha', you don't?"

"I might be enjoying presswork more than I remembered," I say, "but my love will always be for the numbers."

He gets that lusting-over-wooden-type look again.

It's not far from the way his green eyes went hazy when I ran my hand under his kilt.

Yanking at my collar—*why the fuck is my tie so tight today?*—I open my laptop on the end of the worktable, opposite from where he's standing. Unlike when I arrived, the place is spotless. I want to keep it that way, put our best foot forward for our potential new hire.

Auden shucks his coat and goes down the back hallway. When

he returns, he's exchanged his outerwear for a leather apron. That, plus his long-sleeved, checked shirt and jeans... Jesus, it's a good morning.

He looks at me, a self-conscious smile tilting his lips. "What? I wasn't going to put on a tie or anything for our meeting—no point in setting unrealistic expectations—but I thought you'd appreciate it if I wore something a little on the nicer side."

"I do." My mouth is dry. I suck back half the water from my bottle of Evian. "You look really good."

"You do too?"

"I thought so." Not too sure why he posed it as a question, but I'm guessing it has less to do with how I'm dressed and more with him not wanting to give me a compliment. "However, if it's in doubt..."

"It's no'. I'm sure the candidate will be impressed." He lets out a sheepish chuckle and walks around the table. My pulse kicks up as he stops a couple of feet in front of me. "Inadvertent pun."

"Still a good one."

"Here." He straightens the knot in my tie with careful fingers. "You must have been fussing with it."

My stomach turns to jelly. "Well, if we're playing that game—"

I brush the front of his hair into place, then run both hands through the rest of the thick mess until the sides lie somewhat flat and the top strands are all swept to one side, as I'm sure his stylist intended.

His eyes flutter closed.

And I slide my fingers back into his brown waves, wrecking all my work. When I tilt his head down so our lips can meet, he moans.

"I cannot get enough of making you make that noise."

He does it again.

"Asshole," I say, knowing I'm unraveling, not entirely caring.

"Your turn." His hands land on my ass, pulling my body close to his.

He tastes like tea. Which I can't stand drinking, but on his lips, it's my new favorite thing. As are the indents of his fingers, ten shocks of pleasure pressing through the seat of my pants.

I whimper.

"Close enough." He grinds his front against mine, the unmistakable ridge I could happily rub against for hours. "Carter, this is irrational. I told myself we wouldn't do this again."

"We can stop," I promise, but tighten my hold on his hair and devour his mouth as if I starved myself all weekend.

In a sense, I did. We haven't so much as touched since Thursday when he washed the ink off my hands.

Ask me if I'm keeping track.

(I am.)

"I'm cautious, not stupid," he says, slicking his tongue against my lower lip and sliding one of his hands lower on my ass.

The bell on the front door jingles, and a frigid gust of air sweeps over us. We jump apart.

I have to catch my breath. Jesus. Making out at work. Good thing shop rules apply and not OfficeMart's—if I'd kissed an employee there without running it by HR and filling out some hefty paperwork, I'd have my VP title yanked for violating the company-standard fraternization clause.

Our interloper doesn't look like he cares about technicalities. He's average height, white, in his midtwenties. He stands in the foyer, watching us with contempt. Chances are, this is our job candidate, and he just got a hell of a show as a welcome.

I sure as hell hope his attitude is over our unprofessional conduct, not because he witnessed two dudes kissing. I didn't have *ejecting bigots from the shop* on my to-do list today, but I'll never hesitate to follow through on it when necessary.

"Are you Wayne?" I tug on my cuffs and try to fix my tie and adjust my pants without drawing attention to the NSFW situation behind my fly.

"Yes. Is one of you Carter Prescott?"

"Me. Sorry, you caught us by surprise. Should have anticipated you'd be early." I motion at Auden. "My dad's assistant, Auden Macarthur."

"Gotcha. Mixing business and pleasure. Happens sometimes," Wayne says.

He's trying to alleviate the tension, which I appreciate, but I'm not sure I like his tone. It's one part patronizing and two parts annoying as fuck.

"You know Vermont. Not exactly the hub of corporate expectations." Auden goes over to the swinging gate to let Wayne past the counter. "Welcome. Can I take your coat?"

My mouth hangs open. Look at my ex-boyfriend, being Little Miss Sunshine.

"Thanks," Wayne says.

Auden hangs the leather jacket out front on the rack by the customer consult table. "We should give you a tour of the shop."

What? That wasn't my plan.

I don't correct him. We'd look even more disorganized if I contradicted him. I follow along, listening as he and Wayne discuss the various machines. Better that Auden's doing this part, really. He'll be able to recognize gaps in Wayne's technical knowledge more than I will.

"You use photopolymer?" Wayne asks, ducking to check out the underside of the Vandercook press.

Okay, I know that much. Even my dad is willing to use computer technology for the sake of creating the hardened, plastic plates that allow us to print images and text not covered by our metal and wood type.

"Of course," Auden says. "Francis and I take turns with the design work. I do most of the press work, at this point. What's your skill set?"

Oh, look at him, being all boss-like. God, it's hot. Our gazes connect for a second. Wayne's facing away from me, so I wink at Auden.

He rolls his eyes, listening intently as Wayne goes on for what feels like fifteen minutes about being a gofer at a PR agency in

Boston before moving on to a midsize print shop in Montpelier. Since he came to Burlington, he's been working two part-time jobs. He's throwing in enough keywords to give OfficeMart Carter a stiffy.

Except I'm yawning, not getting excited about team strategy. Maybe Auden kissed the jargon-lover out of me. Maybe the one percent of me that's similar to my father is taking charge of my brain. Maybe it's because we're standing near two pieces of century-old printing equipment.

Whatever it is, Wayne's *synergy* and *key learnings* and *visionary blah, blah, blah* are falling flat.

Dad would hate him.

I kind of do too.

"I'd love to get in on the ground floor somewhere, take a business from small to successful," Wayne says.

Uh, excuse me?

"What makes you think Imprescott Designs isn't already successful?" I ask.

Auden's in the middle of taking a sip of his tea. He coughs, holding a fist to his mouth but not totally managing to stop himself from spraying Scottish Breakfast at Wayne.

Jumping back, Wayne looks between us both. His eyes are wide. "That's not what I meant. When you emailed, you said you were looking to expand, so I thought—"

"You're right. I misspoke." I want to keep defending what my dad and Auden are doing with their work. It's so foreign I don't know what to do with the urge. "I did mention growth. What would it look like to you?"

Wayne's expression is wary. "Letterpress printing makes for a nice luxe option, but print shops tend to do better when they offer digital products as well. I'm particularly loving what's happening with water-based inkjet work. It gets close to letterpress quality but faster and cheaper."

He isn't saying anything I haven't said myself, but I don't have to work with this guy. And for that comment alone, Francis

Prescott would have slapped a Soulless Big Paper™ label on Wayne and ushered him out the door.

Is this what I sound like when I argue with my dad?

No. No way. I gave up on proposing an artisan/digital mix for the shop long ago. My ideas will only grow what they're already doing, not take it in an entirely new direction.

Auden blinks at the guy. "This is a *letterpress* shop. It's… it's in the name."

"And letterpress is great," Wayne says. "I have experience running a number of different machines."

"That's good." I cross my arms. "This shop isn't going to expand into digital. Employees need to expect to be operating the letterpresses only."

"I can learn anything I don't already know."

Auden's green gaze narrows, percolating with questions. I give him a few seconds to formulate.

He rubs his beard. "Wayne, I'm wondering—"

"Auden?" A feminine voice interrupts from the back entrance. "Carter-Farter? You there?"

Wayne snorts.

Auden groans.

"Oh, you're shitting me," I say under my breath.

My older sister. Her timing is impeccable as always. "We're up front, Jill!" I leave off the *The Pill* of our youth, despite her having thrown out her less-than-flattering childhood nickname for me.

She floats into the room, wearing tights, knee-high socks, and boots, and what's either a corduroy skirt or overall dress under her puffy coat. She's always stuck heavily to her granola-kinder-garten teacher motif. I give her a hard time for it; she teases me about sleeping in a three-piece suit—it's what we do best.

I tilt my head to the side. "No school today?"

"Lunch break." She comes up to me and pokes at my tie before giving me a big hug. "So formal."

"Yeah, we're doing a job interview, Jilly," I say quietly.

She stiffens and whirls to face Wayne and Auden.

Auden winks at her.

"Uh, hi?" Wayne says.

"My sister, Jill," I explain to him. "You don't need to be worried about her giving you a juvenile nickname"—*Wayne the Pain?*—"because she does not work here."

She turns to look at me. "And this guy does?" she whispers.

"Job *interview*," I repeat in a patronizing tone.

"Dad didn't mention any job interviews."

Oh, for fuck's sake. "Let's discuss it after this one is done."

She pulls me to the side. "I get you know how to run a business better than Dad, but I don't think he would be on board with you hiring someone without him."

"And I don't think you said that as quietly as you think you did." I'm clenching my teeth so hard my jaw aches. *Serenity, serenity, serenity.*

Wayne looks downright lost. "Look, uh, should I come back another day?"

I make a simmer-down-everyone gesture with my hands and glare at my sister. "Dad's given me leave to make decisions."

Auden chokes on his tea again.

I smile at Wayne. "Despite how this may appear, I am in the position to hire a new employee. Things have been moving quickly, hence my sister not knowing about this interview." I look back at her. "Because she *doesn't work here.*"

"Neither *do you.*"

"I do right now!"

She glances at Wayne. "I guess that's true."

Oh Jesus. How did this go so sideways? I'm supposed to prevent shit like this from happening. Take control of situations.

"Jill, do me a favor? Come back at the end of the school day once we've finished up with Wayne's interview?"

"You know what, I'm good," Wayne says. "I don't think I'm the right person for this position."

I don't either, but not getting to be the one to point that out pisses me off.

Auden gets his coat for him, and my fastest way to get out of Burlington and back to Montreal—with my parents' marriage and finances intact anyway—escapes out the front door.

"Well fuck, Jill. Thanks."

She crosses her arms. "If he can't handle a little Prescott drama, this isn't the job for him. And seriously. Dad is going to kill you if you hire someone without him."

"That's what I said," Auden mumbles around the lip of his mug.

"Dad. Knows." I explain my plan to Jill—do the groundwork, *then* involve Dad. "And it's impossible to keep him in the loop with Mom banning him from talking about work."

"Oh." Her lips flatten.

Waving my hand in a hurry-up circle, I say, "Make more sense now?"

"I guess." She shrugs. "Really, none of this is relevant to what I came here for anyway. I wanted to make sure you were still good to have the fam over for Cypress's birthday tomorrow."

I freeze. "What? You said her party was on Saturday."

"Mmm, yeah, it is. With her daycare friends. For family, it's easier to do it separately. It's tradition for Mom and Dad to host."

Of course it is. And of course I don't know about it.

I can no longer tell. Am I not part of it because I've never fit into the family mold? Or am I separate because I keep myself that way, because I left? It's a chicken-and-egg scenario I'm not sure I'm capable of answering.

"Do I need to point out they're not here?" I say.

"No. I'm well aware. We all are. Including Cypress. She knows it's her birthday, and things are weird enough with having to explain why her grandparents split—"

"It's not permanent."

"Whatever helps you sleep at night, Carter."

"Couldn't the aunts host?" I'm careening toward pleading.

She squeezes her eyes shut for a second. "Look, you don't have to do much other than show up. Maybe hang a few decorations. It'll be us, the aunts, and my in-laws. I'll bring dinner and cupcakes."

"Vegan impostor cakes, you mean," I point out in true asshole fashion. I know I have no right to an opinion on Jill's eating habits, and I agree with several of her arguments about animal husbandry. But she just wrecked my interview and hijacked my Tuesday afternoon and evening. My petty side is rearing its head.

She pretends to wind her middle finger up using an imaginary crank. "Cupcakes free of animal cruelty, and tofu dogs. Cypress's favorite junk-food dinner. Though maybe we'll run out before we serve you."

Auden, who's busy looking at something on his phone, chuckles.

Jill looks at him. "You're welcome to come too, Aud." She focuses on me. "Can you knock off at four tomorrow? We have bedtime to deal with, so I want to eat at five."

Another day of leaving the shop early. Super. Normally I'd be fine with throwing around some balloons and streamers, but Jill's assumptions are grinding my gears. "You say that like we have nothing to do here."

"Priorities, Carter."

"Easy, kids," Auden says. "I'll come, but not until after we close up. Carter can get out of here early and won't miss a bite of vegan glory."

"Great!" She hugs me, then Auden. "And by the way—I don't think you thanked me well enough for the interruption. It took me disturbing the peace to scare that guy off. If he thinks I'm out of line, he'd never be able to handle Dad."

She leaves.

Auden half sits on the worktable. He crosses his arms, and I am not complaining about the cotton-over-muscle view. "Jill's cupcakes are delicious."

"I know. I was being a prick on purpose."

"You're good at that. I also think she's right—it was lucky, seeing Wayne's true colors."

"I think, between you and me, we would have figured him out without my sister embarrassing us."

"Maybe. Saved us time though."

"I was impressed by your interviewing style," I say. "You know what you're doing."

"Of course I do. I love this place."

He does. Can I say the same about OfficeMart? It provided me with a landing place at a time I desperately needed one. Facilitated my becoming who I am today. I love the success. I love the people and pushing them to reach higher.

Do I love *the company*? Maybe not.

Oh shit, he's still talking.

"Sorry, I missed that," I say.

He lifts a dark eyebrow. "I said, I want to work with someone willing to wallow with paper and design. Tease out the one-of-a-kind magic."

His voice is quiet, soothing. It demands I take a deep breath and get out of my feelings.

"I've been reminded of how much of an art it is," I say. "And that I can get by, but you—you have a gift."

Rosy splotches bloom on his cheeks. "You know what you're doing too."

"I don't have the rhythm of it like you do. The innate... mastery, I guess. The relationship."

Auden tilts his head and looks out the front window.

"What?" I ask. "He's not coming back."

"I know, but hearing the words rhythm and mastery and relationship when it comes to using a press... I'm looking for locusts, frogs, horsemen—any sign of the apocalypse."

"Fuck off," I mutter.

Rhythm, mastery.

When he repeats the words like that, I'm not thinking of cast-iron machines—I'm thinking about sex.

I can't believe he didn't call me on how filthy that sounded.

He's biting his lip, still a little pink in the face.

Okay, maybe he's thinking it at least.

"I could show you," he says.

Meeting his gaze is like swimming in a lake, when you dive down, down on a bright day, and you have the dark depths below and the streams of light from above, and it blends around you like you're wearing a crown of green water and sunlight.

Holy fuck. He's too much sometimes.

"Come here." He crooks a finger for me to meet him at the Chandler and Price.

Definitely too much.

I join him anyway.

He takes my left hand and places it on the small shelf on the front of the press where we'd normally collect the cards during a run. The wood is smooth. And it would feel exactly like palming a flat piece of wood always does, except his big hand covers mine.

"Artisanry demands that relationship." His voice is insanely low, but he's only inches from me, so I don't miss a syllable.

"I'm not an—"

"You have the artistic talent. You just need a little patience." He puts his other hand on my right hip and positions me square to the press. He taps his toe against my heel, a silent command to put my foot on the treadle.

"We're missing some parts." Paper. Ink. The frame. Everything that actually turns into a product.

"We're not making anything." He's at an angle to me. If he leaned forward three inches, his dick would be pressed into my hip. His left hand is still holding mine to the shelf. The other is a heavy weight just below my waist.

"I don't understand," I say.

"Just watch it, Carter." He sounds amused. "You want to know every quirk. And not to try to learn when you're rushing through eight jobs at once. When you have time to go easy."

"Really."

"Really," he says. "Grip the wood with your other hand too."

"*Grip* the *wood*? You're fucking with me."

"A little." I can't see his face from where he is behind me, but I hear his smirk.

A little? A lot. I grab hold of the shelf anyway.

"Just work the treadle," he says.

I press my toe into the pedal, making the flywheel whir.

"And listen," he says. "Watch."

I obey.

I've been so damn busy since I got here—paper in, paper out, paper in, paper out—I haven't actually watched anything I've done.

The rollers, mesmerizing as they glide over the circular, iron platen.

"What color's the ink?" Auden's hand tightens on my hip. His breath tickles the side of my neck.

There is no ink.

"Green," I say. I can't get that sunlit lake off my mind.

(I don't want to. Ever.)

My tie… Why am I wearing something meant to restrict my airflow? I want to loosen it, but Auden told me to keep my hands on the shelf, so I'm keeping my hands on the goddamn shelf.

"Hear anything in the flywheel?" he says.

Just the whir and clicks and whuffs it normally makes. "Should I be?"

"Nothing unusual, but the more you know the sounds of it, the more you know exactly when to feed the paper." He taps the top of my hand once. Twice. Again. Matching it up to some sensory memory that's so ingrained in him he probably dreams in that rhythm.

Anchored by his touch, I'm the one who leans in the three inches. My shoulder, touching his chest. His breath, much more than a tickle. A caress.

"It's a pulse," he murmurs, so gruff the consonants and vowels mix together. His fingers brush the hollow above my shirt collar. My knees wobble.

"A pulse." I tilt my head to the side, exposing my neck.

"Aye." Bending his head, his lips land on the same sensitive spot.

My head's turning faster than the flywheel.

"Auden."

"See? You know the rhythm."

Oh God, I don't know *anything* right now.

I straighten, stumble away from him.

My breaths are short; my skin is just exposed wires, side by side, snapping and shorting out.

And I could have sworn the underwear I put on this morning was the right size, but now it feels like it shrank to an extra-small in the wash.

Could be because my dick's harder than the concrete floor.

Auden's is too, going off the bulge in his jeans. At least I'm not alone in my agony.

He stacks his hands on his head, chest rising in a long, deep breath.

As the machine quiets, the awkward silence grows, and the pressure builds in my core. Normally, I'd jog off to the office at the back, escape into planograms and marketing keywords, but ducking and hiding isn't going to fix this.

Dropping his hands, Auden glances at the clock. He stiffens, swearing under his breath. "I, uh, have a meeting to go to in a few minutes. A maple wine tasting."

Maple what? I blink, shaking my head a little to try to focus on something that isn't Auden's hands on my body. "Sorry?"

"My friend Brody wants me to come try out his product and talk about label designs. I wanted to do it at his distillery to get a feel for what he's doing there. Do you want to come?"

I shake my head. "I'd better stick around here."

I lobbed him a soft one with that. A few days ago, he would have snapped out a "There's a first time for everything."

He doesn't.

Disappointment flickers at the corners of his mouth. With a quick nod, he goes to get his coat. And he's gone.

The momentary sense of loss swamps me.

Key word, Prescott: momentary.

I yank at my tie until it hangs undone around my neck. I need to get my head on straight. Get some work done.

But Jesus.

All I want is another lesson.

10

AUDEN

I trudge down the gravel path that runs down the side of Carter's parents' house. It's after six, too late to participate in any of the actual birthday festivities. Not a bad thing, actually. The shorter my visit, the less time everyone will have to suss out my lingering, unaddressed, unwelcome feelings for their prodigal brother and nephew. I'll drop in for politeness's sake, make sure the birthday girl loves the notebook I made for her with her name printed and debossed on each page, and scoot.

Scoot somewhere that *doesn't* involve being in the same space as Carter Prescott.

Touching him yesterday, having my hands on him as he let himself dwell in the intangible for a few precious seconds—

It was foolishness.

Wonderful, shattering foolishness.

I shake out my hands, trying to rid my skin of the memory. I can pretend yesterday didn't happen, right?

Birthday party. Cypress, present, scoot.

The outside of the clapboard farmhouse is on the shabby end of shabby chic, but the inside is warm and full of love. It takes me back to what my house on my long-ago-liquidated family farm in

Scotland could have been, had bankruptcy and my da's tendency toward wankerdom not been our reality.

The main floor is mostly living space, with the bedrooms upstairs. Entering through the garden mudroom in the back—I stopped having to knock years ago—I shed a few layers and make my way into the cheery, cluttered kitchen.

Wait. Not cluttered. Spick-and-span. Carter's clearly been organizing his parents' house as much as he has the Imprescott workspace.

Decorating too. Swags of yellow and navy streamers and some of those colored cardboard springy things with number fours dangling at the bottom brighten the pale-blue painted cabinets and the windows. The streamers extend into the dining room and beyond.

Huh. Earlier today, during the one awkward moment when Carter had deigned to leave the back office, he'd grumbled about the lack of notice he'd had to prepare. I got the impression he was going to buy a bouquet of helium balloons and be done with it.

Chatter spills out from around the corner, the direction of the living room. I'm about to head toward the crowd, gift bag in hand, when a sexy, masculine form trots down the stairs connecting the kitchen and the upper level. Carter's still wearing the charcoal-gray slacks and burgundy V-neck sweater he had on earlier. The cashmere knit fits over the dress shirt underneath with no bulging lines or creases, and I kind of hate him for that. It's a style I find bonkers-sexy but can never pull off.

I also feel a titch underdressed, as I'm only in jeans, one of the dozen MAKE AN IMPRESSION T-shirts I own, and a thick, hand-knit cardigan. Chances are the rest of the family won't be as dressed up as Carter though.

"Escaping the familial horde?" I ask.

He scrunches his face and pushes up his glasses. "I had a call I had to take."

"And you're feeling guilty about it."

"I am, actually." He snatches up an empty wineglass from the kitchen table and dumps the remainder of an uncorked bottle into it. The rich red liquid reaches a finger's distance from the brim.

"That good a party?" I say.

"Silly to leave a splash in the bottle." He drains a good inch from the glass.

"Let me look at the label."

"Argentinian Malbec." He passes the bottle over.

I take it with my free hand and read the description. Oak, jammy berries, a hint of licorice—sounds about right for this varietal. I send him a cheeky smile. "I'd have given you my professional opinion had you not hogged the rest."

"I have another. Want me to open it?" He sips again and licks a drop from his lip.

I lean in, tempted to nip at that lush mouth like I did when he tilted his head and silently commanded me to kiss his neck.

No. That's exactly what I'm *not* here to do.

Yesterday. Didn't. Happen.

I step back.

Disappointment flits in his brown eyes, matching the twist of my gut.

He opens a second bottle, takes a clean glass from a cabinet, and pours me a healthy serving.

Hand clenched around the stem, I follow him into the living room.

"Hi, everyone!" I lift my wineglass. "Cheers. Good to see you all."

There's a discordant mix of hellos from the crowd—Bee and Grace, Jill and her husband, Will (a never-ending source of family harassment, that rhyme), and Will's parents. Cypress and her little brother Odin are lying on the floor, cake-drunk and covered in lavender frosting.

Will and his family seem unfazed by my presence, but Bee and Grace examine Carter and me with a level of detail usually saved for doing lice checks on a preschooler.

I pretend not to notice. "Where's all the Christmas stuff?"

It might be getting to the end of January, but Caro usually leaves her Christmas decorations up until at least the day before Valentine's Day, claiming it makes her too sad to take them down. Streamers, cardboard springs, and three clusters of yellow and foil balloons occupy the spots where holly and fir swags hung for the holidays.

Carter shrugs. "No one with a January birthday deserves to share their day with a December celebration."

"Doesn't explain the multiple balloon bouquets though." I also suspect the birthday girl tiara tilted haphazardly in Cypress's blond curls and the glittery, bestreamered wand in her hand are Carter's work. He jumped in with both feet here.

"Kids like balloons," he says.

And he loves his family. My heart skips at his efforts to show it.

There's nowhere to sit—the rest of the family is taking up the two love seats and armchairs. Carter and I stand to the side, not quite touching but closer than platonic friends.

"Auden, honey, I want your sweater," Bee calls out.

"You'd swim in it, love. Maybe if my mum's in the right mood, I could convince her to knit you one too."

"Time for presents!" Jill announces. "Sorry, Auden, we ran out of dinner. There are cupcakes on the dining room table, and I see Carter's taken care of your grape-related needs."

He could take care of a lot more than just my drink, if I was daft enough to suggest it. The back of my neck gets warm.

I lift my glass and add my gift to the mound on the coffee table. "Always the priority. Presents and wine. Dual priorities, I mean. And obviously not wine for the kids." I'm talking too fast. Going back to where Carter's standing to the side, I add, "You know what I mean."

Jill smiles and gets the present-opening started by handing Cypress a neatly wrapped package. Pleated paper, homemade bow, the whole shebang.

"From Uncle Carter," she announces.

"Wow, Harrison really went to town when he wrapped your gift," I whisper.

"I did it," he says.

He's sheepish.

He's *adorable*.

Yesterday left me… it left me raw, quite frankly. And shifting from that to awkward moments in the shop today to him being sweet now… I don't know what to do with him. Or how to feel.

I swallow my confusion. "You pulled out the full Caro Prescott treatment tonight, even though Jill was less than gracious about dropping this on you. I'm impressed."

"Deadlines don't faze me."

"I'm glad. It's come in handy for getting caught up on all the projects your dad let slide."

His laugh is brisk, unforgiving. "Both my parents left loose ends."

"They did." I know Caro deserves to see parts of the world she's dreamed of visiting for years. Her decision to follow her heart was necessary and likely overdue. I doubt anything else would have gotten Francis's attention.

Which pisses me off.

Them taking off on their family, taking off on *me*—I'm angry they let their relationship fall apart to the extent they did.

Christ. Do I have the right to feel mad or abandoned when I could have been the one to throw up a red flag about Francis's bad habits years ago?

A lump forms in my throat. I take a big gulp of wine to try to clear it.

"Something on your mind?" Carter's question is quiet, for my ears only.

I shrug, shoving away the urge to ask him to hold me while I untangle my thoughts.

Cypress finally gets through all of Carter's ribbon and paper artistry. She squeals appropriately at the books and bounces over to hug her uncle's knees.

He crouches down for a kiss and whispers something in her ear. Two blond heads bend together, plotting some kind of conspiracy, based on their grins.

Well, then. That's *also* adorable.

He stands and straightens Cypress's tiara for her.

Feeling Bee's gaze measuring the space between us down to the quarter inch, I shift to the side a few steps.

His eyes narrow. "Are you hungry? I'm worried you're hungry. The cupcakes are, admittedly, delicious, but they're not a meal." Carter motions toward the kitchen. "I could whip you up something. A meat product even."

I'm not the only one whose words are running together.

"Later."

A flouncing mass of ruffles and little girl limbs pounces on me before I can figure out how to best ask Carter what the hell's going on in his head.

"You put my name on the paper!" Cypress crows. "I love you, Uncle Auden."

"Love you too, squirt." I steal her glittery wand and tap her on the head with it.

"Nice gift, *Uncle* Auden," Carter says, watching his niece as she bounds back to her pile of loot.

"Enh, Jill's into the honorary aunt-and-uncle thing. Pretty sure Cypress uses the honorific for half of Burlington."

He only looks half convinced.

After presents, we all drift into the kitchen, where Cypress and Odin successfully wheedle another cupcake out of their parents. I have one too. Carter disappears up the stairs again, cell phone glued to his ear.

I can't decide if this crowd is easier to navigate with him at my side or without.

Bee sidles up to me. She takes a drink of buttery yellow wine and sends me a knowing look over the rim of the glass. "You make him smile."

Oof. Play dead, Macarthur.

I jam the rest of my cupcake in my mouth, mumbling, "So good. Might have two," around the crumbs.

"He doesn't smile enough."

Christ. Put three glasses of cheap chard in Bee, and she's a freight train.

"He smiles tons," I say.

"Nope," she says. "So, I got some more answers out of him today on the changes he wants Frank to make at the shop. Heard yesterday's interviewee crashed hard."

I laugh. "An understatement. Glitches from the moment he walked in the door."

"Inevitable, when a guy walks in and catches my nephew with his tongue halfway down your throat."

Carter told her that? Shite. "No more than a quarter-way."

She lets out a single *ha*.

"Wayne was a prick," I say. "More importantly, he doesn't love actual press work. We need to hire an artist who understands spreadsheets, not a business major with an artistic bent."

"Which is what it would have been if Carter had stayed," she says.

"I know," I say. "Proof it wouldn't have worked."

His willingness to stand in front of the C&P and feel what I feel though… Maybe I've been underestimating him.

She takes a drink of her wine. "Seems to be working okay this week."

I jam another half a cupcake in my mouth.

She holds up a finger. "I've got it. I know a few people who work in the Fine Arts department at the university. I'll see if they know of a go-getter senior or master's student with experience on an antique letterpress."

"Not a terrible idea." Pretty sure the university still has a platen press and a Vandercook kicking around somewhere. "Don't worry about making the call. I'll shoot my senior project advisor an email tomorrow. If she's still on staff."

"Tenured and everything," Bee says, grinning.

It has an *I am here for this* edge to it that I suspect goes beyond her approval of me contacting Professor Sharma.

"What?" I say.

"You could make a killing off personalized notebooks like the one you gave Cypress. People love shit with their kids' names on it."

"Okay, but why are you looking at me like I'm a lab experiment?"

"Because my nephew just came down the stairs and can't take his eyes off you."

"He's not—"

"Stop," she says. "I'm far too deep into middle age to have to explain my flights of fancy to someone who's going to scoff and tell me I'm wrong."

Yup. Chard-Bee, pulling into the station at full steam.

I risk a glance at Carter. He took off his sweater upstairs, undid another button on his shirt too, and the V of skin at his neck is a magnet for my gaze.

He lifts a corner of his mouth and winks.

Seriously? With his aunt watching?

Then again, she can probably tell I'm thirsty for a few measly inches of chest. Also for the sparkle in Carter's eyes when he lets himself relax. Who am I to point fingers?

Those pretty eyes—they were always your weak spot.

Christ. I don't need my mum's voice in my head tonight. Not when I'm in Caro and Francis's house and feeling more wrecked about their situation—and my part in it—than I realized.

Carter comes over, bottle of Malbec in hand. He refills my glass. "Did I do okay tonight, Bee?"

She cups his cheek. "Of course, sweet pea. You always do okay. And we always love you. Even during your worst fuckups."

"Bee!" Jill hisses from across the room.

"Oops," Bee says.

Carter's frozen in place. Probably not from his aunt's f-bomb.

"What?" I whisper.

He shakes himself. "Nothing."

"That's a lie," I say.

"And this isn't the place," he says, teeth clenched.

My earlier worries about people watching us seem less important. "Look, I get it. It's weird not to have your parents here. And to be worried about them, even mad at them—"

"Not all of us can fix our relationships with our dads."

I rock back on my heels. "You think my relationship with my da is *mended*? He walked out on me and my mum. I haven't spoken to him in years. There's no coming back from that. From someone *leaving*."

Whelp. Now every eye on the place is on us.

I might as well hang a World's Biggest Bawbag sign around my neck.

Carter's throat bobs and his eyes glisten. "Excuse me."

He leaves out the back door without putting a jacket on.

"He'll be cold without a coat," I blurt.

Bee strokes my upper arm. "I'm sure there's something in the mudroom you could take him."

"Right." I go look, but Carter's wool coat isn't on the rack. Grabbing a thick flannel jacket of his dad's, I toss on my own coat, unzipped, and head out into the chill.

He's standing by the post-and-rail fence. Half leaned over, gripping the top board. A foreign, polished object in the middle of winter-blackened, curling brambles and sleeping plants.

My boots slip on the cornstarch-soft snow as I follow his tracks across the lawn. I drape the jacket over his tense shoulders, then back away. He's only in dress shoes.

"You're going to wreck your loafers. And get rather cold ankles."

He doesn't move.

"Sorry I said that in front of your family." I zip my jacket and jam my ungloved hands in my pockets.

"Shouted, you mean."

"Right." Anger simmers in my gut. He's not innocent here.

Even so, the Prescotts didn't deserve to have their party interrupted by my unmanaged childhood issues.

You weren't a child when Carter left…

Fine. Unmanaged issues, period.

"I'd really hoped to be chill in front of them tonight," I say.

He laughs, but it's dry. "Eventually you get used to fucking up in front of my family."

I want to hold him so badly my arms ache. "Like Bee says, they still love you."

"Do they? Always?"

"Yes, they do. If they didn't, your dad wouldn't have called you for help. Your aunt wouldn't think your shite doesn't stink. Your mum wouldn't text you every day."

He hangs his head, arms still braced on the fence. "I'm afraid…" He smacks the wood with one hand. "Fuck. Never mind. It doesn't matter."

"Doesn't it?"

He wipes his eyes with a bent knuckle. "I can't tell if I'm a sore fucking thumb because of them or because of me."

"Probably both," I say quietly. I join him at the fence and lean a hip on the post a couple of feet from his clenched hands. "It was with my dad. Partly him. Partly me and Mum."

"You were a child."

A child who missed the mark.

It was so, so much easier to have lowered expectations.

A lesson Carter's never learned.

"I was a teenager, not a child. And I'm still mad about him leaving. Might always be."

"I left you too." His voice breaks.

"You did," I say. "And I was mad at you, darling. Furious."

I shiver.

From the cold. Or from holding in the endearment for so long it caused a tremor when it came out.

"Was?" he says. "You're going to tell me you aren't still mad at me?"

That truth swirls between us on a chilly gust of wind.

"I probably am. At you, and at myself. You had to leave," I admit. Nor was I fully honest with him about why I decided to stay.

He blinks in surprise. "You sure didn't think that back when we broke up."

"I'd like to think I've matured, at least a little."

His gaze blazes a trail from my face down my torso. "I'd say you have."

"Not that kind of maturity."

"I know," he says, voice dry. "Just trying to cut the tension."

Or trying to avoid how we're careening toward hashing out why it hurt so bloody much when we broke up. Spending all this time working on avoiding the emotional, it's impossible not to feel the physical.

Over a decade later, and I can still picture every pixel of what his face looked like when I made him come.

Thinking about that is easier than coming up with the words to explain how it felt to aim for everything with him and miss the mark.

Because of my shortcomings, as much as his.

"Maybe," I venture, "if we stop beating ourselves up over still liking to kiss each other, it'll be easier to leave the emotional shite in the past."

He straightens, and the almost-full moon spotlights his expression. The curious tilt, one brow high up above the frames of his glasses. A small smile I want to cover with my own.

"Who says I still like kissing you?" he teases.

"Your hard-on yesterday, darling." It rolls off the tongue a little easier the second time.

Earns a soft "oh" from Carter too.

I steal another one of the breathy sounds when I bend my head to his.

He hitches up onto the top railing, sitting with his knees wide and his feet hooked behind the middle board. He spears his fingers into my hair. The coat draped on his shoulders falls to the ground with a swoosh.

I lean to pick it up.

He keeps me in place, strong hands holding my head and thighs squeezing my hips. "You can warm me up instead."

"Christ, you're corny." His eyes are dancing. He likes it.

I laugh along with him and let my body run ahead of my logic. I open my coat wide, snugging him inside the fabric as much as I can.

He grins and slides his hands around to my back, under my cardigan and T-shirt.

Frigid hands.

I start. "Oh hell, your fingers are icicles."

"Mm-hmm. My feet too," he murmurs against my mouth. "Ask me if I give a shit."

His fingers tuck into the back waistband of my jeans. The cold shocks my warm flesh. Need rips through me. I want those fingers lower, under my boxers. I'd be dropping my jeans to the ground if it wasn't bloody January and there was a risk of frostbite.

I lose track of how long we kiss.

It's long enough for his hands to warm up, for him to undo my belt buckle and tease me between my arse cheeks, just above my rim.

Long enough that Jill sticks her head out the back door. "Carter? I need to get the kids home to bed."

"Fuck." He tips his head back and bites out another curse at the winter-black sky.

I tilt my hips against his, stealing one last reminder of how blessed he is in the cock department.

"Just a sec," he calls to his sister.

I do up my belt and go to step back so he can get off the fence.

"Wait," he says, voice rough. His fingers tuck into the front pockets of my jeans on either side. His eyes are luminous and

115

dark, full of heat and absent of reason. "Once they're gone—stay. I want more of you."

Can I give him more? More than kissing?

It might require fully explaining why I had to let him go.

Or would it? I picked security over a risky, luscious, kaleidoscope life with him. That I did it partly for my mum's sake doesn't fix the choice I made.

And Carter knowing the whole truth isn't going to help anything.

I clear my throat. "Uh, maybe I was sending off the wrong signal by letting you get your hands in my pants. I need more time to think before we... Before I stay."

His face dims and he releases me. "Before we fuck."

"If you want to call it that."

"No point in calling it anything else," he says.

"Uh, yeah. Obviously."

And no point in baring my reasons for letting him go either.

He jumps off the fence and reaches through the boards to grab the now-snow-crusted coat. Shaking off the fabric, he sighs.

"Nothing's obvious with you, Auden. Other than how I can't get you out of my head."

(11)

AUDEN

The minute Carter barrels into the studio space the next day, shirt pressed and hair just so and posture executive straight, I can tell things are going to be awkward.

Not because he's acting strange.

Because he's acting like nothing happened at all.

This is a skill I do not have.

All I can think about is the brilliance of his lips on mine. Years of working to forget that feeling, erased in a few moments of frantic hands and need.

And I'm thinking it was worth it.

"Auden?" Carter's across the table from me, staring at me from behind his glasses. "Did you hear me?"

I straighten on my stool, almost knocking my tea mug off the worktable in the process. "Right. Sorry. Wha'?"

"A rush job. Can we fit one in this week? I got an email from a bride in Concord a few minutes ago. The printer she hired to do her stationery fucked it up, and she doesn't want to work with them even if they fix it. She's asking if we could have a suite done and expedited to her by the weekend. She's willing to pay through the nose."

I take a drink of tepid Genmaicha and pretend to care about this contract. Pretend the hand currently holding up a sheet of loose-leaf for me to read wasn't fondling my arse cheeks yesterday.

Pretend my heart isn't twisting in my chest like an orange peel on an old-fashioned, deciding what our best way forward is.

My hand shakes as I set my mug on the table. "Depends on the design details and color work."

"Line drawing and type. Three colors."

Adding up the time for each print run to dry, I shake my head. "It'd take until next Wednesday, at the earliest. A full suite requires an arseload of design work, which, sorry to say, I don't think you can manage. Not quickly. If I'm creating mock-ups and plates for the next day, day and a half, that puts you running the press for our existing orders. Especially since we have to cut out early on Friday to go check out the Golding."

"I can run the press."

If he says so. We have a finicky job on the go already, needing two days because of the blue-over-yellow design.

Maybe my ill-advised "lesson" the other day will help him be speedy.

All it did for me was make my cock hard.

He sets us up on a Zoom call with the bride on his laptop at the main worktable. After saying hello and confirming our deadlines and price, he leaves me to figure out the design details. She knows what she wants, which speeds up the process. I sketch as we talk about the motifs she's insistent on having on her wedding stationery.

Once I have her wishes nailed down, I agree to touch base after I've created the mock-ups. I sit down at the double-monitor computer in the corner. She wants the watercolor tattoo from her forearm—a blush peony—to inspire the suite. And because the shape will affect the dimensions of the text layout as well as font choices, I want her thumbs-up before we move on to anything else.

Half of me is engrossed in pica and line thickness.

The other half is listening to Carter fumble around behind me. If we had a shop swear jar, he would have filled it this morning alone.

"Need a hand?" I call out.

"Not with work," he says.

Oh.

Well. Maybe he's not acting like *nothing* happened.

A couple of hours later, I've gained the bride's approval on the peony motif and the invitation layout. I'm about to dive into designing the response cards when a right racket explodes from the office.

I roll back on my chair and poke my head down the hall. "Sure you don't need a hand?"

"My dad's goddamn filing system"—I can hear the air quotes from his tone alone—"just collapsed on my coffee and then on my lap—"

I hurry the few steps into the office. Carter's standing in the center, arms up like he's being frisked, shirt drenched with the disgusting no-cream, no-sugar brew he prefers. Pottery shards, receipts, a couple of upside-down shoeboxes, and reams of paper —all soaked in brown liquid—litter the floor.

His eyes squeeze shut. "Help."

I wade through the mess, trying to step on as little paper as possible. Threading my fingers through his, I tug his arms down and kiss him. A tender one, something to bring him back from peak frustration.

He squeezes my hands. Kisses me back, first a little frenetic but then winding down to where I started us off. Languid, easy. Lazy morning lie-in kisses.

Breaking the caress, he sighs and rests his forehead on my shoulder. "I hate messes."

"I know."

"Am I a mess though?"

"Other than your shirt?" I say. "No."

I cannot say the same for me. Not when he's using me to hold himself up.

Francis's computer chimes with an incoming video call before we can start cleaning the debris.

"We'll have to deal with this later, I guess." Carter reaches around me to wake up the screen. "My dad. Perfect timing as always."

"I'll leave you to it."

He grabs my wrist. "No, wait." He clicks to answer, and his dad's face pops up on the screen.

Francis's picture is off-center and tilted. It disappears for a few seconds, a pink blob filling the screen in its place.

"Is he tapping the camera?" I whisper.

"I think so. Dad, we can see you. Stop fussing with your phone."

Francis nudges his metal-framed reading glasses and peers down his nose.

"Mom's been trimming your nose hairs, huh?" Carter says, sitting in the desk chair. "Where are you?"

"In the apartment. Your mom's taking a nap before we go out tonight."

"Sounds nice," Carter grumbles.

"Hi, Francis," I say, pulling up a stool.

"Auden!" His eyes light up. "I miss you."

Carter's shoulders slump. I squeeze his knee, out of camera view. *Dammit, Francis. Get a clue.*

When I go to take my hand away, Carter stops me, lacing his fingers with mine, his palm to the back of my hand.

Francis's eyes narrow. "What's this about interviewing some jackass for a job, boys?"

Jill. What a brat.

"Mom gave you the okay to make a work call, Dad?" Carter's fingers stroke the back of my hand. "I don't want to get you kicked out of the apartment."

Francis makes a face. "We're going to the opera again tonight."

"Sorry to hear that," I say in mock sympathy.

"So this jackass—"

"Nothing to worry about," Carter says. "We're not going to hire him."

"Good, but you've got me worried." My boss presses tented pointer fingers to his chin. "Thought you'd be pickier."

Carter's the human equivalent of a shaken soda can right now. He's almost vibrating in his seat. "Between still doing my actual, more-than-full-time job, trying not to complicate Auden's work too much, and bringing in some improvements, I'm working over a hundred hours a week. For you. So, trust I know what I'm doing."

"Hiring your college-age clone?" his dad says.

Carter deflates.

Hell, the air sucks out of the entire room.

"Dad…"

Anger simmers in my stomach. I'm not sure if Francis meant to imply his son is—or at minimum, used to be—a jackass, but it definitely came across that way, and I can't stand the disappointment pulling at Carter's mouth.

"We're not hiring the bloke," I say.

"You agree we should hire *someone*?" My boss's on-screen gaze is fixed somewhere over my left shoulder.

"Not sure I want to, but I think it's necessary." I flip my hand over, line up my palm with Carter's, and squeeze. "Bee had the idea we might find someone suitable coming out of one of the undergraduate or master's programs at Moo U, so I sent an email to one of my old Fine Arts professors this morning."

"You did?" Carter says, looking amazed.

"Yes."

Francis's jaw drops. "You never seemed to want change—"

"We want you and Caro to come home with your marriage intact." My throat tightens. "So yeah, we need to make changes. Even if you and I don't like it. Hell, I probably should have noticed we were in trouble years ago."

The harrumph Francis lets out probably rings through three arrondissements. "In trouble? You don't think I've been a good boss?"

"No. I love working here. You're more than my boss. You're my mentor—"

"But we're not close enough for you to be honest with me? I expected better of you."

A weight presses on my chest. I rub my breastbone. Is this what Carter feels like on a regular basis? His question about his family loving him—"*Do they? Always?*"—rings in my head. I know they love him, but I'm getting a fraction of the disdain he's lived with his whole life. It bloody stings.

Carter lets go of my hand and puts his arm around me, settling his palm between my shoulder blades. My pulse winds down by a few notches.

"Do you know how hard it is to talk to you sometimes, Dad?" he says.

"That true, Auden?" Francis asks.

"Can be," I admit. "Nor have I been sitting here for the past twelve years, wishing we were doing things differently. You know I've doubted Carter's plans. Some of them scare the shite out of me. I won't let him be hasty. Still, I'm seeing his point on a few items."

Carter's fingertips dig into my skin above the neck of my T-shirt.

Francis grumbles some more. "I'd better go."

"Have a good night, Dad."

"Night, Francis."

"Don't kill each other," he says. I'm half expecting him to tell us to stop kissing at work too, but he says goodbye without adding any other advice. Jill must not have passed along that juicy nugget.

The screen goes blank.

Carter braces his hands on his knees and cradles his head in his palms. He lets out a long *fuuuuuuuck.*

I draw idle circles on his back with my palm. "Shh."

"I swear, he thinks of me as a newly graduated kid."

"A week ago, I might have disagreed, but yeah, that call was a bit of a cock-up."

His eyes light up. "I'll show—"

"Do not say, 'I'll show you cock-up,'" I say. "Weren't you just bemoaning being seen as immature?"

"There is nothing immature about my cock, Auden," he says in mock seriousness.

"For Christ's sake," I mutter. I kiss him anyway, then glance at the still-disastrous floor. "We should clean up this mess before we tear any of the receipts or cut ourselves on mug shards."

We start to sort wet paper, binning anything we don't need to keep.

"You had your boss voice on, like you did with Wayne," Carter says. "FYI—it makes me hot."

"Of course you have an office-power kink."

"No," he says. "I just like how you sound when you assert yourself."

"And when I agree with you."

He laughs. "That helps, yeah. Anyway, my dad's lucky to have you as his right-hand man. If he was smart, and if you were willing, you should have created a gradual-purchase structure years ago."

I rock back on my heels, almost tipping over in my crouched position. Taking on more responsibility this week hasn't been all bad. There's a rewarding element to it when things go right. The possibility of it going wrong is what weighs in my gut.

I dump a handful of broken pottery bits into the bin. "Why do you care so much?"

His confident expression falters. "I... I want you to be happy. And reaching for more magnifies happiness."

It's so, so tempting to believe him. Hard, when it's never proven true for me.

It also falls flat considering our past. Carter's brilliant at reaching for more in his professional life. He does the opposite with his heart.

"When you're an aim-high kind of person, you tend to crash hard," I say.

"Only if you crash. Why do you think you would, were you to be the boss?"

"The higher you go, the more uncertainty there is. Where I am now, it's a happy medium. I can pay my rent, help my mum, feel good about the work I do. And save myself the stress entailed in having my name on the sign. Look at your dad, Carter. And you. Are either of you actually happy?"

He stares at the floor. "You should get back to the peony suite. I'll finish up here."

And because I don't push higher, don't push for more, I leave without insisting he answer my question.

12

CARTER

Am I happy?

Why would he ask that?

I work the rest of the Wednesday shift running the press while Auden rolls up his sleeves (hot), sticks a pencil behind his ear (charming), and makes the wedding suite plates. Then I stick around for five hours after the fact, catching up on communications with my OfficeMart team. I hold an online meeting with the West Coast regional execs, and I manage to doodle a whole stack of personal stationery ideas while troubleshooting some of their merchandising concerns. All with a smile on my face.

Would I have done that if I wasn't fucking happy?

My stomach sinks. For the sake of reaching for the elusive brass ring, I might have. And I've gotten ahold of it, my success confirmed by a sparkly new title and office, a team of skilled people who work for me, and a company with healthy annual sales growth. It's great. It does bring happiness.

It's also lonely.

I've been quick to criticize my dad about how much time he puts toward Imprescott. About his shitty organizational skills and appalling record keeping. And though there's no excuse for letting his relationship with my mom disintegrate, he has built something he loves.

I want to help him fix it. Make it so he can have both things—his business and his family.

And maybe it's time I figure out how *I* can have both those things.

Sitting at my dad's desk, headache brewing because I haven't had anything to drink in a few hours and I'm thirsty, I'm still mulling over Auden's question.

I still don't know what my honest response would be.

Wine makes you happy. And it's a drink.

True, though not a particularly effective headache remedy. But grabbing a glass at Vino and Veritas would mean being in the vicinity of Auden's forearms and pencil-bearing ear.

I really want that right now.

I jam my doodles in the pocket of my wool coat and lock up.

The street is relatively empty, but the place is hopping. The only seat available at the bar is on the opposite end from where Auden is crafting something delicious. He's absorbed in whatever he's mixing and doesn't notice me claim the last stool by the wall.

The pencil is no longer tucked behind his ear. But his sleeves are still rolled up, and I'm not the only one at the bar who's enjoying the sight, given how crowded it is at Auden's end of the long, glossy slab of wood.

The redheaded bartender of dropping-a-tray-of-drinks-and-needing-stitches fame sees me arrive though. Molly, according to Auden. She bounces over, singing along to the jazz playing on the speakers.

"You're Carter Prescott, right? I hear you like a Dirty Scot." She leans in conspiratorially. "Want me to get Auden?"

"Nah, just pour me whatever wine you like best. And a water, please. Auden doesn't need anyone in his way."

"Oh, I assure you, he does." She serves me up a glass of a local white blend.

"Maybe so, but not me."

"Disagree." Molly grins. Auden mentioned to me that for all she lacks in bartending skills, she has a heart of gold. I can see what he means. Her smile makes a person feel like they can take on the world.

Or if not the world, at least the shitload of complications inherent in getting closer to the big-hearted hottie tending bar in a black dress shirt and dark jeans.

The clothes would look better strewn on the floor of my parents' spare bedroom.

I like watching him. He's in his element, and it's easier to notice the small parts of him from a distance when I'm not getting overwhelmed by the whole. The flash of silver rings on his hand when he shakes a few drops of bitters into a rocks glass. The tendrils of hair at his neckline. He was made for the needed-a-haircut-two-weeks-ago look.

He moves with efficiency. He does that at the shop too, never wasting an ounce of energy.

I smile at Molly, needing her on my side. "I have a surprise for him, and it's not quite done. So, let's see how long we can keep him from seeing me."

"Got it."

Pulling out my sketches, I add some more detail. A few more leaves to the seasons-in-Vermont set, no text, anchored by a maple tree in its annual variations framing the top and left margins. Another variation of his monogram creation with horizontal rainbow lines on either side of the centered letter.

Design work is really fucking fun. Why the hell doesn't Auden want everyone in the world to see the ones he's made?

"I want that," Molly says, pointing at the rainbow design. She fumbles with the beer the guy next to me ordered. Only his quick reflexes keep the pint from spilling over my sketches. "Oops, sorry. But really—where can I get a set?"

"Talk to your coworker," I say. "He's the one with the gift for multiple colors."

"Auden!" she calls over her shoulder. "I need you to make this for me!"

He turns. His gaze lands on me, and his eyes widen.

And for the second time tonight, I'm gifted with a light-up-the-world smile. Except, unlike Molly's, this one's just for me. For *my* world. It barrels into the dark corners of my soul.

He makes his way over, switching ends of the bar with Molly. "Spying on me?"

Ooh, the full Scottish-accent treatment. He likes that I'm here.

"Figured I deserved a reward after a long meeting."

Bracing his hands on the edge of the counter, he contemplates this. "The wine? Or me?"

"My reward?"

He nods.

"Depends on you, I guess." I reach across the bar and trace a lazy pattern on the back of his hand.

His bearded jaw juts as he pulls his lower lip between his teeth. "I'm working until close."

And I'm running out of days.

"I can wait," I say.

His dark brows knit. "For what, exactly?"

"No fucking clue, but I'm up for figuring it out."

He picks up my sketch. "I can see why Molly likes this."

"Will you do a run of it?"

"For her? Yeah. And for the bookstore, if Harrison wants it."

"And for the website?" I ask.

He rubs the back of his neck, and I want to tuck myself to his side and lay kisses on him until he relaxes.

His throat bobs. "I'll think about it."

13

AUDEN

My Thursday shift at Imprescott stutters to a close just as I finish up the last-minute wedding contract. Perfect timing, really. I'll be home in time for dinner and a soak in the tub to ease the tension in my shoulders.

I'm getting ready to leave when Carter's simple, colorful design catches my eye. It's tacked up on the board behind my computer screen. Molly's hopeful expression from last night is tacked on my brain. And I want to make them both smile even if I don't get home to my bath right away.

You never work late.

I ignore the inner voice that always puts things in perspective.

It's wrong. This project is a favor for a friend, not working. And if it happens to turn into something more... It's Carter's design, not mine. It also won't require me to make plates—I can use existing wood type and blocks with lines. The multiple colors, not the design, will make it more involved, but that's just time.

And both Carter and Molly are worth some time.

Instead of a monogram in between the bands of lines, I decide to place *love* in the center. Lowercase, Bernhard Modern. It's a pretty serif typeface, a titch decorative, but will still look crisp to anchor the letterhead.

And since I'm going through the bother of setting up one round of type and six of the line blocks, I might as well print extra.

I work without stopping until I have a stack of five hundred bright white cotton rag with purple text and the bottom line of the rainbow. It'll look right sharp once I'm done.

The back doorknob rattles, and my heart leaps. Shite, I'm not near cleaned up enough for Carter to see this—

"Carter? Auden?"

Jill.

"Just me," I call out, feeding a few more sheets through the press, one at a time.

She struts into the studio, a curious look on her face. "Where's my brother? At home?"

"Somewhere in between here and Montreal."

"He *left*?" Her voice cracks.

"No. Needed to run up and back for a meeting of some sort."

"Oh." There's relief there but still disappointment. She frowns. "I was going to ask you guys to dinner. I had a rough day at school and reached my limit with my own kids about the time Odin decided to decorate the fridge with a Sharpie he found in my school bag."

I wince. "We have some solvent that might get that off."

"Will's working on it. And he told me to escape for a few hours, drown my sorrows in sushi and Sapporo. Bee's coming."

Smiling apologetically, I shake my head. "Sorry, love, I need to finish up here."

"You don't work after hours."

"This is a labor of love, not a contract," I say.

She glances at the purple text. "Literally *love*."

"Your brother's idea," I explain. "And I want to make a nice stack of them, given it's going to take me a few days to run all the colors."

"You're making him something?" Her tone suggests she's seeing a little project as far more significant than it is.

"It's letterhead, not an engagement ring." *That's* still sitting in my sock drawer, a match to the Celtic-etched, silver band I've worn on my right hand since I moved away from Scotland.

Her jaw drops. "You've been thinking about *engagement rings*?"

"Christ, Jill, no."

"But getting back together—"

"Still no' possible," I say. "And this project is just for fun. Carter designed it. Molly wanted some. And with your brother wanting to sell some more product online, this seemed the place to start."

With one of his projects—when it invariably doesn't fly out the door as he expects it will, I won't have to feel guilty.

"Bee is going to die when she hears this," Jill says.

I start feeding the press again. If I'm fast enough, and if the ink dries, I should be able to get the blue line done tonight. "There's nothing for Bee to hear."

Jill doesn't believe a word of what I'm saying. That's okay. She'll say what she wants to say, and Bee will hear what she wants to hear. The only thing I can control are my own expectations, which are set at a below-baseline height.

I shoo Jill out, promising I'll join her for sushi another time, and get back to work. The stack of partially finished letterhead looks crisp and like something a gaggle of Instagram paper geeks would want to post. Maybe Carter's right. Maybe we can create more buzz and with it more sales. Of something that's still unique and meaningful.

My heart cramps. Thoughts like that careen dangerously close to wanting more out of life.

The press clicks and whumps, a calm heartbeat contrasting with my own jagged pulse.

Reaching, striving... Whenever I do it, fear needles me in my side. If I don't learn from Mum's experience, am I a shite son? If I take heed from her pain, will I have at least made her devastation a little more worthwhile? God knows the time I failed to learn from her experience, I ended up in the exact predicament she'd predicted: alone and hurting.

Don't want for something so big that when you lose it, it wrecks you.

I force myself to take a breath.

Making five hundred sheets of letterhead is not big. Carter trying to sell it isn't going to put the shop in financial straits. And in one more week, things will be back to normal.

If only the prospect of normal filled me with as much excitement as the potential of opportunity.

The letterhead looks even better with the blue line on it. I get the stack tucked away in a place Carter won't look and am in the middle of cleaning ink off the rollers and plate when the back door clicks open again.

This time there's no mistaking the snap of dress shoes on the cement floor. Carter is snow-dusted and highway worn. He takes off his glasses to polish the foggy lenses.

"You're still here. And still working?" He sounds baffled. And almost disappointed, which is odd because he's worked far later most nights he's been here.

"The wedding suite took a long time," I said. Not a lie, exactly. It filled my whole workday.

Finished with cleaning the ink, I wash my hands one last time and wipe them on the towel hanging on a rack on the wall.

He comes over to the sink and strokes my face. I can smell the cold on him. "You didn't have to do that, baby. Especially with the late night we're going to have tomorrow."

Such a silly word, *baby*.

I eat it up, like I always did. "Take me for lunch next week and we'll call us even."

He winces. "Next week…"

My stomach drops. "If you're here."

He takes my hand. A loose link of fingers. Not tight enough to suggest anything beyond casual emotion. Tugging me over to the table, he sits on one of the stools and looks up at me. "Do you want me to be?"

There are about eight answers to his question. They're all partially correct. And none of them are right.

I both want him with me all the time and want him to go back to Montreal and forget I exist.

I don't know how to make sense of that in my head.

I don't know how to explain it either.

I lean a hip on the counter and flatten my free palm against the top, bracing my weight. "Still doesn't seem like your parents are itching to leave Paris."

"Nope."

"You've been home two weeks—I get you can't stay longer. I'll make do. If you manage the website from Montreal, I can inter-view a couple of students and tread water on the incoming contracts."

"You want me to handle everything at a distance?" His voice is measured, a practiced tone. His face is getting more blank by the second.

Of course he can disguise his emotions. He'd have to, having climbed the corporate ladder the way he has. Trading his college T-shirts for suits, vintage Adidas for pristine leather brogues. He might have been in a top-thirty-five-under-thirty-five list in some Canadian business magazine a couple of years ago, but he sure as hell wasn't wearing eyeliner in the picture like he used to when we went to parties on campus.

So yeah, he hides. And his skilled veiling of his feelings leaves me nothing to go off. I'm not sure what answer he's hoping I give.

"I..."

His grip tightens on my hand. "Be honest."

"I don't want you to stay and then run into problems at work," I say. An easy admission. No risk there.

"That came up during the executive meeting today. A few people understand completely. A few others think we should sleep and breathe OfficeMart."

"You'd know something about that," I say.

"Ha ha." He glares playfully. "The company's at least used to people working remotely, and the fact I've driven up twice has helped." He yawns and makes a face. "I could do without the six hours return to Whitingham tomorrow."

"I'll drive." Excitement buzzes through me—we'll have a new toy to play with.

And six hours in the truck with Carter... I'm buzzing about that too.

We had some of our best moments messing around in the cab of the F-150 he used to own.

"And after we get back—do you want me to stay for longer?" he says.

He asked for honesty, which he deserves, even if my truthful answer is rubbish. "I don't know."

Life is easier when he's not here.

It's also less exciting. There's something electrifying about having him crunching numbers in his dad's office or dressed down and working the press or showing up on one of my barstools. Gives me the same feeling I get when I open a box of the handmade paper we get from Europe and the smell of fine artisanry and new possibilities washes over me.

"I like having you here," I admit. More than like. "But 'stay around for longer' doesn't mean 'stay around forever.'"

And if I like him being here too much, it's going to be a whole lot harder when he leaves for good.

The blank expression slides from his face. Only six inches away in body, but an ocean of space in the figurative. He looks tired and rejected.

A feeling I know intimately. My chest tenses, warring with the frustration in my belly.

His feelings are a product of his choices as much as my indecision, for Christ's sake. This isn't all on me giving him a wishy-washy answer.

But the past two weeks have reminded me of how his choices

were a defense mechanism as much as selfishness in action. And our breakup was less about him leaving and more about the two of us having different priorities.

Distance can be overcome. Worldviews, not so much.

"It's hard to line it all up, Carter," I say. "You've been a ghost for years. And now you're very, very tangible." I massage my forehead with my fingertips. "And confusing."

He brushes my hair from my face, then trails his hand along my beard. "I don't want to confuse you."

"Maybe that's not the right word." I turn my head to nip at his thumb. "Contradictory?"

"Inadvisable?" he offers, running a fingertip on my lower lip.

"I think we both know that."

"How much do we care?"

We're facing each other, his legs spread wide on his stool, mine stretched between them. If he shifted forward, he'd be straddling my hips.

Yes, please.

I hook his belt loops with my fingers and tug.

There's no resistance. He shrugs out of his wool coat and eases against me, the hard angles of him sliding against my bigger, softer-around-the-edges body.

He glances toward the front window of the shop and smiles, clearly realizing I closed the blinds when it got dark. His full lips tilt, naughty anticipation bundled in a half smile.

I slide my hands down his back and cup his arse. Hissing out a breath, I hold him in place.

My dick is right on board with having a lap full of Carter. I cant my hips, needing the friction against my thickening length.

He bites his lip.

"Give me that mouth, darling."

He does.

Bossy, plush lips that taste like kissing until the sun comes up.

All the ten-dollar words in the world defining all the ways this is wrong can piss off forever.

14

CARTER

I hope this stool is sturdy, because between the two of us, we're probably topping four hundred pounds.

If we break it, I'll replace it. His hands on my ass, being able to press and circle against his hardening shaft—it's too perfect to care about the furniture. I don't know exactly what we're going to get up to, but we're finally alone with nowhere to go. And we both understand this can't be more than kissing, touching, getting each other off.

"Fess up. You closed the blinds because you knew we were going to do this," I mumble against his eager lips.

"It creeps me out to be watched after hours." He bends his head and kisses my neck. "I didn't *know* anything. Didn't know you'd be in."

I hum my approval. I'm still surprised he's here so late. I just came to pick up my laptop.

"Also…" He loosens my tie further, undoes the top button of my shirt, and tastes me like I'm a delectable petit four. "Define *this*."

His tongue swirls.

"Fuuuuuck." Need pelts my skin. My hips rock.

Auden licking the hollow of my neck is a million times more satisfying than compiling everything I have to send to our web designer.

And this time we're not freezing our balls off in a snowy backyard.

"This," I say, "is sex."

He growls.

"I'm clean. Up-to-date and everything. Are you?" I ask.

"Yeah." He chuckles, and something dirty, needy, flickers in his green eyes. "I'm not fucking you here."

Oof. He saves his *fucks* for when it really matters, and this one turns me on like a light switch.

"You're not fucking me anywhere," I say. "That's my job."

"Says who?"

Gripping his muscular shoulders, I lean back as far as I can without upsetting our teeter-totter balance. "Two and a half years of precedence?"

His biceps tense, stretching his T-shirt as he holds my ass against his quads. Being decently tall myself, I'm used to being bigger than my partners. But Auden... with his thick thighs and upper body the size of a house, he makes a man feel delicate.

"I think a decade-plus separation cancels out any previous patterns," he says.

I sift my fingers through his hair, trying to make sense of what he's saying. In all our time together, I always topped. "You don't—"

"Didn't." He kisses me.

Auden, over me. Controlling my pleasure, taking his own...

Fuck, I'm aching.

"And you want to?" I croak the question.

"We'll see."

Goddamn, I need to flip the tables on him. Get him as turned on as I'm getting from a few kisses and words spoken with those lilting vowels of his.

Climbing off his lap, I spin him on his stool and take his hands in mine. I bend my head, kissing him for a minute. Soaking in his minty taste, his rough groans. He shifts his arms, trying to move his hands, but I keep them at his sides.

"Carter…"

"What?"

"Let me touch ye."

Touch ye. He could not be sexier. "Later."

I spread his arms wider and curve his hands around the edge of the table behind him, like what he made me do to the shelf of the press the day he almost had me coming from a few words and a mimicked heartbeat. "Hold on."

He looks up at me, curiosity and trust in his gaze. He licks his lips. "Wha' 're ye doing?"

"Kissing you some more."

I'm tenting my pants like I stuck a damn letterpress handle behind my zipper. And after his little *I'm not fucking you here* proclamation, I'm looking forward to getting him to drop his *T*s for a week.

"Mmm." Auden licks into my mouth. "I take it I'm no' permitted to let go of the table?"

"You always were smart." It's impossible to tear my mouth from his, but nothing says I must, apart from losing any finesse with getting his belt undone. I fumble with the buckle and the button of his jeans. Slide the zipper down with two fingers. His dick presses into my hand.

I barely touch it. A faint brush against his cotton-covered length with the back of my knuckles.

"Why so hesitant?" His eyes darken. Need, not irritation.

"Who wants to rush something like this?" I delve under the elastic of his boxers and stroke my thumb along his crown, catching a bead of moisture.

"Me." He breathes the word, lifts his hips up, jeans stretching across his thighs. "Hurry up."

I strip his pants and underwear to his shins. "No."

There's a lever on his stool. I depress it so he sinks a foot

138

lower.

He inhales, surprise and anticipation all bound up in one little gasp.

I smile. Just a hitch.

His pupils flare.

My coat will have to sub in as a cushion. Folding it into a square, I lay it between his feet and then kneel in front of him.

He's still holding on to the table, and I'm not going to let him let go, not yet. I might be the one on the floor, but he's at my mercy—arms spread wide, knees fallen open, cock thick against his belly, waiting for me to lick it.

Slipping my lips over the plump tip, I coax another moan from him. A pleasure-filled noise rumbles in his chest.

It's been a long time since I had the weight of him in my palm, the salty taste of him on my tongue. I haven't been a monk since I moved to Montreal. When you live in one of the sexiest cities in the world and only casually date for over ten years, it's hard not to rack up a fair number of hookups. My hand though, it's like it has cell memory. No other cock felt quite like Auden's.

No other man makes *me* feel like I do when I have him in my mouth.

Powerful. And honored, like I'm being given something special, the gift of his consent.

I'm obsessed with his hot, anticipatory scowl. I want to see it once he's gone over.

Once all the need and expectation is washed away by the wave of coming so fucking hard he sees spots.

I need to make sure I still remember how to best do that. I pull back. "Do you still like it shallow?"

"Aye," he says on a breath.

I lick, suck, savor hot skin on my needy tongue.

I'm going to reduce Auden to a heap of sated man, and it's going to be the most fun thing I've done in weeks.

More fun than getting your corner office?

Maybe.

Ignoring the warning bell of surprise ringing in my head, I cup his balls in one hand and jack him with the other, focusing my tongue on the very tip of him.

His hips snap. "Carter—"

Humming encouragement around his thick erection, I take him in halfway.

One of his hands lands on the back of my head and tugs my hair.

Mmm, yes.

I'm aching, but I can deal with that later, on my own if necessary.

Shit, when was the last time I wasn't driven by mutual release?

The last time I let myself get attached to someone, I guess. Which was with this man.

His cock is iron. I glance up, getting a read for how close he is.

Head tipped back, jaw clenching, throat taut… Perfect. I've got him wound tight, and now it's time to spin him back to reality.

One more swirl of my tongue…

"Oh… Carter… Jesus *Christ.*"

His hand is a vise in my hair. I keep him between my lips as he comes, making sure to follow through until he's experienced every bit of pleasure I can give him.

His body relaxes, knees still wide. His mouth is slack, dreamy. He opens his eyes. They're glassy and soft-focused.

My chest aches. I managed to pleasure him, sure, but his gaze lacks the depth I used to crave. I miss seeing affection in that gaze, seeing… seeing love.

Fuck. I can't do this. I can't let myself—

"You always gave the best head, darling," he says, cutting into my rising panic. A rattling noise comes from the back door, and he stiffens. "What the—?"

"Auden!" My aunt's sing-song voice interrupts from the back door. "I brought you dinner!"

15

AUDEN

"Oh shite!" I exclaim under my breath.

The back door slams shut and Bee's footsteps clunk in the hall.

Carter's a blur of motion. He jumps up, bringing his coat with him as a curtain.

I yank up my jeans faster than a kid who accidentally dropped trou on stage during a school play.

Bee appears with a flourish of winter layers and carryout containers. She strikes a pose behind Carter, who's frantically glancing over his shoulder. "If you won't come to the sushi, the sushi will come to you!"

"Wow, thank you," I croak, doing up my belt buckle as quietly as I can. There's a joke about coming in there, but my mind is currently the consistency of mushy peas. "Where's Jill?"

"She had to head home after dinner, so you get me as your delivery gal."

"Brilliant," I say.

"Carter, what's up with your coat?" Bee asks.

"I'm showing Auden the lining," Carter improvises, turning to display the colorful pattern to his aunt.

"Ooh, pretty." She plops the cartons on the table a few feet from where I'm certain I saw God.

I mean, my ears are still ringing from Carter sucking me off. Add in the shock of being walked in on three seconds later, and it's a wonder I didn't have a coronary.

Also, a wonder she hasn't immediately figured out what we were doing. Or maybe she did and is just being polite.

Her mouth twitches.

Yep, polite. Bollocks. We're never living this down.

My brain clears enough to register that the silk stitched into the inside of Carter's coat is actually worth a look. And maybe if we distract Bee, she'll let us off the hook.

"Are those very tiny cows?" I squint at the intricate print.

"Yes. A bespoke tailor friend of mine likes to use me as a guinea pig for his new designs and is perennially amused by my having gone to a school nicknamed Moo U."

Bespoke. Wow. And he was just using it as a pillow so he could get on his knees for me.

He keeps destabilizing me with these moments of selflessness, and I don't know what to do with them.

"And it doubles as a shield when you need to hide your boyfriend's wang from your aunt. Fucking useful," Bee says blandly, opening one of the containers of sushi and helping herself to a piece of spicy salmon roll.

"Jesus," Carter mutters.

"Oh, I'm sure he's proud too," she says. "Took the two of you long enough."

"To what?" I ask.

"To get back together."

"We're not." Carter and I say that in unison.

He sits on his stool, takes the chopsticks out of their paper wrapper, and rubs them against each other to remove any slivers.

"Mmm, okay." She holds out the container. "Sashimi?"

I'm suddenly ravenous, so I accept the offering and grab the chopsticks from Carter. "Thanks for cleaning them off."

"What, I don't get fed too?"

"Didn't know you were here, or I would have ordered more," Bee says.

"I'll share." I hold out a piece of tuna tataki for him.

"It's okay. I had a late lunch." He takes the piece between his lips. *Of your dick*, his eyes say, scanning me, hot and knowing.

"I talked to your mom today," Bee says to Carter. "She sounded ecstatic. Mentioned your dad was acting like he was a twenty-year-old kid again."

He swallows his mouthful and nods. "Paris will do that to a person. Even in January."

"I don't know. I think it's more about your dad working to actually remove his head from his ass and recognize how damaging his choices have been for his marriage," Bee says.

Carter's cheek tenses. I'm not sure the reaction is to his aunt's opinion on his parents' relationship or a flicker of realization that he and his dad share the same tendency to work at the expense of love.

"Do you really think so?" he says. "Dad sure was grumpy when we Skyped with him yesterday."

"His mood was more about you and him being at loggerheads than him and your mom," I point out.

He scowls. "I've been bending over backward for him. Tomorrow's gambit included."

"Ooh, what's happening tomorrow?" Bee asks.

"We're going to fucking Whitingham to check out a press for sale."

Her face lights up. "I have a friend down there, owns an inn. You should book a night."

"We're not going for a romantic getaway," Carter grumbles.

"I dunno," I say, keeping my tone light. "I'm driving. Maybe I'll kidnap you and force you to *not* work for a night."

"We're not going for a romantic getaway," he repeats, eyes slightly wild.

I pretend to be unfazed. "Your loss."

And mine. Loss of pride, mainly. Bee's looking at me, pity on her face.

"You're going home then?" she asks Carter, still watching me.

He sneaks another roll with his fingers and eats it. "Auden and I were talking about logistics before we"—he clears his throat —"got sidetracked. My thought was to manage as much as I can from Montreal, and Auden can carry the rest until Dad gets home."

"Which will mean a backlog for him to come home to," I say.

"Right." Carter grimaces. "Maybe, for Mom and Dad's sake, it'll be better for us to work together for one more week. Might prevent Dad from falling into bad habits at whatever point he gets home."

Bee's smile broadens. I'm thinking she likes Carter's suggestion more due to her whole "get back together" dream than the benefits for Imprescott Designs.

Carter straightens on his stool. "It's probably worth it for me to stay."

My stomach twists.

It wasn't worth it for him to stay for me.

I'm well aware it's not the same, but I can't shake the irrational response.

"One more week?" I sound like I have something stuck in my throat.

Something like years of built-up anger and longing and second-guessing, maybe.

"I think I can make it work. I'm running low on 'you owe me' capital, but what are they going to do, take away my promotion?" His smile lacks his usual confidence.

"Don't do anything irreversible," I caution.

He looks at me, brown gaze piercing through me.

Is what's happening between us irreversible already?

Because I'm feeling things, and I'm not sure they're the temporary kind.

"It's all under control," Carter says.

I swallow. Glad that's the case for one of us.

Bee takes off a few minutes later, leaving us to stare at each other.

I step forward to kiss him.

He presses a finger over my lips before I reach his mouth. "I didn't make you come because I wanted you to return the favor. I just wanted you to feel good."

I palm his muscular chest with both hands. Christ, those lunchtime gym sessions do good things for his pecs. "I want to do the same for you."

"I— Not tonight."

I narrow my eyes. "You sure?"

"Yeah. It just— The moment's gone."

"Uh, okay. If you say so, darling."

His breath catches. Blanking his expression, he shrugs into his coat. "I shouldn't like it when you call me that."

"But you do?"

He pulls me in for a fast, raw kiss. "Too much."

"I felt the same when you called me *baby* yesterday."

He pales. "I... I called you *baby*?"

"Yeah."

"And you liked it too much."

"I did."

Shaking his head, he backs away. "We should stop that. Stop liking it."

He's jittery. It's endearing. And I'll let him off the hook for tonight. "Consider it stopped."

16

AUDEN

Carter arrives at the shop in a swirl of snow and grumpiness the next morning. Handsome grumpiness, mind you. The creases at the corners of his eyes and dark circles underneath do nothing to make him less pretty. He's carrying two disposable travel cups with the V and V logo on them. He puts them down on the worktable next to where I'm sitting and takes his foggy glasses off.

"Good morning," I say.

"Morning." He frowns. "Damn it. I can't see well enough to find a tissue box."

I take the glasses out of his hand and gently polish them on the hem of my T-shirt, then slide them back onto his face. "Better?"

His mouth softens into a smile. He runs his thumb from my temple to my jaw. "Yes."

My throat tightens. I fight the urge to tilt my face and kiss his palm. I don't want to lean into his hand. Not until I know where his head is at, what he's hoping for.

Shaking his head in something near to self-reproach, he steps back and hands me one of the cups. "London Fog with lavender syrup in it. Sounded good. And you always liked sweet shit."

"And yet I liked you."

"It's a mystery," he mutters.

"I had my reasons."

The shuttered look on his face reminds me he doesn't want to hear any of them. Our time to fix things by talking passed years ago.

Which makes spending six hours in a car together sound grand.

"Still want me to drive this afternoon?" I say.

"Yeah, your truck's in better shape than my dad's." He glares out the front window at the lightly falling snow. "The weather just had to cooperate."

"It's not forecast to get any heavier," I say. "We can check the highways website before we leave."

"Four o'clock?"

"If we want to meet the guy on time."

"If we're going to bother going, we're not going to be fucking late."

If he's going to be a pissy bastard about it… "I can go myself, if you want."

"Long drive to make by yourself." His gaze goes from irritated to serious. "Do you not want me to come? I mean, I told my dad I'd go, but I suppose as long as you come back with the press, I don't need to be with you."

Talk about our problems from an age ago, summed up in one phrase. He *did* need to be with me. And when I pointed that out, explained it wasn't so easy for me to just up and leave a solid job offer to move countries again, he decided "with me" wasn't good enough.

I know the answer hasn't changed, so I would never ask again, even if I wanted him to. His life isn't here. But spending time with him this week… I'm liking it too much to enforce any degree of self-protection.

"Aye, I want you to come," I say.

He nods jerkily. "I have some meetings to deal with before then." He pulls his phone out of his pocket. "I'm emailing you a

147

list of stores across the country that might be interested in some of your work. Let me know what you think."

He doesn't even surface for lunch.

And I think I'm going to retch. *Across the country. Absolutely not.*

I bury myself in the peony suite. Once I've done what I can with it for the moment, I head out to pick up the trailer and pallet truck I rented. I'm hoping the Golding will be suitable to buy and ready for us to bring it home tonight.

I don't get another chance to work on Carter's rainbow-stripes project until midafternoon when I eke out the time to add the green and yellow ink.

And as I'm working on it—and admiring the combination of Carter's simple design and my skill with the press—I can't help but think about how much more we could accomplish together.

Things on that email he sent you.

Things that I never would have thought of had he not planted the seed. National reach... I know I'm good at my job. I do some right pretty presswork. It *could* garner attention if promoted with a deft hand, like Carter's.

You're being daft, son. Don't set yourself up for disappointment.

Mum's solid advice filters through the nonsensical feelings swelling in my chest.

My fist clenches, crumpling the sheet of cotton rag paper in my hand before I can add it to the stack of five hundred.

Four hundred ninety-nine now. Damn.

I make a ball out of the wrecked sheet and send it flying into the nearest recycling bin.

I stack the paper in my chosen hidey-hole behind a rack of metal type and imagine it in one of the clear-topped boxes I chose to package the sets I already made for Harrison. If it got placed as far as Carter suggested we should aim for, I could fly across the country and visit my work in boutiques on the West Coast.

My stomach can't decide whether that daydream is thrilling or nauseating.

Column B, stomach. Column B. I don't need to be known in some random rubbish store in California. I'll finish the gift for Molly and Carter, enjoy the smiles on their faces. Sell the remainder in stacks of fifty at V and V. And if Carter wants me to make him a few special designs to hock on the website, I'll do that for him. Not more than that, not expanding beyond our little niche. Stroking my ego isn't worth the financial outlay and the potential failure and bankruptcy.

Speaking of egos, I haven't seen Carter and his healthy-sized one in a few hours. He's been holed up in the office, mostly on Zoom calls, so we've barely had the chance to talk about last night.

About why he was so willing to blow me but wouldn't let me reciprocate. I can't tell if he's avoiding intimacy or just selfless.

Probably the first. Carter's a lot of things, but he's made a few selfish decisions in his time that are impossible to forget. Then again, recently, he's been on the giving end. It almost seems like he's learning the definition of the word compromise.

And tonight I'm going to get six solid hours with him and his newfound generosity in my truck as we venture down to the Mass border.

He won't be able to avoid me like he did last night.

At 3:58, I stroll into Francis's office.

Carter is sprawled in the chair, head resting on the high back with his eyes closed. His glasses sit on the pad of legal paper in front of him on the desk. With an unbuttoned collar and rumpled hair, he looks the opposite of a driven executive.

Or maybe this is the shadow side of that, the reality of working without a break.

I walk over to the desk and step between his legs. The large antique can hold my weight, so I lean on it. I rub my knee on the inside of his, finally earning his gaze.

It's full of heat and regret and frustration.

If he'd let me, I could ease some of that.

149

"Need me to take the edge off before we head out?" I say. "Suck some of your long day out of your cock?"

His eyes widen, just a fraction. He licks his lips. "I— No, we should go."

I blink, lifting a brow at him. "If I didn't know we had somewhere to be, I'd be insulted you keep blowing me off."

He snorts and leans forward a little to stroke his fingers along my thighs. It's like my jeans are made of tissue rather than denim. "Pun intended?"

"Let's pretend it was."

"I'll take a rain check. We don't want to be rolling back into town at midnight, especially if we're towing a trailer with a press on board. How's the snow?"

His thumbs creep higher. If I didn't have jeans on, he'd be sneaking inside my boxers. I wear them snug on a good day, but they get tighter, like they always do when any part of Carter is touching me.

"Still light." I straighten, shifting away from his hands.

He pulls back, expression blank.

Maybe he doesn't want me as much as I want him.

A rubbish feeling, that.

"I'll bring my truck round back," I say, voice tight. I don't know how to manage what's happening here. Wanting him, wanting to give as well as take. Wanting to blurt out all my desires, my fears.

Knowing that would make things infinitely worse.

It's going to be a bloody long drive, making sure I keep my mouth sealed shut.

17

CARTER

"Carter. Love, wake up."

I do, but slowly. The burred words swirl through my chest, muddling me worse than I already am from sleep and the heat blasting from the vents of Auden's truck.

My neck is pinching like a lobster's gotten ahold of it. I rub my eyes and stretch my complaining muscles. A few rolls from side to side and the pain eases.

Auden's word choice doesn't fade so easily. *Love.* He calls a lot of people that. So why does it feel different when it's directed at me?

More of my sleep fog dissipates. I blink, trying to focus. The world is blurry. "Shit, did my glasses fall off in my sleep?"

"No, I've got them. I didn't want you to wake up with sore ears." He slides a vaguely glasses-shaped blob out of the breast pocket of his flannel shirt and hands it to me.

I jam the frames onto my face, and the world comes into sharp relief.

His face comes into sharp relief.

Soft expression, tender amusement… I've woken up to that before.

151

Fuck, I used to enjoy waking up to Auden. He's a nuzzler. And with that beard of his, I can think of a hundred parts of my body I would be A-okay with him nuzzling.

In a fantasy anyway. I don't want to hurt him, and I don't want to *get* hurt. We're careening toward that so fast I'm not sure we have time to brake.

Figuratively careening. The truck is stopped, the engine idling. Large white flakes land on the windshield, big and thick enough that they don't melt right away.

"Where are we?" I ask, feeling guilty for having dozed off. I scan the snowy surroundings outside the truck. A gas station off a rural road. Could be anywhere in Vermont.

"Whitingham."

I jolt to attention. "What? Why'd you let me sleep so long?" Last I remember, we were just outside Montpelier. And I don't feel like I slept for two minutes, let alone two hours.

"You needed it," he says quietly. He doesn't look at me, stares at his knuckles, white and gripping the steering wheel. "I need to fill the tank. Want anything from the"—he squints through the snow at the sign—"First Stop Convenience?"

My stomach growls. "I can get myself something."

"No need for us both to get covered in snow."

"Surprise me then."

Ten minutes later, he returns, hair and beard looking like he made a trip to the North Pole. He shakes his head, clearing the flakes before getting back in the truck. He clutches a medium-sized paper bag in one hand and has two wine-bottle-sized ones notched in the crook of his elbow.

"What's with the hooch?" I ask.

"A couple bottles of red from the winery down the street." He reaches over the seat and puts the wine in a plastic grocery box sitting on the floor of the crew cab. "I've never heard of the place. Too bad we got here after business hours—I could have done some reconnaissance for Tanner."

It's the kind of thing I'd suggest we take a weekend road trip to enjoy, but I'm not going to be here as of next weekend.

I swallow the regret that bubbles in my throat and catch a whiff of whatever else he managed to rustle up. "Going off my nose, I'm going to guess you got us some nachos with plastic queso."

"Maybe." Unearthing a foam container of instant ramen and a cardboard tray of corn chips covered in lurid orange cheese sauce, he holds both up for me to choose.

I take the nachos.

"Still your guilty pleasure?"

I lift one eyebrow and shrug, shoveling a stack of gooey chips into my mouth.

He smiles, which makes me smile, and we're just two dudes wearing stupid grins in the cab of a truck that smells a whole lot like his dorm room used to whenever I brought over snacks for an all-night cram session.

You didn't make this trip to eat crap convenience store food and stare at each other like fools.

Checking my watch, I wince around a mouthful of salty junk food. It's past seven. "We're late."

"I texted the guy, said we were having to drive carefully because of the snow. He said not to worry."

"Good." After I initially gave in to my dad's demands to buy the press, and Auden agreed to drive, I let him make the arrangements with the seller. It only made sense, given he's the expert.

He eats his soup in record time. He's also still wearing a smile the size of Lake Champlain.

"You look so happy," I say.

"A Golding Pearl, Carter. A new precious."

My heart lurches. The words could have been stolen out of my dad's mouth. "I, uh, hope it lives up to expectations."

It does.

When the seller unearths the press from under a canvas tarp, Auden's face approaches postorgasmic levels of joy.

I hover on the sidelines, completely out of my element. I know how to run a press, but fixing them, looking for flaws, knowing if one's in good shape or not—my knowledge is rustier than the antique tractor taking up most of the seller's detached garage. The aroma of my go-to college snack clings to my coat, noticeable even over the sawdust and metal scents in the cluttered space. It's too bad my dad couldn't make this trip—he and Bob could have had a verbal game of "bet mine's bigger" over Bob's stacks of tools and farm equipment. I've tried to bring some sense of order to the shop and Dad's office, but no fucking way am I setting foot in the workshop around back of my parents' house.

"We'll need to order a new treadle from Francis's ironworks contact before we can get it up and running," Auden announces. "And the rollers need replacing. You willing to knock the price down for that?"

The upper-end-of-middle-age man crosses his arms over his barrel chest. "Well, I dunno. I thought I'd priced it fairly—"

Auden whips a stack of papers out of the inside pocket of his ski jacket. "For a machine in better shape, aye, but not one that needs repairs."

I hold in a snort. It's a hundred years old. Of course it needs repairs. Auden's done his research though. He cares about details and getting things right more than he'd ever be willing to admit.

The back of my neck crawls. Was I wrong when I accused him of being satisfied with mediocrity?

I've been blown away by some of his work.

The things he could do if he was willing to shoot higher...

He and Bob continue to dicker over the price, and Auden proves every stereotype about cheap Scotsmen true as he refuses to budge from his initial offer. The older man eventually caves and accepts Auden's low-ball price. I almost feel sorry for Bob.

Almost.

My inner businessperson is too busy being turned on by Auden's sexy AF negotiating skills.

"So, we'll bring it home tonight?" I ask.

The seller scans me, gaze turning judgy as he takes in my wool coat, jeans, and Chelsea boots. Oh, for fuck's sake. We have a pallet truck to do the heavy lifting—it doesn't matter what I'm wearing.

Auden's mouth quirks before I'm able to defend myself. "Let's get the new love of my life strapped in."

"Kinky," I mutter as we head out to back the truck and trailer into place.

His cheeks, already pink from the cold, redden further.

They don't fade while we trailer, secure, and cover the press. Auden's light mood does though. When we finally ease out onto the road, his face is lined with worry. He squints into the near white-out conditions.

I reach over and rub his shoulder. "We can take it super slow."

"Mmm." His hands tighten on the wheel.

We pass back through Whitingham, tires catching periodically in the ruts on the uncleared road. Auden's brow is glistening with sweat. He slows, easing into a pull-off. His breathing has that slow, forced-calm rhythm.

"Want me to take a turn?" I offer.

"When was the last time you drove with a trailer?" He sounds like David Tennant at his most Scottish, and my God, it tickles every *Broadchurch*-loving bone in my body.

"Years ago," I admit.

"No fucking way then."

"So, what do you want to do?"

He tips his head back on the headrest and exhales, eyes shuttering closed. Hitting the Call button on his Bluetooth speaker, he tells the system to call my aunt.

"What, Bee's going to come rescue us?"

He rolls his eyes and greets her when she answers. "How's the weather, Brenda?"

"*Brenda*," she says, mimicking his rolled *R*. "Everything okay, sweet pea?"

"No, the weather's shite and the extra thousand plus pounds

in the trailer is pulling my truck around like we're on a carnival ride."

"Be careful," she cautions, concern spilling into her tone. "It's snowy as anything here too."

"Bollocks." Auden scrubs his hands down his face.

"Where are you?"

"Outside Whitingham," I say.

"Want me to call my friend for you, the one with the inn I mentioned, see if she has room tonight? You're only about ten minutes away from her."

Spending the night with Auden?

Oof.

Yeah, I know I sucked him off yesterday. And I enjoyed every second of having his smooth, thick cock in my mouth. I can do that, make him feel good without being vulnerable myself.

Letting him do the same to me?

I'm not sure I can manage the emotional fallout.

Wind buffets the truck, and Auden's eyes widen. He looks at me, silently asking my opinion.

I shrug. A short jaunt to Jacksonville is better than crawling all the way to Burlington. I have a Saturday-morning meeting I should be at home to attend, but if it's unsafe to drive, I'm not going to suggest we push on for the sake of a debrief with A-E. "Safety first, right? And will it hurt the press if it's outside overnight?"

He shakes his head. "It'll sweat when we warm it up, but it should be fine after a spell back indoors." He lets out a sigh of relief. "I— Would you, Bee? I can't handle three more hours of this."

The look on his face makes me want to scoot closer and hold him until he relaxes. I will once we're somewhere it would be safe to take our seat belts off.

She tells us she'll get right back to us and hangs up.

I reach over and rub him between his shoulder blades. "If her friend doesn't have room, we'll figure something else out."

When I check my phone, I have one bar of call service and no data connection. "Did you see anything back in Whitingham? Might be our best bet." Though rolling up to an unknown, unvetted establishment is never my favorite option.

"Or we huddle in the crew cab and hope it lets up soon," Auden says.

He yawns deeply, like his body just realized he's been taking too-short breaths and is desperate for more oxygen.

Either that, or he's as bone tired as I was before I crashed on him for hours.

Fuck, I have to take care of him.

Can I do that without giving up the last few strands of control I have over my feelings?

Maybe this inn will have two rooms available. Or we'll decide not to continue what we started yesterday. When he offered earlier, I said no. I can do it again.

Bee calls back a minute later. "Good news, children. Budgie has a vacancy."

"Budgie?" I say, crossing my fingers that more than one room will be free.

"Well, Bridget to you, I suppose. She's a delight. Retired biology professor, and she'll be nothing but welcoming."

That's good at least. Avoids us having to worry about coming upon a random motel staffed by a bigoted front desk clerk and ending up in a whole lot of trouble. Vermont's liberal, but not so much that we can afford to be entirely carefree.

Given we can't count on Google Maps, I scribble directions from Bee on the paper bag our convenience store dinner came in.

Auden takes a deep breath before braving the road again.

"Go slow. We're in no rush," I say.

"I'd really hoped to be in a bed the next time you said that," he grumbles.

"Better to avoid that tonight, don't you think?"

He sends me a quick, hot look.

157

Okay then. (A) he doesn't think that at all, and (b) I need to figure out a way to adjust my jeans without him noticing.

Bee's friend Budgie is a woman in her sixties with deep brown skin, close-cropped silver curls, and a smile that could power an electrical grid. She ushers us into her foyer with the consummate hospitality of a person who runs a B and B because they love it, not out of obligation. She insists we call her by her nickname and tuts over our bedraggled appearances.

"Darn good thing Bee called me on your behalf." She closes the door behind us, shutting out the swirling snow.

The reception space is airy with farmhouse decor. Though where a person would expect there to be little touches of cow prints or chicken figurines, there are… parakeets? No. Budgies. Of course. They're the pattern on the roman blinds flanking the door, and a cluster of colorful ceramic figurines line a shelf behind the antique kitchen countertop that serves as her reception desk. Tasteful and whimsical all at once.

She pats Auden's arm before plucking a key from under the counter. "Bee prepaid for you, so there's nothing I need from you on that end. The two of you look ready to fall over. You likely would have driven off the road had you gone any farther."

"Possibility," Auden croaks. He's not exaggerating. It took us a half hour to drive what would normally be a ten-minute jaunt. I catch his hands shaking out of the corner of my eye. He shoves them into his jacket pockets. "And that was nice of Bee."

Nice. Ha. As if my aunt doesn't have ulterior motives.

"Your face is as white as the snow outside," Budgie says to Auden. "Were you the poor soul who had to drive in this? There's a kettle and pot in your room and tea to brew. Herbal or black."

"Herbal at this time of night. Last thing I need is caffeine," he says at the same time I ask, "Room? As in, not plural?"

A wrinkle forms between her dark brows. "You wanted two?

Bee seemed to suggest you were traveling together. I'm afraid I only have the one."

Of course she does.

Weariness creeps into my leg muscles.

Fuck it. I need a bed even if I'm sharing it with Auden.

"We'll be fine with the one," I say.

"Wonderful. I'll show you to your suite." She eyes the two of us with curiosity. Who knows what my aunt told her about our relationship?

Budgie leads us up a curved flight of stairs. Auden grips the wrought-iron railing as if he's afraid he's going to tip over.

"This is the only room up here," she says. "The other door is for my office." She puts her hand to her mouth like she's going to tell a secret. "And my reading nook. You can take the professor out of the university, but you can't take the books out of the professor."

"I understand," Auden says. "This little detour means I'm going to be missing my 'stroll through the shelves' Saturday morning at the bookstore connected to the wine bar where I work."

"You're welcome to peruse my collection instead, if you like," she says. "Nothing a bookworm likes better than to share her treasure trove."

I glance at him. His gaze is broadcasting his intention to peruse *my* treasure trove.

"I'd love that," he says, talking to us both at the same time.

Uh-oh. Giving him a quick blow job allowed for compartmentalization. Sharing a bed with him will not.

I need to distract him.

"The wine," I say, nudging Auden. "It'll freeze overnight."

"Shite, that's true," he says. "I'd better fetch it before we get too comfortable to venture into the cold again." He winks before jogging down the stairs, a spring to his step that wasn't there a minute ago.

Budgie leads me into the room.

My jaw drops. I'd bet all the cash in my wallet that it's the fucking honeymoon suite. A Jacuzzi tub nestles against the window, a basket of high-end bath products at the ready. Two armchairs face a gas fireplace next to a sliding door. Pristine, pale blue bedding covers the bed. It's a queen mattress though. Unless one of us takes the floor, we'll be jostling elbows all night.

Budgie catches me sizing up the bed. "I sacrificed a king to create more room for the tub and the sitting area," she explains. "Figured that anyone coming for romance wouldn't mind cuddling close anyway. I hope it won't be a problem." She screws up her mouth. "I could set one of you up on the sofa in my office, but it's only a love seat—"

"We'll be fine."

"You're not together?" She's clearly puzzled. "You have that look about you, like you're well accustomed to each other."

"We were. A long time ago." And that's all the detail I'm in the mood to give. "If you'll excuse me, I think I'll make a pot of that tea you mentioned to Auden."

"Of course," she says. "Have a good night now."

I seriously doubt that.

But I hold it in, smiling as she leaves.

I set the water up to boil and buzz around the room, exploring what we have to work with. There's a glassed-in shower, sink, and toilet, and all the toiletries we need. We're at least solid for keeping clean, despite not having a change of clothes. It's weird, checking in without any luggage. If I had my own room, I'd wash my underwear in the sink and let them dry overnight. Sleep naked.

Not tonight. No way am I stripping down to nothing around Auden.

I don't want to return to Montreal all mixed up about my college ex-boyfriend.

Tonight my boxers are staying on.

18

AUDEN

Snow whips my face, sneaking under my collar and chilling my neck as I head back to my truck in the B and B parking lot. It's a night that's begging for a warm fire and a glass of wine, so of all the places we could have landed, this one is stellar.

If only I was certain of what Carter wanted. His quiet, closed-off routine is getting old, and I'm still not okay with his rubbish no-reciprocation routine from the other night. He seemed completely into it, before he pivoted into the opposite, and I need to know why he changed his mind.

It's not that I'm under any delusion that having sex will magically make solutions appear.

It will, however, feel terribly good. After that drive and the back-and-forth between us all week, I'm craving the stress release alone.

After checking to make sure the Pearl is secured and as sheltered as I can get it, I grab the wine and a few just-in-case supplies from my glove compartment. In keeping us safely on the road, I earned one of these bottles of wine for sure. My blood's still singing in my veins, my thoughts tumbling like a gymnast with vertigo.

I jog the rest of the way upstairs.

The room smells of chamomile tea. Carter is lounging in one of the chairs by the fire, phone in hand.

"All well?" I ask.

"Just letting Anne-Emmanuelle know that I'll have to attend our meeting on my phone instead of my laptop tomorrow morning. Mind sticking around here until eleven or so?"

"Fine with me. My shift at V and V doesn't start until five."

He nods. His eyes turn curious. "What took you so long?"

"Making sure the press is as covered as possible. It's a disaster out there. Not the two inches that was forecast." There's a long bureau along one of the walls that separates the bathroom from the room. I set the wine next to a small tray of glassware, along with my small plastic bag of goodies.

Carter's gaze rakes my back.

I would pay a month's worth of tip money to know what he wants from me right now.

I take my time shedding my various layers and work boots. After rolling up the sleeves of my flannel shirt, I crack open one of the bottles of wine.

"God bless screw tops." I pour a few inches of the rich, red Syrah into two glasses. Shuffling over to the seating area, I hand Carter his portion. I sit on the carpet next to his chair in front of the flickering flames.

It gets me closer to the heat.

Closer to him.

Anticipation flashes in his eyes behind the clear frames of his glasses. His body is tense, as if he's fighting how easy it would be to reach out and touch my shoulder.

I take a large slug of wine. Between the fire warming my outside and the wine working its magic within, I'll be toasty in no time. More so if he decides to put his hands anywhere on my body.

"Thirsty?" he says teasingly, sipping from his own glass.

Hell yes, I am. The way he holds the wine in his mouth, savoring it… Christ.

"What's your expert opinion?" he asks.

"It's damn good wine. I can see why it's a medal winner." I'll have to let Tanner know so he can order some for V and V. Then again, at the moment, it could be rotgut and I'd still drink it. "I'd meant to decant this and taste it properly, but I don't much give a shite at the moment."

He chuckles.

After sniffing and picking up leather notes, I take a smaller sip and play with it around my tongue. "Pepper, jam, dark chocolate —true to a Syrah. And fits the criteria of being alcohol."

With a lazy hand, he combs back the hair from my forehead and idly strokes the side of my beard. "Still shaky?"

"Not from the drive."

His hand stills on my cheek. There's the tiniest vibration to his fingers. "What from?"

"You really need me to waste breath explaining it?"

The gas fireplace fills the room with that manufactured-flame sound, but it's not so loud that I miss Carter's sharp intake of air. He withdraws his hand.

It's a palpable loss. I toss back the rest of my wine and put the glass to the side.

I stroke the back of my hand along the top of his socked foot. Warmth seeps through the material, a magnet for my still chilly fingertips. "How many nights did we spend in my dorm room, me spread out on the floor in a mess of paper and you working all efficient-like with your laptop on my bed?"

"Made sense to keep the bed clear for when we were done studying." His eyes flash, as if the memory's filtering in against his will. "Miracle we got any sleep at all, squishing onto that fucking single."

"A single that saw a lot of fucking."

That earns a real laugh. "Better than waking up my parents."

Francis and Caro had been nothing but supportive of our relationship, but Carter had lived at home when he was attending school, and his bedroom had been right next door to his parents'. When we spent the night together, it was at my place. I got many a look of jealousy from dormmates over having a hot-as-hell graduate student do the walk of shame from my bedroom on a near-daily basis.

I sneak my fingers under the leg of his pants. His socks are low cut, and I draw circles around the knobby joint.

"Trying to get me to show off my ankles like an old-timey chorus girl?" he says.

"You'd have to shave, but you could pull it off."

He plays with the stem of his glass, not making eye contact. "My drag days began and ended with that one fundraiser revue back in grad school."

"Too bad." He knows his way around a vocal run, and his Marilyn was more than half-decent. I cup the lower part of his calf and massage lightly. "What do you do for fun in Montreal?"

Convincing him to open up about other parts of his life seems as good a plan as any. If I can get him to relax, to remember that we used to be each other's safe space, he might be willing to revisit some of the things we did together, shut off from the world in our Carter-and-Auden cocoon. Let *me* make *him* feel good.

"I work," he says. "Have drinks with coworkers. Play ball hockey at the rec center close to my house, go to the gym, volunteer for a theater nonprofit."

I clear my throat. "Dating, probably?"

"Not lately." Something flickers on his face.

I pull my hand away. "If you don't want me to touch you, I won't."

"I don't know what I want." He shoots to his feet and strides across the room, disappearing into the bathroom.

Ouch.

He erected that emotional wall faster than I could blink.

The sound of the shower competes with the whoosh of the fireplace. Spray sluicing over Carter's slim, strong body... Christ.

164

The bulge behind my fly goes from *approaching interested* to *deal with me right goddamn now.*

Carter was nothing but game to make that happen yesterday. He'd probably drive me off the oblivion cliff again if I asked, but another round of no reciprocation sounds pure depressing.

Best hide under the blankets and pretend I'm not aching for him. I strip down to my T-shirt and boxers and slide under the covers on the left side of the bed. I'll go deal with my teeth and such once he's out of the bathroom.

He eventually emerges, hair damp and golden skin flushed. His tight, silky-looking boxer briefs peek out from under the hem of his white, V-neck undershirt. And his chest... I could cry. It's a work of goddamn art, and I suspect I won't even get to see it bare.

It takes all my effort not to check to see if he's sporting a semi like I am.

For all I know, he wanked in the shower so that he wouldn't need anything from me.

I frown.

"What?" He stands at the foot of the bed, appraising me lying on one side and the untouched covers opposite me.

I wanted to be the one to make you come. "Uh, I was going to wait until the morning for a shower."

He lifts a shoulder. "Whatever you like. I used the purple toothbrush."

He goes to his side of the bed and stares at the duvet as if it's made of woven snakes.

"I'll go deal with my teeth while you get comfortable." One of us might as well be.

I wasn't expecting to get much sleep tonight. Was wondering if I'd be too busy running my mouth along all the angles and hollows of Carter's beautiful body. I'm thinking now it'll be from sensing every inch of him next to me but not getting the in-person reminder of what his face looks like thoroughly ruined from sex.

So be it. I'll respect the boundary he slapped between us. I give him a wide berth as I get out of bed and head for the loo myself.

I take care of the necessities. The knot in my chest tightens.

Goddamn it. Sex or no sex, I need to lighten the mood. Two white, terry robes hang from the back of the door. Hmm.

I strip down to my underwear and shrug into a robe. Crossing the foot of the bed with a right pathetic jazz walk, I pose.

One corner of Carter's mouth twitches. He's sitting up, leaning against the headboard with his knees drawn up so he can scribble on a pad of paper he must have found somewhere.

His glasses do awful, awful things to me.

As does the fact he lost the T-shirt he'd put on.

Shite. The robe material's thick but not enough to hide my stiff cock from view.

His gaze dips, and his eyes widen in appreciation.

At least I hope it is.

I spread my arms wide to draw his gaze up and leap sideways onto the bed.

"Jesus!" He laughs and springs to his knees.

The mattress shifts, and I roll backward with a garbled shout.

I land on the cushy carpet with a floor-shaking thud.

Ow.

"Baby, what the hell was that?" he cries out, scrambling over my side of the bed to crouch next to me.

Squeezing my eyes shut, I take stock of my body. I landed flat enough that it was jarring, but not enough to hurt. "Graceful leap. Rubbish dismount."

"Hopefully Budgie doesn't think we broke the bed."

I wince at the thought of Bee's friend coming to investigate. Rolling my shoulders to check for kinks, I stare up into Carter's concerned gaze.

He scoots a hand under my neck and prods with gentle fingers, slowly traveling up to the crown of my head. "Everything feel okay?"

"Aye. I just like the feel of your hands on me."

His breath hitches and his cheeks flush. One fingertip trails down my jaw. "I ever tell you this beard is hot as fuck? Drove me to distraction every time I saw you on a visit home."

"Liar." The word catches in my throat. "You've been looking through me since the day you left."

"You really think that?"

"I did until this visit."

He splays a palm on the bare skin of my chest, between the two gaping halves of the robe. "Surprised you didn't catch on that it was an act."

An act? Him brushing past me with barely a hello whenever he ran into me, over years of visits? "Mighty talented thespian then."

"I can't believe you didn't see it. You always knew how to read my mind, even when I was hiding shit."

Instead of standing and returning to the bed or offering me a hand up, he curls into a comma by my side, laying his head on my shoulder and seaming himself down my body.

Oh. Oh shite, that's good.

I loop my arm around him and pull him closer, soaking in the weight of him. Running the fingers of my free hand through his hair, I drop a light kiss on the top of his still-damp head. The herbal shampoo isn't his usual scent, but it suits him.

"I don't read minds. Least of all yours," I say. "If I did, I could have predicted you'd leave." Could have prepared myself for the heartbreak.

I should have predicted that anyway. Trusting love is asking to be made a fool.

"I chose to leave... You chose to stay. We both had a hand in it."

"You're... you're not wrong." Twenty-two-year-old Auden would have denied every inch of that claim, but present me can't ignore the truth. Other men, faced with the cards I'd been dealt, would have gone all in and chased after their love.

Having him against my chest, being in a snowbound hideaway, it feels like we're drifting out of reality. Safe enough to expose truths that I've kept secreted away from him.

"My mum drained her savings for me to attend Moo U."

He lifts his head just enough to catch my gaze. "Yeah? Wow. Generous of her. Maybe ill-thought-out too."

"I was furious when I found out."

"That why you help her financially?"

"Aye." I tighten my hold. "She screwed over her senior years to give me a good start, and I'm not sure I'll ever be at peace with that."

"Parents are supposed to support their kids, Auden." His hand's resting on my belly, and he's worrying the end of the terry cloth belt like it's a child's comfort toy.

"At the expense of everything? Future health? Future poverty?"

He sighs. "Maybe not at the expense of *your* future though?"

"I called to talk over the feasibility of moving to Canada—"

He rears up on an elbow, fast enough to make my head spin. *"When?"*

"The night we broke up. You'd been crying. Cried yourself to sleep, remember? While you were sleeping, I went outside to talk to her. Needed a rational perspective."

His face is a storm cloud, seething turmoil darkening his gaze. "And she told you not to go with me."

"No, but she told me about her finances and that she had nothing left if things went haywire for me in yet another immigration process. Between that and knowing I had a steady job with your dad and that she and I both needed that paycheck…"

I stare at him, expecting he'll pull away farther.

He doesn't. He strokes my face, slowly shaking his head. "You didn't tell me all that."

"I was in shock. You were hell-bent on a bigger life, and then Mum's admission—everything I'd counted on seemed tossed around. Except for my job. It was the only life preserver in sight. When you walked out before I could fully explain, I was too hurt to chase you. And after, it faded into irrelevancy. You knowing or not knowing wouldn't have changed the outcome."

"I—" He scrambles up to sitting, leaning against the edge of the bed. Strong arms loop around splayed knees. Incredulity and reason chase each other around his face, dark flashes and flinching muscles.

I sit too.

And wait. Not like we're going anywhere tonight.

And as delicious as his biceps look, straining the sleeves of his undershirt, it's obvious his brain is whirring too fast to be rushing into anything sexual right now.

"I want to disagree with that," he says. "That the outcome was inevitable."

"But you can't?"

He shakes his head. "Doesn't change anything now either."

I shift closer, kneeling between his spread thighs. Taking his hands in mine, I kiss his knuckles. Left, right. Tiny affirmations of agreement.

"Who's asking for anything to change?" I ask. "I'm sure as hell not."

Fingers tensing around mine, he shoots me a confused look. "I thought you wanted more. Sex."

"I do. Not the kind requiring commitment though," I say. "I just want to give you a goddamn orgasm."

He worries his lip. "That's it?"

"Yes." That's all I'll let myself want anyway.

I lean in and nip at the soft, pinkened flesh. An elemental need churns through me. Like something about this man will realign a long-ago shift in my cells, my body, my very existence.

"Carter. Let go with me. Just physically."

He groans. "Fuck. Fine."

"Not fine." My breath is short, jagged. "Necessary."

He was then, and he is now, and he might always be, but in the face of that impossibility? I'll take his surrender.

Long fingers spear into my hair, pulling oh so good. He tilts his head to gain better purchase.

The crash of our mouths carries an edge to it that only time and pain can hone. Not the reckless need we used to experience, the scrape of skin on skin that I used to crave all the time. The ache in my belly is bound by caution, by awareness. His grip is sure, his taste is sheer lust, his moan is grittier.

The desperation of youth, that selfishness, is gone. Because touching him, it's about consuming him, setting him on fire. Making sure I don't burn to a cinder alongside him.

Our tongues lash, harsh strokes of pent-up frustration.

"Keep kissing me like that," he says, voice rasping against my skin, "and you're going to end up on your stomach with my dick in your ass."

"Told you I wanted to top."

"No." His voice is quiet, but iron-hard.

I lift a brow. "Imperious, much?"

"Yes." Carter bites my lip, and my balls tighten.

He wants to pretend that topping means being in charge? I can go along with that charade. "Another day then."

He doesn't challenge the implication that this is going to last for more than one night.

Confident fingers tug at the belt of my robe.

It doesn't loosen.

I chuckle and kiss him. His low, sexy rumble of complaint hums against my lips.

"Think I'd make it that easy?" I ask.

"You should."

"Why hurry?"

He gets to his knees, using both hands to undo the stubborn knot. Victory flares in his eyes as he exposes my chest and tight boxers. He traces a fingertip just under the waistband. "Because the date I had with my left hand last night was useless."

My breath catches. "Your bloody fault."

"Who's keeping track?"

"I am," I say. "You're the one who turned me away the other day."

"Well, I'm not now. Get on the bed."

I peel back the fluffy comforter and scramble onto the plush mattress.

Carter stalks overtop me, straddling my legs and leaning in to claim my mouth.

Pressure builds in every inch of my body and my erection swells. I want release, but I want this play too. Want to be pinned to the bed and teased.

"You feel different," he says.

"Time's a bastard."

"No." The word is solemn. "It's been a gift to you."

I let out a sound that's bloody close to a squeak.

He grins, hands busy, tormenting my exposed skin.

I want to explore him just as much. I roll him to his back, savoring the sheer rightness of being nearly naked and close to him.

He lets out a startled sound.

"You were getting too comfortable overtop of me," I say.

His breath shudders. "Not going to fool myself that this is comfortable."

"Good discomfort, or bad?"

"Neither." Rising on his forearm, he cups the nape of my neck, pulling my mouth toward his. He nips my lower lip, soothes the sting with his tongue. "Just not easy. Holding back, it's been…"

I get on my hands and knees over him and start out on a lazy trail, tonguing the hollow at the base of his neck. "So, stop holding back."

A moan heats my temple. "I will. I have plans."

"What are they?"

He threads his fingers through my hair. "You'll find out."

I dot my lips over his pecs to the trail of hair bisecting his abs. "Think you're in charge, do you?"

"I'll let you play around first."

I've half a mind to have him shouting my name in the next ten seconds, just to knock his ego down a peg or two, but that'd be punishing myself as much as him. I really want to get him moaning and pliable.

Prove he's as needy as I am.

His thick, shiny crown bumps against his happy trail. I kiss my way down, ignoring it, nibbling the V of muscle that he must do an impressive number of sit-ups to maintain.

"Jesus, Auden, just suck me already."

I make my way down to his balls. Cupping the underside, I tease the sensitive skin between his sac and his hole with a fingertip. His hips buck. I smile, press open lips to the warm, soft skin at the base of his cock. He smells of bar soap and need and a whole lot like two and a half of the horniest years of my life. My dick pulses at the memory.

"Not what I was asking for," Carter says, teeth gritted.

"You keep thinking I'm in the mood to let you set the terms," I say, slipping my tongue down to his rim.

His hands flatten on the sheets and he arches off the bed. "Jesus Christ."

Humming, I keep licking, the taste of just-showered man flooding my tongue. Heat spirals through me, twisting, proving false all my lies about staying in control.

A garbled moan comes out of his mouth, and he reaches for his arousal.

I catch his hand. "No. My job."

"Well, you're fucking late for work!"

I take his thick shaft in my fist and draw a slow circle around the head with my tongue. He swears again. "Finally."

Finally, indeed. He's salty and hot and everything I ever wanted to taste in my life.

Instead of sliding my lips down his length—I might prefer to be played with shallowly, but he likes to go gag-reflex deep—I withdraw, leaving a featherlight kiss on his tip. "And you were trying to avoid this."

"You... You do things to me, Auden. I'm still not sure this is smart."

Oh, I'm sure it's not.

Now that I've had a taste of him, I'm never going to get him out of my mind. But if we're going to be stupid, it might as well be bloody perfect stupid.

Easing my throat open, I take more of him in with every thrust. My eyes water, but I can do this, relax and enjoy pleasuring him.

"Fuck me." It's got a worshipful tone to it. "Do you even know how good you look right now? I could watch you do this for a goddamn year."

My heart skips a beat at even the briefest allusion to anything long-term.

Not happening. Take this. It's all you're getting.

Making sure my thumb is wet with saliva, I circle his rim with the fleshy pad, pressing against his hole enough to tease.

His hips snap. My lips wrap around the hilt of him.

"Aud—" He gasps. "Slower. Don't want to be done."

If my throat wasn't full of his straining dick, I'd tell him I needed the magic words.

"Please, baby. Don't want to come yet. Please."

There they are. Finally. Didn't even need to ask.

I suck one last time and then release him, getting up on my hands and knees over him to see if his face looks as needy as his voice just sounded.

His chest rises and falls with jagged breaths. A flush pinks his neck and cheeks, and his pupils have swallowed most of the pretty chocolate brown.

I kiss the corner of his mouth. "Next time I get to finish you off."

"Okay." The word shakes. He locks gazes with me, his dark, wild eyes consuming any pride I gained from making him beg.

Because I'm about to do the same.

"Get on your back." He grins, a predatory curve of lip and desire. "I want to see your face. You have a fucking great face."

Shite, my cheeks are heating.

"You're blushing," he says.

"I am."

"Good. Roll over."

I do.

He rolls with me, settling between my spread legs. I'm honestly glad I'm on my back. I'd be shaking otherwise.

He heads for his discarded jeans, digging around in the pocket.

"There's lube and condoms in the plastic bag on the dresser," I say.

He grins, grabs the first and rolls on one of the second. And then he slides back over me, and my heart's ready to burst. Having my ex-boyfriend staring at me, all lusty and bossy, is seriously the best.

Ex-boyfriend.

It's accurate.

Sort of. We are each other's past. But we're part of each other's present too. Not boyfriends. Not *just* exes.

Carter catches my jaw with a gentle hand. "Lost you for a second there."

"So keep my attention."

"Done." He kisses me, fists me, strokes me long. His palm is slick with lube.

I groan. "Christ, that's—" Pressure builds, insistent, clawing inside. "Get on with it."

"Shh, I'm busy keeping your attention."

"Cheeky." I shake my head, making our lips brush and our noses touch.

One wet fingertip presses against my arse, slides in an inch.

Biting my lip, I lift my hips, trying to get him to give me more.

"You had me pleading," he says. "My pride wants to make you do the same—"

Lips land on one of my nipples, then teeth, worrying my flesh.

"You won't."

"Nah. I just want to make you feel good."

The finger slides in farther.

I hiss my appreciation, the hint of a burn. "Good place to start."

He adds another.

My balls tighten. "Oh shite."

"Too much?"

"Never."

His mouth hovers over my chest. "A third?"

"No. Your cock."

I grab the lube and slick it down his covered length. His blunt, heavy head nudges my hole. I relax as much as possible, enough for him to get in an inch or two. "Love, yes—"

A fist thumps the mattress. "Jesus." It's through clenched teeth.

I dig my fingers into his rock-hard arse muscles and pull him in farther.

And I'm the one swearing, hissing at the stretch, the too-full-never-enough sensation that screams through every cell of my body. "I missed…" I whimper. "I missed…"

"Me?" he murmurs.

Yes.

I can't get the word out. "Your dick."

He stills, gaze latching onto mine. Something thrums in my chest that I don't want to name.

"My dick," he repeats, driving his hips until he's buried to the hilt. The rude slap of flesh rings in my ears.

I close my eyes. I can either give him my gaze or my words, but not both. "And you."

"Auden. You—"

Strong glutes flex under my palms. The pace is tantalizing, punishing in its lazy rhythm. His stomach presses against mine, wedging my aching erection between us. I want to demand that he take me in hand, but I know I'll be lost if I do.

Arms circle my shoulders. His mouth lays messy, rough kisses on my cheek, my beard, my lips. Our tongues duel, mimicking his commanding thrusts.

"You're a tease, Carter Prescott."

"You— I could stay like this forever."

Forever.

The word latches onto me. I shove it away, give him a hard look.

His jaw clenches, and with a strong, persistent fist, he strokes my length from root to tip. I strain under his weight, my body unused to being folded at his will.

"I'm close…" The need to come shimmers in the distance, then rushes at me like a wave, dragging me under. And I hit the sand, upside down and right side up and tumbling, shooting sticky ropes on my chest. Crying out something even I can't make sense of.

Carter's face is pressed to my neck. His body tenses over mine.

"Fuck yes." The shout is muffled against my skin.

My hands skate over his sweat-slicked back. I need to straighten my legs, but his lips are moving silently over my too-sensitive nerve endings as if he's muttering state secrets and I'm not allowed to hear them. He's nowhere near close to softening inside me.

"Carter." I'm not sure if I'm asking him to move or stay still.

"Mmph," he grumbles, holding the hilt of his dick as he slides out.

I ease my leg down, sighing at the rush of relaxation, the buzzing in my ears, the endorphins frying every one of my neurons.

Carter doesn't move, stays draped across me.

"You all right?" I say.

His hand is still jammed in my hair, cupping the back of my skull. His fingers tighten. "No. I'm not."

"Shite, it wasn't good for you?"

He lifts his head to look at me. To kiss me. Soft, infused with an emotion I haven't seen from him since long before he walked out on me. "It was so fucking good."

"But you're not all right."

"No, I'm not." His mouth is an uneasy half curve. "I missed you too."

19

CARTER

Auden stills under me. Leashed power, anticipation in his frozen form. His fingers dig into my back, holding me to his broad chest.

"When?" It's a bullet of a word, cased in doubt.

"When, what?"

"When did you miss me?"

Whenever I let my guard down.

I can't admit that without admitting too much. Or inviting pity, or disdain. Either of which would be worse to accept than his current, obvious disbelief. I already know I irreparably broke his trust.

"If it's that hard to answer, I'm not sure I want to hear it." He slides out from under me and heads for the bathroom. His retreating form is blurry, but his slumped shoulders are clear enough.

Fuck. This is the problem with admitting small bits and pieces —it casts light on the vast remainder you want to keep hidden from view.

I snatch my glasses from the nightstand and put them on, then get up and deal with the condom. An uneasy, jittery guilt erases my sex-satisfied mellow.

I need to give him more, but I don't know how to explain myself.

The shower comes on.

It's loud.

He's left the door open.

An invitation?

I peek through the doorway. Steam and water droplets obscure the glass, reducing my view to a hazy shape of an ass and thighs and cock to spare.

"Want company?" I ask.

Limbs shift, and a spray of water hits the clear panel.

"I want to know what you're thinking." His voice is barely audible over the drumming of the shower on his flesh and the floor.

I step over the low lip. Residual drops hit my calves, but his bulky frame shelters the rest of me from getting wet. He's immersed in the spray. Suds slide down his body from his hair.

Shuffling closer, I work the lather in further, massaging until the unhappy crinkle between his brows relaxes.

"Sorcerer," he says with a hint of a smile. "Making me forget why I flounced in here in the first place."

"I wasn't being forthcoming," I say.

His eyes darken. "Maybe if I was *actually* coming again, I'd care less."

I doubt it. We'll have to have this conversation eventually, to admit that it's impossible to find pleasure together without digging up our history.

He started it, really—the details about his mom shined a light into the shadows of something I spent years trying to understand. Eased some of the sting of what I'd always defined as his stubborn choices.

I'm not going to dig us deeper by spilling my guts too.

Exposing the twisted knot in my chest would complicate things worse.

His breath shudders out through full, parted lips. A wet lock of hair slides down his forehead. Water trickles off the end.

"Love touching ye," he says, hands busy skimming my chest, arms, hips. As if he's relearning the sum of my parts.

I'm doing the same. Because we weren't exactly kids when we broke up, but he sure wasn't the man he is now. Broader, more muscled. Marked by a seriousness, gravitas, that carries a heft of its own. It holds me in thrall, the weight of experience.

I loved him once. I don't know if I appreciated him. Not like he deserved.

Grouted stone bites into my knees as I kneel on the shower floor. His cock is getting thicker by the second. His stomach's mostly flat with some softer, kissable parts that are begging for attention from my hands, my mouth, before I get to the main event.

His sexy-beast body has me feeling delicate. I want to strip him of all logic, all reason.

I look up at him. "Lean against the wall."

"Oh really." His words hitch with gravel and honey and the need to give in.

"You're going to fall over, otherwise."

He presses his brawny shoulders against the tile and spreads his legs to make room for me. "Promise?"

"You know it."

I wake up with a start. Auden's arms encircle my chest. Heavy, solid, an anchor helping me bridge the near illusion of last night and the sharp reality of morning. Sun glares through the inch-wide gap in the blackout blinds that we failed to fully close when we stumbled back out the shower and continued what we started under the water.

By the time we finally passed out, I was an unformed mass of bone and muscle, barely able to lift my head off the pillow.

That languid peace is gone this morning, despite the cozy, warm man at my back and the plush comforter that cuddles around us both.

Jesus. How many times did we wake up like this?

Not that it's the same. The bed, his body, my body, all recognizably different enough that it's not like we're shifting back into old patterns.

It's not us being in love, and me leaving, and him choosing not to be with me.

It's a fling. It's all it can be.

Yeah, right. I groan to myself.

A sliver of sun hits my retinas, jump-starting my internal day planner. I never sleep in. Today it's all I want to do.

Anne-Emmanuelle. I've asked for too many favors from her these past two weeks, and begging for one more is going to cost me something, I know it. But I have to stay as much as I can this week and help Auden hire someone for the shop. I'll drive up to Montreal on Wednesday night in time for Thursday's presentation.

Parallel lists of what needs to be done for Imprescott and OfficeMart this weekend roll out in my brain.

Wait. What time is it anyway?

I fumble on the nightstand and pull my phone toward me until the face recognition registers and opens the screen. Nine twenty-four? Shit. My pulse skips. My meeting's in six minutes.

It almost kills me to slip out from Auden's arms. I brush a kiss across his forehead before getting up.

He's a sound sleeper, barely stirring from the movement. I want to climb back in and wake him up slowly, tease him with my lips and teeth and tongue until he's moaning his first words of the morning.

Fucking work.

This is why I don't let men sleep over when I'm back home.

Saves me from resenting having to get shit done, from wishing I had time for lazy mornings. I don't. People don't make CEO by the time they're forty by lolling around with their lover until the clock shifts past noon.

I pull on my clothes sans underwear, telling myself that there's no way for A-E to know my shirt and jeans are a day stale. A quick teeth brush and I'm headed for the library across the hall, hoping it's unoccupied. I don't want to wake Auden with a scintillating rundown of OfficeMart's new merchandising strategy.

Or with a ripping argument between me and my second-in-command.

No one else is in the room, which is tastefully decorated in grays and whites with dark wood furniture. An impressive set of built-ins run down either side of the room. I sit in one of the two love seats by the bay window and set up my phone for a video call.

Anne-Emmanuelle's face fills my screen at precisely nine thirty. A bookshelf is behind her too, the one in her office.

"Tell me you're going to be here on Monday," she opens with in lieu of a greeting.

I wince. English again. Shit.

I clear my throat. "Well—"

"Do not do this to me, Carter. Every regional team rep is going to be here for Thursday's meeting—"

"As will I. Bright and early that morning."

"*That* morning?"

I nod.

"Not before that? Not for the three days of polishing?"

"No. I'll be working from Burlington."

Her dark eyes snap with disappointment. "You're letting us down."

That hits me right in the spot my dad's kept primed since I moved away. Staring at the screen, I keep my face neutral. Inside, I'm churning.

Unlike Dad, Anne-Emmanuelle's right to be calling me on this.

And she wouldn't like the answer I'm tempted to give.

I don't even want to be in Montreal for the big reveal. I'd rather attend it remotely so that I can get as many hours as I can, chipping in with the peony suite and finding a good employee. And Auden. I want to wake up next to him again, just one more time. I need to relive seeing his eyes drift open, his lips quirk as they land on my skin.

"Carter?" Anne-Emmanuelle jogs me from my thoughts. "I understand you need to take care of your family, but this has been garbage timing."

"You and the team have it under control. I trust you." This is exactly why executives have 2ICs—so that they're ready to parachute in when something serious comes up. "I'll check anything over that needs checking, but we've put hundreds of hours into this. Everyone knows what they're doing. I'll oversee from here, and you'll take care of the in-office fires, and we'll all be ready for Thursday. Run me through what you got."

She screen shares her slide deck and takes me through it, follows it up with the promotional videos we've prepared. Seeing all our months of work summed up in a flashy, concise presentation is the kind of professionalism I've built my career on.

"It's gorgeous. The whole thing. The slides, the footage, the modeling—the rollout is going to catch us some major attention."

"I know." Her eyes glitter. "I want a raise, Carter. And a reassessment of my duties. Tack executive in front of director."

I pause. "Noted."

"The correct word is *promise*."

"You know I can't do that unilaterally," I say quietly.

"How about 'I promise I will do everything in my power to make it happen.'"

I nod.

"What the hell is taking so long down there anyway?" she asks. "You said it was a bandage situation. A quick in and out."

"I'm overhauling the business. Bit more than a bandage."

"Didn't you say you were hiring someone to help your dad?"

"First interview bombed."

She looks at me like I'm wearing Bjork's swan dress as a hat. "And you're holding more when?"

"When we find a suitable candidate."

The door to the library opens.

"Ah, there ye are, darling."

Ye arrrre. Auden's voice is gruff. Like he spent half the night calling out my name. The sound rasps across my skin.

He's carrying a tray with coffee, toast, and some scrambled eggs that look like they're part white, part yolk, and part cloud. "Sorry, I didn't realize you were still in your meeting. You missed breakfast."

Anne-Emmanuelle's eyes widen.

Oh fuck.

"Breakfast," she echoes, brown eyes suspicious.

"Necessary meal, A-E."

"And a waiter with a hot accent."

"Not a waiter."

She grits her teeth. "And not the reason you're staying in Vermont?"

"No," I assure her. "It's family leave. Honestly. Auden's my dad's assistant. We got stuck in the sticks yesterday because of a snowstorm. We were picking up a new press for the shop."

"Right then. I'll let you get to… breakfast."

"Thanks." I sign off.

Auden sets the tray on the coffee table in front of me.

"Could've woken me up," he says, slinging himself next to me on the love seat. His hand strokes my thigh.

My cock offers itself up as a breakfast alternative. Exactly why I snuck out of bed without waking him.

I take a sip of coffee. Picking up the plate, I shovel a forkful of eggs into my mouth. "Only had six minutes to make my meeting on time," I say around the heavenly bite.

"How'd it go?"

Thick fingers trace tantalizing patterns. My body heats like someone cranked the old-fashioned radiator under the window. After taking another bite, I put my hand over his, stilling his touch so that I can at least marginally focus on what he asked me.

"Everything's ready for the presentation on Thursday. I'll need to drive up for that but can work the rest of the week from Burlington."

He looks surprised. "They're far more understanding than I would've expected."

I roll my eyes and finish off the eggs. "Why does everyone think working for a large employer means giving up everything you value? I'm not going to sell my soul to a company that doesn't treat me like a human being with human realities."

"Okay. I'll accept that last part."

"But…"

Auden stares at the floor, biting the inside of his lip. After what seems like a full minute, he takes a breath and says, "But you did give up parts of yourself. When you started working for them."

The accusation lands like an anvil in a Road Runner cartoon. Except nothing about being told I compromised who I was is funny. And my heart doesn't bounce back as easy as Wile E. Coyote.

Fuck this.

"Giving up the shop wasn't giving up who I was. I always wanted success. I found a new way to get it." I put my plate down with a clatter and jump to my feet. "Maybe you didn't get what mattered to me."

"Maybe I didn't. And maybe I wish I could have mattered more than success." He pales. "Sorry. That came out wrong. You deserve to succeed, to be fulfilled."

He falls silent but doesn't look like he's done talking.

I wait.

"Even so, I felt like I wasn't enough," he finishes.

My stomach cramps. The anguish of not quite being good enough for the people you love… It tears at you, stealing strips and chunks, leaving holes. That's how I felt when I made the decision to leave, knowing my dad would never see where I was coming from, would never understand or accept me as I was. And then when Auden took Dad's side, I questioned every time he'd told me he loved me.

It doesn't mean my past pain justifies hurting him now. "I left because of me, not you."

He chokes on a bitter laugh. "It wasn't you; it was me? Seriously?"

Yeah, seriously. Because his whole "I wasn't enough" routine —it applies to me as much as him.

My legs feel heavy. I don't want to sit but can't quite stand properly. I lean back against one of the built-ins.

"My decision to leave..." I let my head loll on one of the wooden shelves. "For all that I wanted someone who dreamed as big as me, I couldn't be what you needed either."

He sobers. "Yet you told me you thought we were good for each other. Or at least disagreed with me when I said we weren't."

"Somehow it feels like it's both."

"It can't be both," he says.

"I know." This man deserves more than I could give him.

No matter how much I wish there was a way to have him in my life.

I freeze at the thought. Do I want this to be more than an interlude, a brief fall into the past?

Blood rushes in my ears. "This isn't nostalgia, is it?"

"You thought it was?"

"Would have been a nice excuse." I lift a shoulder. "But I can't pretend you're the guy you were in college."

It's him now, arms straining the sleeves of his gray T-shirt, stretched along the back of the small couch. His talent, the skill necessary to create gorgeous, modern designs using ridiculously archaic technology. And his heart, big and generous.

"I know I pale in comparison." He's trying to joke, but his worried mouth ruins his delivery.

I slowly shake my head. "Except you don't."

He rises, lumbers over. Braces one hand on a shelf above my head and one on my hip. Warmth curls between our bodies, singing from the inside out.

I groan.

"Neither do you." He kisses my temple. "Except that you're still easy," he says.

When it comes to him? I really am.

"You're complaining about how much you turn me on?" I dig my fingers into his firm ass.

"Christ, no. I love it."

"I do too. You're… special." Always was. Is even more now.

His lips dip and dive along my neck, pulling impossible thoughts from places I've long ignored. Could I somehow make both things work? Now that I've progressed enough in my career and the business world is more adapted to a remote workforce, could I cobble together a two-city existence, enough to try again? It's not unheard of for executives to work far from where their company is headquartered.

"Auden, what if I—?"

No. I can't say it. No one's going to benefit from me heading down brambly rabbit trails. We have a plan, and it involves me leaving after next week.

Which sucks. I'm so used to being the fixer. Why can't I fix my own life?

Auden cups my jaw and kisses the breath out of me. When he pulls away, his eyes dance with satisfaction. "You lost your train of thought."

Got caught up in a dangerous train of thought is more like it.

"You're a fucking distraction," I say.

"You fucking need it."

His lips are so damned soft but insistent. I sift my hands through his hair, deepening the kiss. Tasting the sweetness of the spoonfuls of sugar he insists on insulting his coffee with.

I could taste it all morning.

I'm so damn jealous of my parents, whiling away their time in Paris. I want to take Auden there, sit on a sidewalk in a wicker chair and argue about it being sacrilegious to sweeten his *café au lait*. And then steal away to a little flat overlooking the Seine and screw him until his eyes cross.

The shelf behind me digs into my back. He wedges a thigh between mine, rubbing hard muscle against my thickening erection. Our mouths spar, a blur of tongues and lust.

"Hang on to the shelf," he commands.

Oh Jesus. Yes. "When did you get so bossy?"

"When I decided you needed to be bossed around."

He might be right.

"It's never been our thing," I say.

"This isn't going to last long enough to require a 'thing.'"

The truth lands with a wallop.

And that's how I want it.

I'm going to take Auden at his word that he doesn't want anything more than a few fucks over the next week or so.

And the first one is happening now.

"Someone could walk in," I point out.

His face falls. "Bollocks. Right. No need to scandalize Bee's friend's guests."

"It's as if you forgot we have a room."

"We do," he says, smile wicked.

"So, take me there."

20

AUDEN

V and V has a vocals/acoustic guitar duo playing during my Saturday shift, and it helps with the dragging time. My head—and heart—is in my apartment, cuddled up against the hottie who promised he'd be spending the night, working on my couch while catching up on *The Crown*.

I have some definite opinions about the existence of the British aristocracy knit tight into my Scots crofter DNA, but even I can't resist some pretty costume porn when it's accompanied by a bowl of popcorn and Carter in sweatpants.

"Where's your head at, sweet pea?"

"On an email I got today." I'm completely lying to Bee, who showed up with Grace a half hour ago and has been not so subtly fishing for info on my impromptu romantic getaway with Carter.

My head's been nowhere but on her nephew.

A tidbit she wants to hear, so it's not what I'm going to tell her. "My project advisor got back to me today with a small list of students who would be good candidates for the shop. Carter emailed them this afternoon, and I'm curious to hear if any have responded."

"I'm sure that's all true, but there's no way the wistful look on your face is related to job interviews."

I point a double jigger at her. "Do you really want to go there? When we checked out this morning, Budgie admitted she had another room and that you paid for an extra night so that she wouldn't tell us."

Grace, still dressed up in the business suit she wore to whatever work function they came from, gives her wife a look that makes me think they already had words about this.

Bee grins, guilt-free.

"Look at you, all proud of your meddling," I say, topping off their glasses.

"Did it work?" she asks.

"No shame," I say.

She narrows her eyes. "Did it *work*?"

As if I'm going to give in so quickly. She needs to suffer.

Not that I suffered last night. The opposite, really... When he got down on his knees in the shower, I nearly evaporated along with the steam from the water.

Heat rushes into my face.

"Auden Macarthur, you're blushing! Was it that good? Of course it was," she says, answering her own question. "You wouldn't be glowing like an emergency flare otherwise."

"Yeah, it was that good," I admit.

"Ha!" The crow turns heads on the opposite side of the bar.

"Easy, killer," Gracie chides, stroking an idle hand down Bee's spine. "You got what you wanted. No need to rub it in."

"No, *Carter* got what he wanted. Namely—" Bee wiggles her fingers, indicating me from top to bottom.

"Hey now." The printer spits out four drink ticket orders in a row. Molly's standing by the point-of-sale, face screwed up in concentration. I check my watch—ah, last call. I pour a few local beers and a pint of Shipley cider while shaking my head at Bee. "I didn't give you specifics on what 'that good' meant."

Gracie snorts. "You didn't need to, sweetie."

I cock a brow and serve up the two glasses of winter ale from the second ticket. "The room was lovely."

The glee on Bee's face as she rubs her hands together is a sight to behold. You'd think she just found out she'd successfully rid the world of polio. "My work here is done."

"You're wasting your effort," I say.

"Lies," she replies. "Why isn't he here?"

"Because I'm bartending. Or trying to. Good thing the two of you drink enough wine for us to keep the lights on, otherwise I'd be getting side-eye for the amount of time I've spent entertaining you."

"He was here the last time you were working," Bee says.

I'm about to tell her she's wrong, but she isn't. He *was* here on Wednesday, at the other end of the bar. "Might have been."

"You're keeping track then," Grace says, getting in on the action. Her smile is small but knowing.

I shake my head. "You're both being ridiculous. I'm cutting you off."

"Empty threats. It's after last call anyway," Bee points out, taking a long swig of chardonnay.

"Do you two need a ride home? I could give you one once I'm off."

"And keep you from meeting your love wherever he's waiting for you? Never," Bee says.

I fist my hands on the edge of the bar.

He's not my love.

I don't need him to be. Don't *want* him to be.

I'm not careful, I might go there.

And if I admit my feelings to Bee and Gracie, they'll try to help and make things worse. "You're seeing things that aren't there, Brenda, love."

"You're *ignoring* things that *are* there."

I stiffen. "Wrong. I'm paying attention to what needs to be paid attention to."

Namely how Carter won't be here come next Saturday.

Bee's face goes serious, and she twirls the stem of her wine-glass. "I know my nephew isn't perfect, Auden. And I'm not unaware he hurt you, which doesn't always deserve a second chance."

"Exactly."

She holds up a hand. *"But."*

There's nothing she can say to help here. Shaking my head, I start cleaning up my station.

"But you're smarter now than you were then. So's he. And he's not fucking fulfilled, which I hate."

"And what do I do when he leaves?"

The question comes out jagged. Too loud. People sitting at tables halfway across the bar turn their heads in my direction. As does Tanner, who's over by the entrance, talking to his boyfriend. Probably about how they're going to go upstairs and fuck till their eyes cross. Tanner sends me a look somewhere between concern and warning. Jax's smile goes the you-poor-wanker route.

Shite.

I twist my bar towel in my hands and stare into the ice well.

"He's looking for a reason not to leave," Bee says, voice pretty much as soft as she can get it and still be heard over the mellow music.

My eyes sting, and I blink rapidly. Nothing Carter has said over the past few days has indicated he'll want to stay. And even if he does, I don't have it in me to believe him. "I can't be his reason. Not anymore."

He might be waiting in my flat for me tonight, but it's temporary.

An hour later, I'm tiptoeing into my entranceway. A pair of polished brogues are lined up on the drip tray next to my work boots.

My heart twinges. Ugh, why do the bits of domesticity always get to me? The extra coffee mug out on the counter. Our tooth-brushes side by side. Or this morning, waking up to his note on the B and B's dresser:

SLEEPING BEAUTY:
I'M WORKING IN THE LIBRARY.

He didn't claim to be the prince, but the abstract he'd sketched of the two of us left no doubt as to where his mind was when he left the room.

I'm almost disappointed there isn't a follow-up written on the pad of sticky notes on the little table next to my front closet.

The hallway light's on, but the rooms beyond are dark. Carter's in bed then.

I clean up quietly to avoid waking him. When I go into my room, the bed is empty, the covers straight.

I find him on the couch, too fetching for his own good with my plush navy blanket pulled up to his chin and his dark lashes looking miles long on his cheeks. His laptop is in sleep mode on the coffee table, and the half-finished mug of tea next to it— peppermint, by the smell—is cold to the touch. Speaking of adorable signs of domesticity—

Bollocks. Enough of this.

No matter how adorable it is to see him occupying my space like a contented house cat, I've got to keep my urge to snuggle up to him under wraps. He's here for sex, not sweetness.

It's a good thing I have a fixed end date. If I didn't know, if it was open or uncertain, it would be impossible to keep the last few parts of myself gathered close to my chest. I'm essentially like a kid trying to clean their room in one go, carrying everything precious to them in one precarious armload. Dropping bits, one by one, as I move through my day.

Not everything though. I can steal my last few moments with him, focusing on getting him naked in my bed instead of spooning with him on the couch and not have everything crash to the floor.

With how damn skilled Carter is with his hands and tongue, it shouldn't be at all complicated to stay busy. Last night was almost too good. And I might be swaying on my feet after the drive home this afternoon and a night of bartending, but if Carter's willing, so am I. Screw the late hour.

Wait. Saturday night… It's past two, and I was too distracted today to leave my mum a message and let her know I wouldn't be calling. I'd better ring her quickly now, else she'll worry. After facing the Bee-and-Gracie interrogation, I don't have much left in me for anything but the sinful promises Carter made before I left for work. Sadly, my mom hates texting. I'm better off dialing her up and keeping it short.

I switch places with the pillow Carter's using, settling his head on my leg. I play with the soft strands of his hair. He doesn't stir. Christ, he's a heavy sleeper.

Even so, I make sure to keep my volume low when I get through. "Morning, Mum."

"You're late calling," she says, voice rife with accusation. "I'm about to head out with my walking group."

Having her in my ear and Carter in my lap transports me back to college, to being tangled up in him and having Mum call. Even back in the day when people bothered with voice mail, she never did, would just call again immediately. So I usually answered and hung up as quickly as I could. Unlike then, she doesn't know he's here. And I'd best keep it that way, lest she lose her ever-loving mind.

"I'm tired anyway, Mum. I just wanted to check in."

"Better not be too tired," Carter murmurs from my lap.

"Who said that?" Mum says suspiciously.

Oh Christ. I sigh. "I said I was tired."

"No, someone else said something."

"I turned on Netflix."

Carter rolls onto his back and stares up at me, brows raised, and whispers, "Hiding me? Really?"

I shake my head at him. Two or three humdrum questions and I should be able to hang up without more suspicion.

"How's everything at work, Mum?" She must not be terribly late for her walking group, because she launches into the latest office drama, something about a coworker who keeps eating out of Mum's jumbo container of yogurt.

Oh my God, hang uuuuup, Carter mouths.

"Mix it with something bitter. Make it look like strawberry flavor or something," I suggest.

Carter glares at me, pouting at first. Then a sly smile creeps across his face. He tosses the blanket back. He's wearing a rather familiar-looking plaid shirt. Mine. It's loose on him and open at the throat, framing a sprinkle of chest hair. His gray sweatpants showcase every inch of the bulge in his underwear.

My mouth goes dry.

His hand slides down, under the waistband of his pants. I can't totally tell because he keeps his hand under the fabric, but it looks like he grabs himself and strokes.

Ungh. My cock throbs behind the fly of my jeans, stealing all my attention.

"Auden!" Mum snaps. "I asked you if Carter was still in town."

Oh shite. I completely lost focus. "Right, uh, I'll let you get to your walking group."

"Without answering my question?"

"Carter—" *Is giving me a come-hither look that might just kill me.* "Don't worry about him. We can talk about it—"

"Hi, Betsy," Carter says, louder than necessary. He pulls his hand from his pants and stretches his arms over his head, draping himself farther over my lap. "Yes, I'm still in town."

Oh, he didn't. Hot anger bolts through me. I cover his pretty, cheeky, infuriating mouth with my hand. Lightly, but it gets the point across.

His eyes sparkle, and he smiles against my palm, then nips the fleshy base of my thumb.

"For Christ's sake," I hiss.

"*Auden,*" Mum cuts in. "He's at your flat? In the middle of the night?"

"I'll talk to you tomorrow. Bye, Mum."

"Be *careful*."

"Love you." I hang up, toss my phone on the coffee table, and glare at Carter. "And you, I'm going to throttle."

He faces me and rises on his knees. "Promise?"

Glaring at him, I shake my head. "That's not your kink."

"No, it's not. You are," he says, unbuttoning another button, exposing another two inches of skin.

The tips of my ears warm. I'm so here for having my lover wear my clothing. Especially when it's bloody easy to remove.

I spin, facing him with my back against the arm of the couch and my legs open with him kneeling between them. The position pulls my jeans tight, making it obvious I'm right turned on.

"Oh yeah?" I say. "What do you want me to do for you?"

Carter shakes his head. Teasing heat spreads on his face. "I want you to sit there and watch."

"Watch what?"

"Me."

"And wha' are you planning on doing?"

His mouth quirks at one corner. "What do you want me to do?"

A Carter show? Hell yes. "Touch yourself."

"Here?" He flattens both palms to his chest and skims them down, pressing my shirt against his skin and giving me a hint of defined muscle.

"It's a start. Unbutton your shirt. *My* shirt," I command. "Slowly."

"Maybe I'll keep it," he says as he flicks open a button. "Gets just as cold in Montreal."

Having him hold on to part of this fling… I'm not sure that's smart. "Stealing my shirt seems dangerously close to hanging on to the past."

"Not all memories need to be discarded." His fingers ply another button, then two more.

The sliver of exposed skin grows. Spreading the sides open, he waits.

I drink him in, every inch of his rippling abs and carved pecs. The golden trail of hair arrowing under his waistband. God, he's hot. I mean, I find all sorts of bodies sexy. Soft ones, hard ones, curvy or angled or average. And the superfit look doesn't do it for me when it doesn't come with intelligence, humor, a smile.

Carter's got all that. All on his lips at once. I can't take my eyes off him.

For each moment I stare, his dark brown gaze turns more molten. He grips the sides of the shirt.

"You're not touching yourself," I say.

After staring at me with the dirtiest intent, he rises on his knees just enough to shove his sweats and underwear down, freeing his cock. It springs to attention. His tongue darts out and he licks his lower lip. "Tell me exactly what to do."

The words settle low in my belly.

I jerk my chin at him. "Stroke yourself."

He obeys, jacking himself off like he's desperate for release. He sucks his lower lip between his teeth, the flesh whitening as he bites down.

"Too fast." I unbutton my jeans and take myself in hand, setting a slow pace. "Like this."

It's torturous, but it's worth it to hear him whimper.

"Aud…" His pupils flare. "Baby, I need more. Need it fast."

Pumping my fist even slower, I let my mouth widen into a teasing grin. "No, you don't."

His free hand lands on my knee and squeezes. "Watching you… It's too much."

"Savor it."

I don't need to explain we should relish the time we have before it's gone.

Sadness flickers on his face, belying his flushed cheeks and pleasure-twisted lips.

Damn it, what am I doing, ordering him to put on a show that keeps him separate, at arm's length? We need distance emotionally, not physically. I want to be together, touching, caressing as much as humanly possible for the few remaining hours we have.

"C'mere." Bending my leg that's not sandwiched between Carter and the couch, I use my calf to pull him toward me.

He falls against my chest with a groan of relief. "Fuck. Yes. I want to be close to you. Touching you, not me."

"Both of us." The building pressure in my body makes my voice shake. I let go of my cock so he can take it, snug against his own in his hand. The heat of his skin, the strength of his grip. Leisurely, teasing strokes.

"Thought you wanted faster," I say, thrusting my hips up. My body's demanding release, but now that I've given over control, Carter doesn't seem like he's in a hurry.

Bracing himself on an elbow, he works us over. He lays soft kisses on my neck, little bites, tiny stings of pleasure.

"Driving me mad," I grumble. I palm his ass, creeping my fingers toward the center of his cheeks.

"Good," he says. "I'm there with you."

I rise on my own elbow, just enough so I can reach his tight hole, press in with a single digit.

He swears between gritted teeth. "Your finger fucking belongs there. I'm—"

I push in farther. My vision narrows as his hand grips harder. The smell of sex and his shampoo is sharp in my nose, and the friction of his body against mine crystallizes everything around me, the utter perfection of knowing he's going to fall apart in seconds, and it's because I'm with him for this wild moment—

"Oh fuck, baby."

Bliss, low and growly, spills from his lips. He shoots on my belly, half on skin where my T-shirt got shoved up, half on the fabric pressed between our bodies.

I follow him into the abyss, ignoring the instinct to keep some sort of barrier between us. Letting myself slide into the space where it's impossible to tell where he stops and I begin. A haze settles, the tang of our release tickling my nose. There's a faint ringing in my ears.

That loss of time when you swim in a postsex fog, unable to properly move your muscles.

Carter's in jellyfish mode on top of me, somehow covering all of me despite his slimmer frame.

He stacks his hands on my chest and rests his chin on them, staring at me. "Look at you. You'll be useless for a week."

I chuckle. "You'd better hope not. We're going to be busy at work."

"Yes. Starting Monday—we have an interview lined up."

"With whom?"

"One of the candidates your professor recommended. Olivia Yang. She got back to me within minutes of me sending the inquiry email—I took it as a good sign."

"Oh… great." I force a smile and trace a finger through his hair.

His mouth turns down at the corners. "You don't sound like you think it is. Aren't you on board with the new hire?"

"I am." But this weekend—the drive, the night with this delicious, frustrating man, too many people chirping in my ear—has left me unsure of what I'm on board with. "Just tired, love."

"Then let me take you to bed."

And I let him, trying to focus on the lines of his body instead of the reality of his words.

(21)

AUDEN

"Is that a Pearl?"

I chuckle, following the force of nature that is Olivia Yang into the corner of the shop where Carter and I stashed the new press when we got home two days ago.

She's as enthusiastic as her email suggested. She also knows the difference between the Pearl and the C&P, and I have to admit, I'm getting hopeful she might be a good fit.

Her high ponytail bounces as she walks around our newest acquisition, examining the mechanisms. Her velvet Vans squeak on the cement floor. She's not dressed up for her job interview—nice jeans and a sweater—but neither am I.

Carter's in a suit, but he likes to show off like that, and I'm pretty sure he's doing it to tease me.

"Ohhh, she's so pretty," Olivia gushes. "I did the presswork for my senior exhibition piece on a Pearl. The Fine Arts department has one."

"I went to that show," I say. "I think I remember your design—a layered collage of faces, right? Found-family theme?"

She blushes and nods. "Flattering you remember."

"It was insightful. And stood out between the still-life made of the artist's hair and the wall of parking tickets meant to represent time."

Carter shakes his head.

I put my hand to my mouth and pretend my words are for Olivia only. "He has a business degree."

She laughs and glances back at the new press. "Can I give her a try?"

"It's not in operation yet—needs repairs."

Our interviewee strokes the machine like it's a new kitten, murmuring praise and whispering how lovable it is. "What's her name?"

"Haven't decided on one yet," I say.

Carter snorts from behind me.

Olivia braces her hands on her hips. "She needs a name."

"So my dad insists." Carter's lips twitch. He's taking in the graduate student's brimming energy with the practiced eye of someone used to evaluating personnel. "He probably spent more time thinking of a moniker for the Vandercook than he did naming my sister and me combined."

She lifts a black brow. "And what did he pick?"

The look on her face makes me suspect her interest in the position is one hundred percent contingent on our answer.

"Presley," he says.

She looks across the shop at the press in question, narrows her eyes for a few seconds, then nods.

"I need to understand the machines I'm going to work on. I can handle a press named Presley. Probably temperamental when he's too cold, sticks a little when there's a full moon, but overall a reliable workhorse."

Ha, I like her. I hope she's as talented as she is passionate. I was impressed by her senior project, but she needs to be good at day-to-day design work too.

"'*Going* to work,'" Carter echoes. "You're confident." He scans the one-page, precisely laid-out résumé Olivia brought with her.

"I am. And you like it," she says. "You got where you are with OfficeMart by being confident."

Carter blinks, clearly surprised. "You did some quick research."

"Of course. I want this job. I'm not going to walk in here uninformed about the people interviewing me."

"You won't be working with me though," Carter points out. "This guy's the heart of the operation."

My jaw drops a bit.

"Not your dad?" Olivia asks, taking the words out of my mouth.

"Dad's the foundation. But Auden… He's the one you want to look to as a mentor."

Between Carter's quiet praise and Olivia's impressed gaze, it's my turn to be the one with warm cheeks.

"I'd do my best," I say. "I like teaching. I know you have experience, but there would still be training involved."

"Of course." She screws her mouth up. "You're seriously looking to hire someone to run letterpresses all day?"

"And some admin work," Carter says. "It'll be Saturdays and part-time during the week at first. Can you manage the hours and your schooling?"

"I already work twenty-five hours a week at my current job. Give me two weeks so I can give them notice, and I'll be yours."

Carter looks at me, and I know where his head's at. Francis and Caro still haven't booked tickets home, so if Olivia can't start right away, I'll be on my own as of the weekend. I give him a brief nod.

He waves a hand at our two working presses. "Show us what you've got."

She blinks. "Like, make you something?"

"Yup," he says. "Impress me."

Her chin lifts, and she grins. "Gladly."

We chat for a few minutes about business card design and the stock we have available for her to play with. After confirming she's familiar with the quirks of the Chandler and Price and pointing her in the direction of the ink, type, furniture, and frames, I leave her be. I'm not planning on babysitting a future employee, so I'm not going to do it while she makes her sample. If she could complete the senior project I saw, she's not going to have a problem running through a simple project.

Carter looks ready to hover beside her, but I flag him over to the front counter.

"Leave her be, darling," I say in a low voice.

He braces his hands on the Formica. "Right."

"Auden?" Olivia asks from over by the metal type. "This box here—is this some of your work? It looks similar to the sets of stationery at V and V."

Carter and I both turn.

She's holding my half-done rainbow project.

"Yeah, uh, that's Carter's design. I'm not done printing it yet."

A strong hand grips my arm. "Auden…"

My heart jumps into my throat.

"He's got a good eye for a corporate stooge," I say lightly.

"I bet it'll sell," Olivia says, understandably oblivious to having exposed my surprise. She puts the lid back on and shelves the box.

"I hope so," I say. Though in reality, all I want is a smile from the man digging finger-divots into my biceps.

And he's not giving me one.

His face is carefully blank.

His hand isn't though. The muscles and tendons snap with emotion.

I cover it with my own.

"It's just letterhead," I murmur. "And it's not even done. You don't get to see it until it's done."

He pauses, mouth open, then shakes his head.

Good. I don't want to get into this in the middle of a job interview.

Because it's not "just letterhead." I'm trying things, going along with his ideas, and I know it could wreck me. I'm doing it anyway.

The letterhead is a small step. This interview with Olivia is not.

She'll mean a significant change in the shop, implementing Carter's broader goals, opening us up to more risk.

My gut roils. What are we doing?

It's all great to love my designs and to bring someone on who can work her own magic, until a recession hits and people's ability to buy exquisite, but right frivolous stationery, implodes. Leaving us with the debt of having put in our initial outlay to pay for costs and Olivia's salary. Putting us under for good. Market forces were what did my parents in. They were farming before slow food and local providers became a thing. They tried their damnedest to keep my da's family farm profitable. In the end, it collapsed on them. And then their marriage collapsed. And my life did.

The press clunks and spins as Olivia runs it dry, looking to get a feel for it. The rhythm speeds up.

My breathing follows suit.

If this plan comes to nothing, Francis and Caro could break up for good. Carter and Jill would have to live through the repercussions, the pain of it.

Of waking up in the morning and knowing you weren't enough to keep your parents together.

All right, Macarthur. Be real. People can't stay together for the sake of their kids. And Carter and Jill aren't young, vulnerable teens.

But people can put in the safety switches necessary to protect themselves.

The writing's on the wall with Olivia—a new hire is inevitable. Carter's convinced it's the only way to get his dad to reduce his hours, and I see his logic. Even if the idea of failure is specter-grade frightening. I'll have to keep a close eye on things as plans become actions, look for the red flags Francis might miss because of his abhorrence of details, and Carter might not see because he won't have his hands in it anymore. He'll be back in Montreal, consumed with corporate branding and planograms, whatever the hell those are.

He won't have time for Imprescott Designs 2.0.

Or for me.

So, yeah. Safety switches.

A big old red one when it comes to Carter Prescott.

We can fool around a bit more between now and the end of the week, but I'm not giving in to any of the emotions trying to surface since our night away. The ones I've seen on his face too.

Carter excuses himself to the back, leaving me to casually monitor our prospective employee. I glance at Olivia at the work-table. Her face is screwed up in concentration. She's finished putting together her printing block and is mixing ink with a prac-ticed eye. She's chosen a rich, dark blue. It reminds me of the midnight sky the other night. When I had Carter up on a fence and we hadn't given in to the temptation to strip each other naked. When he was still pretending nothing was happening and I was still telling myself that kissing each other would help us leave our baggage in the past.

Bloody hell, we need to get back to that.

Carter emerges from the hall, carrying what looks like some of his sketches from the other day, the ones showing how we might rework the front area to increase the amount of product. He slaps them down on the counter in front of me.

"I want to see what Olivia thinks about these," he says in a low voice. "It'll give me an idea of her business knowledge."

The press starts up again, clacking and clattering behind us. Makes it easier to keep our conversation private.

"She's making a better impression than Wayne," I say. My mouth twitches at the memory of the man's disdain when Jill walked in throwing around childish nicknames.

"I like her. And I can tell you like her too, which matters the most," Carter says. "I really want her to work out."

Okay, but as if his urgency to hire her is entirely for my benefit. "Makes sense. If she works out, it's easier for you to leave."

"Easy to leave…" He snorts, crossing his arms, making his dress shirt tighten on his chest.

My mouth waters. I'm a thirsty, pathetic arse for this man. Can I manage just sleeping with him until he leaves?

Calm down. Just because you want him doesn't mean you want to be *with him.*

He tilts his head in thought and pokes at the bridge of his glasses. "I was wondering…"

"About…"

He flicks a hand, as if dismissing his own idea.

"Now you've got me curious," I say.

Sucking in a breath, he leans closer to me. "On the trip home from Whitingham, when we were chatting, I was thinking about how it's not unheard of for executives to have two residences. Split their time."

I rock back on my heels. Someone else might be able to come up with a two-city, back-and-forth plan, but it's not going to be Carter. He's all-or-nothing. "You can't be serious."

His mouth quirks in disappointment. "No?"

"No," I say.

"I honestly thought all I had was my drive and my career," he says, sounding on the verge of dropping some sort of personal revelation in the middle of the goddamn office in the middle of a goddamn job interview.

"What do you mean, two residences?"

"I mean finding a compromise. Do my job there *and* here."

Christ. If only. My pulse skips. I want to touch him, get closer to him, but Olivia's here, and even though there's no way she can hear our quiet conversation, I think one job interview where we get caught kissing was enough.

Not that we need to kiss right now. We need to talk. He needs to listen.

"You know you wouldn't be happy here, Carter. Not even if

you were here part-time and still working for OfficeMart. And if you were so convinced you only had your career, I don't think you'd be happy changing. You've never compromised in your life. Something I know too bloody well."

"All done!" Olivia announces, breaking into our conversation.

I'm breathing hard.

Carter's red in the face, jaw tight.

"Uh, is everything okay here?" our interviewee asks. She holds out a small stack of cardstock circles about three inches in diameter. "I riffed off something you mentioned, Carter, the coaster idea."

I accept the stack calmly, as if my ex-boyfriend didn't just tell me he's suddenly willing to relocate and as if I didn't just have to point out to him there's no earthly way for us to make it work.

Olivia's created a circular design with varying fonts and a snippet of a poem:

HERE,
With my beer
I sit,
While golden moments flit

"It's from a nineteenth-century poet. Obviously, we'd need to use the right weight of paper. The 110-pound isn't thick enough for coasters. Though," she says, tapping a finger to her lip, "maybe for food festivals and markets and stuff, it would be enough, given how disposable they'd be. Anyway, I thought it would be something you could propose to the local craft breweries."

"It's brilliant," I say, voice gruff. Her mocked-up, fake logo is precise and eye-catching.

"Fantastic work. I love what you brought to the table today," Carter says in a more even tone than I was able to muster. "Give Auden and my dad and me a day to chat."

Olivia grins. "Thanks."

Carter pulls a business card from his pocket and hands it to her. "This has my cell number on it so you know when it's me calling."

She toys with the ridiculously thick piece of smooth, red-edged stock. "Thank you. I can't wait to hear your decision."

The minute she's out the door, I hold out my hand.

"Give me one of those," I say.

He hands me a copy.

I flip the card between my fingers. It's a double thickness. "Oh my God. This is the stationery equivalent of windmilling your dick."

"And?"

"You're hung, but not that much," I say. It's hard to joke, but I need to pretend everything's okay right now.

He snorts.

"If you wanted a fancy business card, you could have just asked."

"As if, Auden. I had them done before I got here. We'd spoken nothing of consequence in years."

And now he's spoken a metric ton of consequential things.

Things about living here half-time, and what the hell would even be the reason for said suggestion if not to *be together* for half the time too?

I can't go there.

I hold up the card. "I can do better than this."

"I know you can."

"Maybe I will. A goodbye present," I say.

"And if I don't want to say goodbye?" His voice is rotgut rough, like the feelings coming out of him are too new and strong and burn his throat.

It's an audacious question.

"We agreed we wouldn't—"

He takes one of my hands in his. "I know, but I"—his chest rises as he inhales deeply—"I'm falling for you again, Auden."

Every word in my vocabulary explodes in my brain, a scattering of thousands of letters, like a shelf of type was knocked on the floor. I can't get a sound out.

For a minute we stand, my hand limp in his as I struggle to put two syllables together. He squeezes my palm, staring at me in resignation. He knows. Knows what he just said goes against what we'd agreed to.

My chest feels like he's taken an ax to every board and shim I've nailed and shoved into place to keep upright. To keep going after he fucking walked out of my life and confirmed everything I'd ever known about love but was too naive to believe.

"We weren't going to *go there*," I croak.

Lifting his hands upward as if to say *what else was I supposed to do,* he makes an apologetic face.

As if he's sorry he's feeling things for me.

Yeah, I'm sorry he is too.

For fuck's sake. I'm not an idiot. The hollow parts of my chest that want to soak up all his goodness… I know full well what that is. The pull in my gut, my inability to take my eyes off him. The way my heart is lying to me, telling me the only balm for my wounds is to let Carter love me.

If it was just my feelings, the suspicion I'm falling for him too, I'd deal. Keep it to myself, keep it safe.

But he opened his pretty, pretty mouth and said things he promised not to say, and now I need to say things back, and I can't.

I know how this ends.

"We planned on a few nights together," I choke out. "I can't do more."

Face paling, he pops his lips together a few times. He slips his glasses off and rubs his eyes. When he puts the clear frames back in place, his expression is blank.

"If that's the best you can give," he says, backing away a step, "I'll have to learn to live with it."

22

CARTER

Tipping back in the chair in Dad's office, I fidget with one of the mock coasters Olivia made, admiring the artisanship. She has an eye for proportions and a precision with the type that shows she's no rookie.

I'd hire her in a second, but it feels like something I need to run by my dad, so long as Mom'll give him the go-ahead to talk about work.

It's after dinner in Paris, but I don't feel like waiting until tomorrow to call. Hell, with how he and Mom have been carrying on, they're probably in the middle of a four-course spread of duck-a-la-all-the-things. I don't even want to think about what this trip is doing to their bank account. It's not my problem to worry about. As long as the Imprescott books are balanced and any temporary debt we're taking on will be matched by future returns, I've done my job.

I dial his number.

"Carter!" There's a slurping sound. "Your mom and I are sharing a bottle of Cab Sauv on the terrace." He proceeds to read me the label in stumbling French. "Have you heard of it?"

"That's like when people ask me if I know their cousin who

lives in Montreal, Dad." I chuckle. "Bring a bottle home with you, and we can share it sometime."

"Home, yes." He sounds thoughtful.

"Any plans there?"

He hums noncommittally.

"I can't stay past Saturday, Dad." I explain my week ahead, the jaunt up to Montreal for the presentation. "Will Mom let you talk about work for a second? I have someone who I want to hire."

There are a few seconds of muffled conversation. "She says to tell you, 'only because you're her favorite son.'"

A classic Caro Prescott line. I smile, then launch into a long description of Olivia's many talents. "She's a gem. I think you'll love her."

There's a long pause.

I can't decide what's worse—his silence or having to rehash the same argument about how necessary it is for him to have more support.

"You're sure she's the one? You don't want to look at more candidates?" he asks.

Wait, no pushback at all? What? It's my turn for silence. My tongue is stuck to the roof of my mouth.

After a few seconds, Dad says, "Carter? Did I lose you?"

I swallow down my shock. "No, I'm still here. And yes, I'm sure she's the one."

"Auden agrees?"

"On Olivia? Yes."

On everything else, no. His unwillingness to step out of his comfort zone—with work *and* with me—is coating my heart like a layer of lead.

"Go for it then. Unless you want to wait for me to do it."

The hairs prickle on the back of my neck. His agreement came too easily.

"But…" I wait for whatever wild-ass thing he's going to throw at me next.

He sighs. "Your mother and I were going to surprise you, but it's probably easier not to keep secrets. We're flying home tomorrow."

"Oh. Wow. Okay. Earlier than I expected."

"I thought you'd be thrilled," he says, sounding puzzled. "And for your timing, it's great. You can head home tomorrow. It'll give you an extra day to organize for whatever you're doing on Thursday."

"Whatever I'm doing? As in, the biggest presentation of my career to date?"

"Yeah, that," he says.

My throat tightens.

I get it. I've brought a lot of this on myself. But up and leaving, keeping up the walls between Auden and me, and the distance with my dad—it's not what I want anymore.

If I leave tomorrow, I won't get my one last Friday night with Auden. Or my last chance to drool over him while he mixes me a drink with his talented hands. No stumbling home to his place after his shift and reliving the striptease he ordered me to give him two nights ago.

"I was planning to come back," I say lamely. "I still could. Spend the weekend with you and Mom."

"Nah. Go take care of everything you've been putting off while you've been my placeholder."

Placeholder.

Ouch.

If he doesn't want me around, I'm not going to beg. "Sure. It'll be easier to leave early."

My voice cracks. Shit, did he hear that?

"Exactly what you wanted," he says.

I guess he didn't recognize the emotions breaking through my words. Good. He also has no clue how our usual patterns, worn into grooves through years of his pride and stubbornness rubbing up against my own, aren't doing it for me anymore.

If close to three weeks of me busting my ass for him hasn't

proved I'm worth listening to, worth accepting as is, then nothing will.

Easier to keep the father-son status quo in place even if it's not what I want.

I jam a hand in my hair and tug, counting on the sharp sensation to center me, to remind me I need to salvage my dignity here.

"I want you to succeed, Dad, but in a way that won't interfere with your and Mom's happiness."

"I've *agreed* to *hire* someone," he says, tone sharpening. "Like you told me to. Hopefully the extra productivity will bring in enough profit to cover both the new salary costs and me working shorter hours."

He seriously still thinks hiring Olivia is the only change we need to make? My skin heats. "I have a lot to show you when you get home—"

"Don't push it," he says. His words sting like bits of gravel flying out from under truck tires.

"What happened to 'do what you need to do?'"

"While I'm away, yeah. Not once I'm home."

My voice is going to come out weak, and I hate that. "What if I—?"

Oh. Oh *shit*. I've started to think of Imprescott as mine again. I was too deep in numbers and hiring and to-do lists to see it for what it is.

I want to be part of this again.

"What if you…" Dad gestures for me to continue.

"What if I want to keep contributing?"

Silence.

Long enough that I check the screen to see if the call dropped.

The seconds are ticking. He's still there. Somewhere in Paris, Dad's sitting and drinking wine. And… laughing?

Wait, what?

I put the phone back to my ear. "Are you laughing?"

"Yeah. You're funny. Keep contributing. Talk about a recipe for misery—for both of us." He chuckles. "We're a small business with heart. I appreciate the offer of more help, but it isn't needed. Keep your expansion ideas for your own company."

Prickly heat rushes over my body from my scalp to my feet.

"I've kept that heart beating for you," I say quietly.

And in doing so, mine got battered.

I can't listen to any more of this, listen to how I'm not needed. Hanging up, I toss my phone on the desk and drop my head to the back of the chair.

I'm done trying to get Francis John Prescott to see things he's too stubborn to acknowledge. I'm not going to be enough for him. I need to stick to my plan of making CEO by forty, because it's clear I'm not going to get the fulfillment I want out of life from my dad's approval.

And as for Auden?

Same goes. It's futile to hold out hope he'll change his mind, be willing to find a solution that works for the grown-ass people we are now.

Seems he was right—when you aim for it all, you end up on the floor.

The bruises in my chest are just going to get worse the longer I stick around. Maybe staying to the weekend is an ill-thought idea after all. I can spend tomorrow working with Olivia, then make a quick exit the day after. No need to drag things out, risk hurting Auden the way I've let myself get hurt.

It's almost quitting time, and I storm out of the office into the main area.

Auden jolts when he sees me and fumbles with the tray of type he's carrying. "Christ. What's wrong?"

You won't love me.

"Dad pissed me off," I say instead. "But good news—he'll be home tomorrow."

Auden leans back against the long rectangular Vandercook press. He grips his tray in front of him, making the muscles stand out on his forearms in tight, sexy ropes. The blue T-shirt he has on leaves nothing to the imagination, hugging every part of his brawny torso.

His expression is guarded. He's not going to give me more emotionally, no matter how much I wish I could get him to reach higher, to risk with me.

"Tomorrow," he repeats cautiously.

I nod, trying to read the uncertainty flickering in his eyes.

"You'll stay in Montreal after your presentation then."

"It's what my dad wants."

He sets the tray down on the press and comes over to stand in front of me. He smells like ink and warm flannel and everything I've ever loved. I press a kiss to his neck, right over his fluttering pulse.

Snagging one of my belt loops with a finger, he frowns. "And what do you want?"

Nothing worth guilting him over. If he can't be emotionally available, that's his prerogative.

Not mine. If I don't leave it all on the table, I'll always regret it. I don't do half-assed work.

I don't make half-assed declarations of love.

I'm falling for you again isn't going to cut it. If I'm going to move forward with a blank slate, I'm going to need to clear out the tangle of words and yearning that have been threatening to consume me since the moment I let Auden Macarthur impress himself back onto my heart.

It's not that I've rediscovered the love I had for him. We're different people now. More worn around the edges, in part because of how we treated each other when we were younger. I don't just like who he is now, I love him. I need to say it. He doesn't have to say anything back, but leaving without being completely honest would feel wrong.

"I'd like another night with you," I say.

Or a fucking lifetime's worth.

I lock gazes with him. I'm met with indecision, deep green and mesmerizing.

He dips his head to my ear, kissing the lobe, then my temple. "Just one more."

23

CARTER

I insist on going to my parents' house instead of his place. I need to figure out the best way to tell him what I feel, and it feels necessary to be on my own turf.

We eat a speedy dinner on the living room couch, two giant servings of steaming, salty wonton soup directly out of the plastic take-out bowls.

Auden takes a slurp of egg noodles and hums his appreciation.

"You still eat your soup the way you did in college," I say. It's easier to look back on those days fondly again. When adding noodles or extra Chinese broccoli to soup was an extravagance, and we'd watch live varsity hockey in the stands instead of throwing the Canadiens-Bruins game on as background noise. Ridiculously cramped dorm room sex too...

I'm going to spread out for him tonight, offer him every part of me he wants to take. It's not what I usually do and definitely not what we've always done, but if I'm going to convince him I'm willing to build something new, I need him to see I'm open to listening and exploring.

He finishes chewing, then swallows. "The only way to eat wonton is to add noodles." He smirks and peeks into my bowl.

"Nah. Gotta leave room for extra barbecue pork." Though I powered through all those slices right after taking off the lid. Only broth and some sad-looking green onions are left. I set my container and chopsticks on the coffee table and weigh my options.

Talk, or fuck?

Auden sucks a few noodles through his lips, *Lady and the Tramp* style, and eyes me warily.

He's obviously not ready to hear romantic confessions.

Fuck before talk then.

"Baby?" I murmur, stroking a hand up his meaty biceps.

He puts down his bowl and sends me a look hot enough to make the dregs of soup boil.

I stand. "Come upstairs."

Before I can take a step, I'm pulled against a hard chest, my back to his front. The fingers of one hand spread below my collar, the other, over my navel, just above my belt buckle.

"Always so bloody fancy." He plucks one button open and traces the skin in the widened V.

I press my ass against his front. Unlike me, he put on a pair of flannel pants when he got here—a size too big on me, the ones I wear once a year when I get a cold and stay home with soup and tea. I grabbed them on impulse when I was last in Montreal, wanting the coziness. Seeing them on Auden is even better than wearing them myself. I feel every inch of his hardening cock through the thin fabric and the wool of my suit pants.

That erection is way too delicious, rubbing between my cheeks, and damn, it's going to feel like a fucking rhapsody when he thrusts in me.

His hand traces an irregular path down to my stomach where he makes quick work of my belt buckle.

"Wait, when did you undo my shirt?" I ask.

"Uh, you didn't notice?"

I grind backward against him. "I was thinking of this."

Delving under the elastic of my underwear, he takes me in his big grip. "Like I was thinking of this?"

One stroke.

One stroke, and my knees are melting, and I'm at his mercy.

I reach up and back, linking my fingers behind his neck. The sides of my shirt hang open. The weight of my belt pulls my pants down to the tops of my thighs.

I'm exposed, undone for him.

A thrill runs through me. Worry. Nerves. Anticipation.

He's stroking me, so slow, so tender.

"I really love thinking about you thinking about my dick," I say, voice half breath, half groan. "What are you planning to do with me?"

My plan's the one that counts, but I'll let him think he's the cruise director.

"Take you upstairs. Let you fuck me one last time."

"Nah," I say.

His even pace stills on my aching shaft. "Why?"

"Let me show you."

I untangle myself from his embrace and pull him upstairs. Tossing my pants and shirt to the floor, I lay back on the queen size bed, rising on my elbows. "Lose the shirt."

He reaches between his shoulder blades and rips it off in one swift movement, then sheds his pants.

My mouth goes dry. At the hot AF way he undressed, at his fuzzy chest, his parted lips.

I bend to kiss his pecs. The hair there is delicious. Trimmed at some point, but not in the past couple of weeks or so because it curls around my fingers, rasps against my mouth. I tease one nipple, scrape my teeth across his skin to find the other. Flicking my tongue on the tight nub, I earn a gasp.

"Make love to me, Auden."

He exhales slowly. "Yeah?"

"Definitely."

"Then get on the bed, darling."

Hot desire jolts through my body. "You first."

"No." It's a verbal hand flick, a get-to-it, and every muscle in my body responds. I ease onto the mattress.

And then he's between my legs, heavy and sure. He nips at my earlobe, and my back arches, the momentary shock passing through my limbs like an electrical current. I can't rise more than an inch. He's holding me down.

He presses his lips to mine, unyielding, demanding my full attention. His hand strokes my side, thumb digging into a hollow of muscle, making me cry out.

Get it together, Prescott.

Except—

That's what he needs from me. For me not to be put together.

Gripping his shoulders, I tilt my hips up, our cocks pressing together through thin underwear. He lays a line of kisses along my collarbone, a tender reprieve.

I run my palms along his sides until my thumbs rest against the band of his boxer briefs. He shimmies, pressing into my hands.

"Take them off," he says.

"These?" I snap the elastic, earning a yelp.

"Those."

I cup his thick erection through the fabric, slide them down until the waistband rests below the base of his hard-on. A bead of moisture glistens at the tip.

"You're so lickable."

"Not yet." It's a growl. A damn command.

"Oh really." I reach to touch him, stroke him.

He clamps a big fist around my wrist. "Not yet," he repeats. "Take yours off too."

I send him an amused look. "And if I'm not ready?"

"You're ready." He hooks fingers in either side of my waistband and yanks them as far as he can get them, just below my ass.

The lack of compression feels too free. I need pressure, friction.

I lean forward, kissing him slow and teasing. Our cocks brush, the searing heat of him branding my oversensitized skin.

"I know what you want." He takes us both in hand.

The snug hold is pink diamonds and platinum in a world of tarnished tin. He pumps easy, a warm-up.

I thrust against his erect length, against his palm. An instinctual movement. "God, yes."

"Tha'? More of tha'?"

"More of you," I admit, groaning as he tenses his hand and pumps again. Tip to base, a cascade of pleasure along my needy flesh.

Work-hardened arms bracket my torso. He kisses a slow, sensuous trail up my chest.

"Auden…" I'm whining. Because I don't like the shift of control? Because I need to give it up to him too damn much? Maybe both. "There's lube in the nightstand."

Abandoning our dicks for the promise of more, he finds the tube I'm talking about. He slicks his fingers, preps my rim. Slides one tip in.

Jesus, yes. I hiss out my approval, pushing against his hand for more. The pressure is perfect and not enough.

It's more than arousal. I love him so, so much.

He inches toward my prostate, adding another finger, hitting gold.

Sparks fly through my body.

I'm all his, a pliable, worshipful devotee of the hand of Auden.

"Baby, I—"

I can't form a whole thought. This is too mind-melting. He's skillful, diligent. Prepping and pleasuring, grinning as he watches me squirm at his touch.

"Enough," I groan.

Though I'm not sure it's literally possible to get enough of Auden's fingers.

He rolls on a condom and makes sure there's enough lube. "Want to be on your back or your front?"

"I want to see your face," I rasp.

Stroking my hair off my forehead, fixing me with a tender, indulgent smile, he nudges my rim.

"I'll go easy," he promises.

"Don't." He's thick and I rarely bottom, but I want to do this for him.

"I'll be careful with you." He eases in a little, kissing me and murmuring sweet, Scottish-burred nonsense in my ear, distracting me with an unyielding grip on my cock until I relax. The burn builds into something all-consuming, incredible. Something I could get addicted to so fucking easily.

Oh God. Being under him while he thrusts… I meet the movements, getting him all in. His green gaze has me in thrall, silently promising to make me feel better than I've ever felt before. That every cell of my body currently clamoring for release can trust him to take me to the edge, over it.

That he'll take me apart and put me back together and I might not recognize who I'm going to be after this, but I'm going to like that man more than I've ever liked who I was before this moment.

Flames lick my skin. The slap of our frantic pace fills the room. My length rubs against the hair on his belly, the friction hinting at euphoria. I grip myself, falling further into the swell of need and heat. "Auden, I—"

I want to confess how much the all-consuming connection feels like love when he looks at me, but I can't yet. He won't believe me, not while he's thrusting into me like a man possessed.

"So tight." He moans. "So good."

I'm reaching, close, closer, my lips and teeth working against his neck, nose assaulted by his masculine, fresh scent.

"Don't want this to end," he grumbles, hand tight on my hip as he keeps my leg wrapped around his ass. His other arm is braced by the pillow, his big hand clutching my hair. "But I'm almost—"

His eyes squeeze shut and he thrusts one last time, hitting my spot, shouting something burred and unintelligible.

I'm thrown off the cliff, tumbling, reaching. Coming hard between our stomachs as he collapses on me.

"Didna—" He clears his throat. "Didn't expect you to want to bottom. Christ, that was something."

"It was." My voice is just as raspy as his. He probably didn't expect me to love him again either. To need him in my life at the expense of logic and reason.

The last time I left, I walked out midconversation. I won't repeat past mistakes.

I love him. And I can't go anywhere until he believes me.

24

AUDEN

Carter's a gorgeous mess.

It's all my doing, which is deeply, deeply satisfying.

He'll be gone by tomorrow night—will probably tag off with his parents like he's passing a baton in a sprint relay.

And I'll be sitting in the stands, deeply *un*satisfied.

With this on replay. Flushed, sweaty skin and tousled hair. His blissed-out smile. Muscled limbs draped across me.

I pull the sheet and comforter over us and hold him. My lips caress his forehead. I taste salt, smell expensive hair products and sex.

A vise clamps around my chest. I'm heavy-hearted and light-headed, and the imbalance is dizzying.

I need to talk about something concrete, or I might spin off the bed and out into the atmosphere.

"What last things do you want to do tomorrow?" I ask.

"Fuck. You too?" he mumbles, words muffled against my shoulder.

"Me too, what?"

"Assuming I'm leaving tomorrow and won't be coming back."

"Why would you need to?"

He lifts his head. His gaze is wrecked, his mouth, haggard. "You're going to ask me that after what we just shared?"

"I wasn't talking about this, Carter." What's there to say about it? "I just meant once you hire Olivia and your dad is back, you're free."

His face crumbles. "I don't feel free."

I tighten my arm around him. "That's rotten."

"Yes and no."

I wait for him to continue.

He nuzzles into my neck and sighs. "I like feeling tied to you, Auden. And I was even getting used to it with the shop."

My heart veers from resignation toward hope. "You sure you don't want to stay on instead of hiring Olivia?"

"I— I've thought about it. Actual consideration."

"But?"

"Dad and I... He's never going to want what I can offer." His throat bobs against my skin. "I'd really hoped you'd see the possibilities in me pushing forward with my OfficeMart plans but exploring living in both places."

"I don't want a half-time relationship," I say.

"So come with me then."

"What?" I blink at him, stunned.

He scrambles out of my embrace, snags his underwear from the end of the bed, and puts them on. Kneeling before me, he's sleek muscle and clenched fists and a desperate, pleading mouth. "If you don't want to consider me splitting my time between here and Montreal... What about you coming there with me?"

I'm lying on the mattress, so I can't fall back farther, but it feels like it's swallowing me. "Are you serious?"

"Very." He takes one of my hands and holds it between his. "I can make room in my life for you there."

I narrow my eyes. "Make room for me? Not exactly a ringing offer."

"You want a ring?" He bows his head, rubbing his fingertip

225

over the digit where he'd slide a wedding band onto my hand. "We could talk about rings."

I shift into a sitting position. The spindles on the bed dig into my back. "How did we go from one last night of sex to marriage? Bloody hell."

He blanches. "I'm sorry. I didn't mean to—" Air shudders from his lips. "I want to find a solution. And if it's me cutting back on hours and prioritizing a relationship, building a life together in Montreal, I'm willing to try. It's not perfect, I know, but it's a compromise, and it's better than being alone. Better than not having you in my life at all."

"You'd be asking me to give up everything I have here," I say. "And I'd be leaving your dad in the lurch."

"I know. I wouldn't expect you to come tomorrow. There'd be a raft of immigration paperwork, and Dad would need to find a replacement for you before you could leave. You wouldn't have to worry about not finding a job there. I have connections in the industry—I could help you find rewarding work. And while you're searching for something perfect, I can cover you. And your mom. My salary… It's enough to share."

My ears are buzzing. Covering for me, helping me find work? Work that wouldn't necessarily be stable. And a relationship that wouldn't be risk-free, because such a unicorn doesn't exist.

"Why?" It's the only word I can manage.

"I love you."

"It might feel that way in the moment, but—"

He leans in and cups my face. "Stop, baby. Fuck that. I actually do."

Fear wrenches through me. If I accept his words as real and valid, then it's going to kill me when he changes his mind.

Because we've been through this before. He loved me once—until things got tough with Francis.

So he can promise to support me, help me with paperwork and finding a job in a new city—a new *country*—all he wants. It's easy to offer those things right now while this feels new and shiny and delightful.

But it'll get dark at some point. If he walks away again, after I've given up my career, my long-term security? I'll be just like Mum, having to start over far too late in life, bitter and unstable. And I'd lose my ability to help her get out of that spot herself. No. I can't. This hurts, but throwing everything to the wind would be irresponsible. Destructive.

I take his hands off my face and run my thumbs along the backs. "You love me *for now*."

He lets out a weird, strangled sound.

I've got to get out of here. I roll off the other side of the bed and quickly dress.

He's still kneeling on the bed, head down and fists clenched on his thighs. "You don't need to leave."

"I do. I shouldn't have come in the first place."

25

CARTER

I shouldn't have come in the first place.

Auden's truth—the truth to him at least—rings in my ears as I enter through the back door of Imprescott Designs one last time.

I'd love to claim the same applies to me. Stomp my feet and say I shouldn't have come home at all.

Not true though. My weeks in Burlington have been nothing if not illuminating.

I now know my dad's incapable of separating the image he has of me as a cocky, bullheaded graduate from who I am today.

Sucks, but it's freeing. I can focus on my own goals, no longer feeling like I have to keep begging for scraps.

Letting things get to where they did with Auden though... My compromises aren't good enough for him.

I'm not good enough.

It's hard to see the bright side of our solar flare of a fling while I'm a walking, jagged wound.

The only solace is I'm not walking away without having tried to find a solution.

When I hunker in the office and call Olivia to officially offer her the position, she's ecstatic. She's also free from school and her other job for the day so is only too happy to come in for training. I spend a couple of hours on office and social media stuff before handing her off to Auden to deal with the artistic parts.

It's nearing on three o'clock when she finishes up and bounces toward the front door, thanking me profusely for hiring her and exuding excitement over getting to work soon. She leaves, a bundle of potential that my dad better appreciate us having found for him.

"I should go home and pack," I say, looking everywhere except Auden.

Hard not to be drawn to him though.

His flannel shirt looks like the softest thing on earth. He's clutching one of the clear-top boxes of stationery he sells at V and V, along with a smaller one.

He hands me the larger of the boxes. It's the rainbow design I sketched out, in its completion. A C monogram is nestled between the colorful stripes—playful without being trite.

It's not the design I saw yesterday. "I thought the set you were making had *love* printed in the middle of it."

His mouth twists. "I couldn't sleep last night. Made a new run of this. For you. Thought you'd get more use out of it than the other… The other motif."

He can't even give me a sheet of paper that says *love* on it?

I finally make eye contact with him. The pain in his gaze is acidic. There's a bit of hope too.

I want that hope to mean more than it does.

I love you.

Just take a risk.

On me. Please.

(He won't.)

"It's beautiful work."

"Thank you," he says, words rough.

I take off the lid to stroke the faint imprint of the lines. "I'll use this."

"Good. It's for you," he says gruffly. "So are these." He holds out the other box.

I put down the paper to take the second offering.

Business cards, a small batch.

Printed with the Imprescott Designs logo, my name, and cell number.

Confusion ripples through me. What part of *my dad doesn't want what I can offer* does Auden not understand? "Uh, what are these for? Is this *your* idea of a compromise? I told you—"

"For memory's sake," he says, wiping a hand down his face. He strokes his beard a few times, fussing with the edges.

I stare at the typeface. *Memory's sake...*

"I don't need a card to remind me of how things could have been," I say.

I fuse myself to him, stealing one last kiss. Hot mouths, frustrated groans. Hands trying to encompass all the moments that will never be and mark them on each other for life.

It ends in our mingled, heaving breaths, our foreheads pressed together.

I take one of the cards out of the box and slip it in the front pocket of his shirt. "I need to go. But I love you. And not the man I loved in college. He was fantastic, don't get me wrong, but now, with your skill and dedication and generosity and being really fucking hot—"

He snorts.

"It's all true. And it's what I want in my life." My eyes sting. "I can't make you want me or love me. I know I'm *not* what you want in *your* life. I tried to prove otherwise. Clearly failed. If you figure out how to take a chance on us"—I pat his chest, reminding him of the business card—"you know my number."

Auden's mouth gapes, and he swipes a thumb down my cheek before backing away a step. Stacking his hands on top of his head, he nods toward the box of paper. "Don't forget that."

I won't.

Not the paper, not the artisan who made it.

He's a fucking part of me. Stitched into my soul.

I'll be trying to undo the threads for the rest of my life.

———————

A half hour later, I'm in my parents' house, scanning the living room for any last phone chargers or work detritus, when the front door flies open.

I brace myself for a wave of maternal love or fatherly grumpiness, but my aunt's the one who marches in.

"So this is it? You're already packed?" Bee brings a flurry of snow with her. She's carrying a suitcase in one hand and a white confectioner's box in the other. She waves it under my nose, and I catch a whiff of sugar and a glimpse of gold lettering. "And here I was going to share my Parisian spoils with you. Now... I think I'll eat them all myself. Stress eating. *Sad* eating."

"Parisian— Wait, did you go get Mom and Dad from the airport? I thought they were driving themselves. Where are they?"

The door opens again, answering my question.

And there's the maternal love I expected, a huge hug from my mom. My dad follows, almost smiling. He pats me on the shoulder, because my mom's still holding on to me like I'm a toddler she lost in a department store.

She's bundled up in a gray winter coat and thick leggings and smells a bit like canned airplane air. "Carter. Sweetheart. Thank you."

"*Merci*, you mean?"

"Oh yes. All the *mercis*. It was exactly what we needed." She holds my face in her hands and studies me. Her smile sags. "Shit. It did a number on you. Why didn't you say something?"

"Bit of a recent development," I mutter, then cringe, because as if a weak excuse will deter her from prying. "Lots of work, Mom. That's all."

"Hmmm." She's always growled like Marge Simpson.

I help with their suitcases. It's blisteringly cold out. I'd love to light a fire in the wood-burning fireplace and cuddle under a blanket and drink a Dirty Scot to warm up, but I want to do it with my own dirty Scot, not my parents and aunt. And given Auden wants nothing to do with sharing fires and blankets and liquor with me, I'm better off to drive back to Montreal. The fireplace in my condo is gas, and the drinks aren't nearly so skillfully made, but at least I'll be alone to wallow in my misery for a day before I have to slap on a smile and make magic at work.

"I have a few things to run by Dad, and then I'll be out of your hair," I tell Mom.

"You're not staying until tomorrow?" she asks.

"You're probably jet-lagged to hell and back," I say. "If I stick around, you'll feel the need to take care of me, and you won't rest."

She frowns and follows me into the kitchen where Bee is cracking into her box of macarons.

"There's some leftover spaghetti sauce in the fridge, if you want," I say. "Auden and I made it—"

Mom's gaze sharpens. "Oh *really*. I knew this"—she circles her hand in the air, indicating my face—"was about more than work."

"It's about more than spaghetti too," my ever-helpful aunt adds, taking a tiny bite of a pink macaron. She moans. "Oh my Lord. Rosewater. That's the best thing to ever touch my tongue."

"Don't say that around Gracie," I warn.

"No relationship opinions from you, not today," she retorts, popping the rest of the confection in her mouth.

I grit my teeth. "You say that as if I'm the one who fucked up."

My mom's gaze bounces between us. She's squinting a little, as if a long travel day and having been gone for a few weeks is making it impossible to keep up. "I must need a coffee."

"Then you'll never sleep. Power through until eight," I recommend before turning to my aunt. "Bee, why the hell would I stay?" I jam both hands into my hair. "Neither Dad nor Auden needs or wants me."

Mom sucks in a breath.

My aunt takes out a gold-dusted macaron and eats half of it. She's still chewing when she says, "They both need you more than they realize."

"I don't think so. I tried to prove myself. Really. And I failed hard." I send my mom an apologetic look.

"Oh, honey," she says.

She doesn't contradict me. It's noticeable, and it slices at me even though she gives me another hug.

Bee's ability to switch from rapturous-macaron hedonism to scorn-the-nephew sternness is startling. She fixes me with a capital-L look. "You don't need to prove yourself, sweet pea."

I raise my brows at her.

"What? I'm serious. You're amazing."

"Truth," Mom adds, stroking my arm.

"Not to them."

Bee scoffs and hands me the other half of the gold macaron. "Here. One bite. That was hard for you to admit. To be clear, it's garbage, but it took effort to get it out, I know."

I take the morsel of sugary art. It's sweet, honey-flavored. "You barely gave me a taste."

"I'll need more than an itty-bitty 'not to them' to hand over a whole piece of patisserie heaven."

I roll my eyes.

She narrows hers. "Since when do you let others define you, Carter Prescott?"

All the tension of the past few days bubbles to the surface, spills into my shouted, "Since when have I not? I've spent my whole goddamn life trying to prove myself!"

Mom squeezes my arm. She murmurs a shush. Not telling me to shut up, but to calm down.

"I'm fine, Mom," I grumble.

"No, you're hurting," Bee says, playing eeny, meeny, miny, moe between two blue cookies.

"Your father and I have had a lot of words lately," Mom says, eyes flashing. "We're about to have some more if this is how you're feeling."

"Don't, Mom. It's not fixable—"

"Want to elaborate on 'prove myself?'" Bee's shifting into psychology professor mode, and she'll be relentless if I don't play along. "You've always had your own drive, set your own goals."

My legs feel like Jell-O, and I sit on one of the chairs across from her. "To try to impress Dad."

"Ah, there it is," she says. She holds out the box for me.

The rainbow effect reminds me of the stationery I carefully packed in my briefcase.

I shake my head. "Can't eat more." My stomach is lurching at the bite I already ate. No way am I throwing more sugar in there while it's busy digesting being rejected by the two most important men in the world to me.

Shrugging, she plucks a brown-and-purple one with two fingers and nibbles the corner. "You're missing out. This one's peanut butter and grape jelly."

"Bee…"

Mom clears her throat. "If you won't let me talk to him, you should, honey."

"Dad or Auden?" I ask.

"Both," my mom and aunt say in unison.

"You say that as if I didn't try."

Footsteps trot down the stairs, and Dad enters the kitchen. He's changed into flannel pants and a plain green sweatshirt. "What didn't you try?" he asks. "Seems like all you've done since you got here is try to do things I didn't want you to do."

"Francis!" Mom glares at him. "Those *things* saved your hide."

"I know," he says, clearly reluctant. He yawns. "Did I hear something about spaghetti?"

"Just sauce," I say. "Auden and I made leftovers on Sunday."

"Managed to get along well enough then?" Dad says.

I warble something unintelligible.

Bee snorts.

"What?" Dad asks.

Oh hell no. I'm not talking about relationships with him. God forbid I give him another reason to take Auden's side. If he found out I tried to convince Auden to join me in Montreal, it would erase all the good work I did here. He'd ignore the fact I'd help him find a replacement and bemoan how I was stealing the man who's been a son to him. More of a son than I've ever been able to be.

"I have a few things to go over with you before I leave," I say, changing the subject.

He grabs a beer from the fridge and waves a hand at me. "I'll figure it out. You don't need to give me a rundown. Or Auden can—"

"Auden isn't the one who's been busting his ass to fix your mistakes!"

Dad stills with his beer at his lips.

I wasn't going to do this. I was just going to give him a quick-and-dirty overview of how things were.

I can't. He needs to see how hard I worked. Not to win his approval—I know I won't—but so *I* can see the worth of my work even if he can't.

"I'm tired of your bullshit," I snap. "I've stuck around for close to three weeks for you. You owe me ten goddamn minutes. I *deserve* your time."

Mom stares at us. Aunt Bee stares at us and nibbles the edges off a purple confection.

And Dad actually sits, taking the chair at the end of the table. "Auden didn't pull his weight?"

I storm into the living room, grab the stack of papers I printed off for him, and return to the kitchen. I'm not sitting. I'm going to spit this out and hit the road.

I slap my first printout on the table. "Auden is a loyal, talented employee. You should give him a raise."

"With what money?"

"With extra internet orders." I slap down a spreadsheet, then my proposal for new products. "And promoting Auden's ideas." Four pieces of his designs, including one of the rainbow ones he made for me. "And Olivia managing our social media, following on what I've done." A sheet of statistics. "Oh, and better—" One drawing. "Goddamn." Another drawing. "Merchandising."

He glances at the top sheet and humphs.

"Carter. Your sketches are gorgeous," Mom says.

Bee nods in agreement.

"Thank you. I know they are. I'm a vice president in merchandising of a billion-dollar company in the middle of a national overhaul. I think I can handle the front of a three-person print shop."

"Hey," Dad snaps. "That three-person print shop got you that fancy-ass graduate degree that got you that fancy-ass VP job—"

I tap the stack of paper. "Drawing up these plans meant more to me than any of the designs my team put together for OfficeMart."

Adding one last stack to the pile—the full, professional proposal I've stayed up late writing—I go for broke. "Redesign the front, and you'll pull in a ton of people from Church Street. It'll work. Just like I know all my ideas would work. It wouldn't take the heart out of the business, Dad. It would help you grow a little, sustain living wages for your employees, streamline operations so you don't have to work late crunching numbers and worrying about red ink."

His jaw tightens. He collects all the papers and passes them back to me. "My name is on the sign, Carter. I'm going to keep running it in a way that works for me."

"It's my name too, Dad. Can't the place have a little of both of us in it?"

"You don't work for me. So, no."

I nearly stumble backward, his refusal hits me so hard. Clenching my fists, I suck in a long breath, willing the stinging at the corners of my eyes to stop.

"Francis," Mom warns. "You're tired. And Carter's a hell of a lot savvier than you are. Don't make any decisions tonight."

"Caro, I'm not going to let him strip the soul—"

"*Francis*. I have ten more vacations on my bucket list, and I won't hesitate to go on them without—"

"It's fine, Mom. I'm done here." I'm so damn tired of hearing no from the people who are supposed to love me unconditionally.

"Thank you, Carter. For everything," Mom says, then elbows Dad.

"Thanks," he grumbles.

"Don't strain yourself there, Dad." Grabbing the full proposal, I scribble a note on the rainbow letterhead, fold and tuck it into the back before handing the duotang to Aunt Bee. "Can you give this to Auden, please? Maybe he'll have more sense."

"On it." She takes the proposal and hands over her nearly denuded box of macarons. "Here. Have the rest. You earned them."

I thank her and accept the box for the road.

What I should have earned is some respect. I guess a cookie will have to do.

26

AUDEN

Beams of late-afternoon sun angle on Lake Champlain, a shimmer of winter-white, iridescent sparkles. I squint and toss another handful of cracked corn into the wire-enclosed run of Bee and Grace's chicken palace.

"You don't know how good you have it," I say to the clucking hens as they pick their way through scattered hay to find their dinner. The run is sandwiched between two wood-sided coops, which are raised off the ground and painted pale blue and roofed in dark gray metal to match the main house. Bee went so far as to add little planters on the sides.

One chicken eyes me with suspicion.

"What, do you also think I'm a grumpy git and am in the way? Keep glaring at me and there'll be no more feed for you, henny penny."

If a chicken could emote disdain, this one just did. And fair enough. I've been a right prick since Carter left. Bee was absolutely right to kick me out of the kitchen. My mood would have soured the chicken and veg pie she was putting together.

"We're having three kinds of pie," I inform the chickens. "And you're all lucky you're not going in one of them."

The birds are singularly unimpressed by my threats.

I lift the lid of the nesting box and snatch the few eggs I see, cradling them in my hand. "That's what you get for your attitude. I'm taking these and eating them."

If anyone has an attitude right now, it's me.

And I don't deserve to be cranky. I knew what I was getting into, messing around with Carter. Knew even a week of sex was reaching too high, for too much.

I was perfectly content before he came along.

"*Bock-A!*" a chicken bloody yells at me.

"Fine!" I snap back. "Maybe *content* wasn't the right word. Maybe *settling* would be more accurate. But I wasn't in fucking pain, so I'm thinking settling was the way to go."

Having less is supposed to mean losing less and being happier.

I'm sure as hell not happy right now. But having had Carter in my life again, challenging each other at work, whiling away the odd lazy moment together, waking up to his smile, I can see I wasn't happy before either.

I was secure, but not satisfied.

I can't see a way to have both though.

I pluck the eggs from the box on the other half of the coop and trudge back to the house.

Once inside, I toe out of my Blundstones and return to the kitchen, holding out the clutch of eggs. "I come bearing an egg-pology."

Bee's brows lift under her dark red bangs. She nods in the direction of a stack of cardboard egg containers next to the refrigerator. "Put 'em in there. You can take them home."

"Thanks."

"And what's the apology for?"

I plop the half dozen eggs in one end of a carton. "For spewing my mood all over your attempt at a lovely family dinner." My throat feels thick, and I swallow. Laughter comes from the front room. Sounds like Francis and Caro have arrived and are enjoying

Gracie's company. I'd put on a happy face and join them, but I don't think I'd be fooling anyone. "For still being my family, despite… everything."

She hums and pleats the pastry around the edge of her pie. Two others sit on the counter, one piled high with glossy cherries and topped with an intricate lattice, the other filled with spinach, ham, and a creamy sauce. "I spoke to 'everything' yesterday, by the way. He's as much of a sad sack as you are."

That doesn't make me feel better.

"I hope his presentation went well," I mumble.

"Call him and ask." She balls up a tea towel and tosses it at my head.

I catch it, twist it in my hands. It's the one I brought her when I visited Mum for Christmas and Hogmanay, blue and white and printed with a dictionary of Scottish profanity. I'm tempted to recite them all five times over.

"Oh!" Bee says. "He left you something, and I keep forgetting to give it to you. Check over by the coffee maker. You might want to read it and then talk to my brother about it."

Draping the tea towel on the bar affixed to the side of one of the hanging cabinets, I narrow my eyes at her. She's wearing an *I'm not plotting* expression, which means she clearly is.

I retrieve the folder and read the print under the clear top sheet. "Didn't realize he made a full-on business plan."

One red eyebrow arches. "Carter was born to make plans and weigh options."

"I know," I say quietly. "He threw about eighteen million of them at me before he left."

"Eighteen million?"

"Well, two," I admit, flipping through the pages, absorbing Carter's thoughtful sketches and skilled projections. "Tossed around the idea of living part-time here and in Montreal, but as if either of us would be satisfied with something so disjointed. And then he asked me to move to Montreal with him."

"He *what*?"

"I know. Don't tell Francis. He'd probably think Carter was trying to screw him over by stealing me away."

"The proposal you're holding doesn't look like he's working against Francis at all," she says.

"True." Carter's work—his labor of love, really—is a thousand times more professional than is probably needed, but it's easy to understand. He's not asking us to go on some wild tangent or even to take on any considerable risk. It's building on what we already have.

Similar to what he was asking you to do with his offer to live between two cities.

Frowning at my idiotic inner voice, I turn to the next page. A note falls out from between two of the back pages. It's one of the monogrammed sheets I printed for Carter. Rushed, larger-than-normal script fills the top half of the white space. Not his usual controlled block printing and written with crappy ball-point ink instead of his preferred fancy fountain pen, but still noticeably his writing.

MAYBE YOU CAN CONVINCE HIM.
AND I REALLY DO LOVE YOU.
THERE'S A HOLE IN MY LIFE WHERE YOU SHOULD BE.
I DUG IT WHEN I LEFT.
I CAN'T FILL IT IN WITHOUT YOU.
~C

Something wells inside me, something I really don't care for Bee to see.

"Handwritten notes are terribly romantic," she says with a wistful sigh. She puts two of the pies in the top half of her oven and the third in the bottom.

"How do you know it's a romantic note?" I say, carefully folding the page and putting it in the back pocket of my jeans.

She stares at me.

"Ah, you read it. Of course."

"Doing my due diligence, sweet pea."

I clear the unwelcome thickness from my throat. "Can't do anything about the hole in his life, but I'll try to see if Francis will listen at least."

"Why do you think I invited you both over for dinner?"

"Because you knew there was no way you and Gracie could eat three pies?"

"That too." She tops up the glass of wine I haven't managed to take more than two sips of because it's the same kind Carter and I shared while staying at the B and B and the rich flavor reminds me of tasting it on his kiss. She pours herself a serving and takes a long drink. "Damn, that's good. Anyway, it seemed like you needed a prod."

"It's Francis who's being resistant, not me," I point out.

"Oh, it's not the business part you needed the prod with. It's figuring out a way to get you in your truck with all your earthly belongings, pointed toward my heartbroken nephew. And to get the truck bit in motion, you have a lot of shit to figure out with my brother."

"You want me to move to Montreal?"

"I want you to live your best life."

"Okay, Oprah."

She pokes me in the chest. "With Carter."

"Got it."

"I'm serious!"

"I know you are." I set my glass on the counter and lean against the marble, crossing my arms. "And you're dreaming. He won't work with Francis." I tick off my pointer finger. "Him living in two cities would be a half-life." I add my middle finger to the count. "And me moving would mean getting a work visa, getting rid of my apartment, giving up reliable income, and eventually ending up broke, alone, letting my mom down, and having to rebuild at a time in my life when I'm supposed to be comfortable and over all the bumps in the road."

She points to my wine. "Drink that."

"What is this, a community-theater rendition of Alice in Wonderland?"

"Going off your rabbit-hole explanation, yeah."

I obediently take a sip. "Currant-forward," I say. "Would go well with cheese. A hard, Italian one." *It paired best with the sweet saltiness of tasting Carter's neck.* Heat floods my stomach. "And I'm not seeing the rabbit hole."

"It's hard to see it when you've been living in it. Trauma, baby. It's a bitch."

"Trauma?"

"Yes, trauma." She mimics my rolling *R*. "Losing your home. Your dad walking away. And then Carter reinforcing that. You can't tell me you don't see it as trauma."

No, I can't. I give a clipped nod in agreement.

"You experienced a lot of pain at a young age," she says quietly. "It explains your risk-aversiveness. As does your wanting to help your mom too. Protecting the family you were left with."

"You're not going to tell me I'm letting her take advantage of me?" A few of my friends had opined on that over the years, informing me my mum should be independent and not rely on me.

"Families are complicated, Auden. Money, even more so. *Does* she take advantage?"

"She doesn't ask for money often. Mostly I help her because I want to. She supported me all the way through college without my knowing it, and I'll always hate that. It makes *me* more comfortable to know she's not struggling." Truth rises in my chest. "She is a rather constant refrain in my ear though. Love's not to be trusted and so on. I've let it color my own relationship choices."

She raises her hands as if to say "Who wouldn't?"

And then she plays the old counselor's trick of not saying anything, waiting for me to add more. It's obvious. And I fall for it every time she does it.

"I suppose what's valid for Mum doesn't have to be for me."

"Handsome *and* emotionally intelligent." She lifts her arms and does a shimmying, celebratory dance. "Put your past aside for a second. This time did he leave you? Or did you push him away?"

I groan and drown my regret with a large slug of wine. "The latter."

She shifts next to me and puts a hand on my arm. "Being with Carter might not work out, but where are the guarantees here either? Businesses fail. People let us down. And if we focus on what we think will go wrong, try to swaddle our hearts from bruises, we miss out on all the precious moments where everything goes right. You're not an island. You've grown your family. People who you trust not to let you down on a regular basis."

"And I need to let Carter be one of those people too," I say.

She nods.

I stare into my glass, at the rich red liquid that reminds me of a remarkable night with a remarkable man—being stuck in an inconvenient situation but mining out the jewels of possibility together. A small, eloquent moment of actual living that mattered more than any feeling of safety, of security. A moment that only came from taking a goddamn chance. A chance I would take again, regardless of my current, battered heart.

I rub my eyes, at the moisture collecting at the corners.

Yes, Carter could hurt me worse than anyone ever has.

Worse than he did the first time.

He also brings me more joy than anyone in my life.

Joy I'm not experiencing on the safe route I've chosen. Which, as Bee so kindly pointed out, isn't as safe as I'd like to think it is. Tragedy could strike tomorrow—fire, death, injury—which could mean having to start over or not being able to support my mum or losing the precious little bubble I've constructed for myself in Burlington.

Carter can fit in my heart but not in my life as I've currently created.

I'm going to need to stretch to be with him.

It'll mean I might not be able to pull out my wallet every time Mum needs something. It'll mean change for Francis.

"He's worth stretching for," I mutter.

"Pardon?" Bee's fingers, still on my forearm, tighten.

"Carter. He's worth it."

My chest cracks, regret spilling out. I reinforced his self-doubt, more than once. I was so focused on keeping my own heart safe I've been ignoring how every time I've resisted loving him, I've been silently telling him he's not worth loving.

"I need to show him I see what he's saying about me deserving more than I'm letting myself have," I choke out. "And that *he* deserves more too. He needs to know he's worthy of every ounce of love I have to give him."

Bee grins.

"But showing him…"

"You know how."

I do. I'll throw security to the wind. And hopefully we'll both end up with more than either of us thought we deserved.

I pick up Carter's proposal from the counter, grip my wineglass for fortification in my other hand, and head for the living room.

"Auden!" Francis says. "Please tell my wife I haven't been overloading you this week with me being home every night by five."

The living room is set up with two love seats facing inward, a low table between them. I smile and sit next to Gracie. Francis and Caro share the other. They're not easy around each other yet. Caro's shoulders are tight. Francis's eyes are a titch pinched. Yet they're holding hands. They're working on it.

I take a deep breath, knowing what I'm going to say won't be well received. I put my wine and the folder down on the rough-hewn coffee table and lean forward, bracing my elbows on my knees.

Turning the proposal to face him, I open it to the index. "Did you look at how comprehensive this is?"

Francis's face darkens, and Caro and Grace stiffen noticeably.

"You need to," I tell him.

"No, you need to respect my position," he says.

Ouch.

Caro's brown eyes, so much like her son's, flare with anger. "Oh, come on, Francis. Don't do this with Auden too."

I focus on Carter's proposal, trying to keep my knife-edge emotions from slashing out at my boss.

"By the looks of this," I say, "he's trying to respect the artisan nature of the business while helping to create steadier income streams."

Francis grumbles something about Carter not knowing artisan if it slapped him in the face.

"You're wrong." I manage to keep my voice level. I flip to the section of Carter's business plan where he's included product sketches. "Look. He gets it." The evidence is sitting in my back pocket, a heartfelt rainbow of inspiration. "And what you and I have done together is fine, but with Carter's ideas in the mix— beyond hiring Olivia—we could be brilliant."

"You think?" He takes a sip of wine and plays with it in his mouth.

"I do." My throat tightens. "I need more of that brilliance in my life."

Concern flickers on the weathered angles of his face. "In the shop, you mean."

Caro swats him and shares a knowing glance with Gracie. "Of course he doesn't mean the shop."

"Yeah, I was afraid of that," he mumbles.

"I love your son," I say.

Next to me, Gracie sighs. Caro's smile turns watery.

"Which I should be telling him, not you," I continue.

Gracie settles a hand on my shoulder. "You haven't?"

I shake my head. "Not yet, but I will. He deserves better than what I've given him."

"And you deserve better than you've been taking for yourself," Gracie says.

"So your wife says."

Damn, I want what Grace and Bee have. Someone to laugh with, be challenged by. To admire and think the world of. To know I bring a balancing weight to their life that were I not in it, they'd be thrown off axis.

There's a hole in my life where you should be.

I have one too. I'm stumbling through my days, crooked and aching and off-kilter from the hollowness in my chest.

"He asked me to move to Montreal," I announce to the room.

There's a collective intake of breath.

I study Francis. It's clear he's budged as far as he's going to when it comes to changing his business. And since it's not enough of a transformation to bring Carter home for good, then yeah. I'm going to build a home with him where he is.

I don't want to live anything less than an incredible life anymore. Maybe I'll fail, but maybe I won't. Love is worth the risk. *Carter* is.

"It's not without complications," I finally reply, "but yes. If he still wants me at his side, I want to be there."

"You're quitting then?" Francis's face is pale, mouth working as if there are a thousand other things he wants to say, but he's holding them in.

"Not until I train Olivia and we look to find someone to replace me," I promise. "I don't want to undo all the good you and Caro found while you were away. But while you were gone, I... I fell in love again. And I can't toss that aside. I need a day to go to Montreal."

Grace's fingers are tight on my shoulder, and the three of us are all watching Francis watch me.

"You'll need more than a day," he says, voice strained. "If my son knows what's good for him, he won't let you go."

I'm not so sure about the "he won't let you go" part, but

Francis is right about one thing—I need more than time. I need a plan too.

I can't show up in Montreal, asking Carter to take me on without knowing what I'll do when I'm there.

When I get home after dinner, I pull his note out of my pocket and read it over again.

And then I examine the letterhead.

He thinks it'll sell.

For Imprescott, but first he thought it would sell for OfficeMart.

I wonder if they need a designer.

Carter had said he'd use his connections for me, but I want to make sure I show up feeling like his equal, his partner, his future.

First thing tomorrow, I'll start making calls.

It takes me a few days to get ahold of the people I need to impress. I keep getting moved up the food chain until I'm referred to Carter's second-in-command. Anne-Emmanuelle. We both pretend she didn't once refer to me as a waiter with a hot accent, and I manage to apprise her of the situation without it being too awkward. She's efficient and kind; I can see why Carter loves working with her. She's also a romantic, so she's fully willing to help me make things fall into place.

Thursday morning, I'm sitting in my truck with the heat blasting, dressed in a white shirt and the navy kilt I wore to my cousin's wedding a few years ago. The coordinating jacket hangs from the hook in the crew cab behind me. I'd have worn a plain suit, but I don't have one. This'll have to do.

"Auden, love, you're sure this is the right decision?"

My phone's to my ear. I needed to call Mum before I left. I did not expect her to hold back in the face of telling her where I'm headed, but I'll take it.

"I do, Mum. I've got to try."

I hear a hiss of air, a slow exhalation. "Pretty uncertain, money-wise."

"Maybe." *Definitely.* I breathe away the twist in my belly. "I think I can survive whatever happens."

"Oh, Auden." Her voice sounds a little teary. "I *know* you can."

"I'm not going to stop helping you, I promise."

"You worry about me too much, love." She pauses. "I've been right grateful for your help, but until you graduated, I did everything on my own. I can do it again."

One thread of worry unravels, easing some of the tension in my chest. "I love you, Mum."

"I love you too. I don't trust most people when they use that word, but I do trust you. And if you think you're making the right decision, then I'll cheer you on from across the ocean."

She holds herself back from saying *though I'm worried it won't work.* I hear it in her tone. I appreciate the restraint.

Hell, I understand it. I'm not sure I'll get what I want today either.

I am sure I won't regret going all out.

I say goodbye and hang up, then stare at the screen of my mobile. Should I text Carter to let him know to expect me? If nothing else, it would guarantee I won't be able to make it halfway and then chicken out and turn around.

I won't do that. I won't turn around.

And I want it to be a surprise. I want to see the unguarded emotion on his face when I show up on his turf. It'll tell me what to expect.

A knock on the half-steamed driver's window has me jumping in my seat, high enough I'm surprised I don't hit my head on the roof of the cab.

Through the fog, I recognize a familiar shape. I roll down the window.

"Francis. Christ. You took a few years off my life."

"Sorry." He smiles, apologetic, fond. Affection gleams in his eyes. "For startling you and for being an ass the other night.

When you were trying to make me see reason. I had no right. I don't want you to leave without knowing—" He makes a frustrated noise. "No matter what Carter says, you're still part of our family. And you have a place in my business for as long as it suits you. Days, years, a lifetime—it's up to you."

My heart fills, and my eyes sting. "Thank you."

"You look sharp." He hands me a sealed envelope. It's thick, weighty. Some of the heavy paper he saves for special occasions. Carter's name is on the front in beautiful script. "Give him this?"

I lay it on the passenger seat. "Of course."

And when he reaches in and cups my cheek, it's a father loving a son, not a boss encouraging his employee. "I hope you get what you're looking for."

I cover his hand with mine and squeeze. "I'll do everything I can to find it."

27

CARTER

A week after I return to Montreal, I drag my ass from the conference room back to my office. The hallway smells of coffee and donuts and industrial carpeting. I wrinkle my nose. It's no Earl Grey tea and cast iron, that's for sure.

I dodge a university intern carrying a stack of boxes.

"Oh, sorry, Mr. Prescott!"

"Carter's fine, Paul," I say, smiling at the kid.

"I just left a letter in your office for you. The door was open. I hope it's okay I went in. I was coming in from getting coffee and the front receptionist asked me to drop it off, and—"

I hold up a hand. "Not a problem. Thank you."

He heaves a sigh of relief. "Thanks, Mr. Pr— Carter."

"Thank *you*. Keep up the good work." I continue on to the opposite corner of the executive floor, chuckling at the intern's nervousness. He's got a real Peter-Parker-around-Tony-Stark energy going on. Nothing like Olivia, who rolled into Imprescott Designs like she owned the place. Hopefully she's settling in okay and my dad and Auden are enjoying training her. Or maybe a miracle occurred and my dad cut them some slack and is letting them run with any part of my business plan.

251

It's taken a gargantuan effort not to call Mom and get her insider perspective this week, but a clean break was the better way to go. Between Auden not being willing to even consider a relationship compromise and Dad making it very clear his Parisian revelations had nothing to do with any of my ideas, I'm better off here where I'm valued.

Plus it hurts too much to see Dad take him and Auden down a dangerous path. My mom's a hundred percent requiring him to cut down his hours now that they're home. If he doesn't commit to creative solutions, he's going to have a hell of a time increasing his profits to justify the new salary and pay for the new press.

Fuck. Why am I worrying so much about this? I have my own shit to deal with. Things have only gotten busier since the merchandising rollout meeting.

Sure, I've been bleeding out at night, alone in my bed for the few hours I'm managing to spend in my condo, but I can keep ignoring that.

"Carter!" Anne-Emmanuelle pokes her head out her office door. She's wearing a jade-green headwrap.

I suck in a breath, trying to keep my lungs from constricting. "Your scarf, it reminds me of—" I stop myself before I say something truly pathetic like "Auden's eyes," even though the similarity is eerie. Like the universe is putting little signs throughout my day to mock my stupidity.

"Reminds you of…"

"River rocks?" I say.

She snorts. "I bet you got all As in your literary analysis classes."

I did, actually, but my brain's working at half capacity right now. "Sorry, I don't know where my head's at today."

She lifts a black brow. "Are you sure it's not with Mr. Calls-You-Darling-and-Brings-You-Breakfast?"

"Nope."

"Mm-hmm. Whatever you say." She holds up a stack of documents. "I have the revised implementation schedule for the Atlantic stores ready for you. Everyone's set for the meeting."

A meeting that could be an email. Why did I schedule it anyway? I lean an elbow on her cubicle wall. "You know, I'm going to send out a memo instead."

No need to inflict my manic need to avoid silence on my team by making them gather unnecessarily.

"*T'es certain*? I swear, you've micromanaged more in the past week than all the years I've worked with you combined. Being around your dad did bad things for your management style. Good thing you're home now."

This isn't home.

I swallow down the truth. This'll have to be home because I sure as hell don't have a place in Vermont.

"I'm going to take an hour to decompress," I say. "Maybe hit up the gym over lunch."

"Don't you have someone coming in soon? A new product line? I think I saw it added to your schedule."

"First I've heard of it." I check my calendar. Sure enough, there it is. Stationery proposal, eleven thirty. "You're right. I didn't see it until now."

Her dark eyes study me, concerned.

"What?"

"*Tu as besoin de dormir*," she says under her breath.

No shit, I need sleep. I'm not sure she meant for me to hear her opinion, but I answer anyway. "*J'ai besoin...*" I need... I need what? "*...de plus que ça.*"

More than that. I can barely remember how to conjugate verbs right now, which is probably why A-E's been speaking English to me all week. I do need more than sleep, more than waking up in the morning and pulling on a suit and coming into an incredible job that in no way feels like enough anymore...

"Fuck."

She snorts. "*Si vous avez besoin de* moi, *criez.*"

"*Merci.*" I appreciate the open-ended offer for help.

She leaves, smile verging on pity.

Criez.

It means to shout, not shed tears, but I'm more likely to do the latter at the moment.

I close my office door behind me and flop into my seat.

How the hell does something symbolic, like a broken heart, lead to actual neck pain and back stiffness and generally make me feel like I'm (a) a thousand years old, and (b) falling apart at the seams?

Because it's not symbolic.

Right. It's the actual people I love in my life, shutting down my attempts to care for them and help them with what matters to them. Fucking hell, it hurts to be rejected over and over again.

A crisp envelope is sitting on my desk blotter. It's the color of skimmed cream.

My name is written on it in the formal cursive Dad saves for condolence cards and writing on the insides of books he gives as gifts.

Huh? How did he get a letter here without mailing it?

I pick it up and rip open the top, pulling out the single sheet of paper, which is folded into thirds, but not at Dad's usual, precise right angles. He might be shit at details but not when it comes to straight lines and paper.

His note takes up most of the page.

Carter—

I'm sorry.

I didn't see your vision. Didn't want to see it, because it meant admitting you knew more—know more—about my business than I do.

Forgive me for my pride.

Your vision intimidates me, son. Always has. For you to go off and be successful by doing everything I'm incapable of doing —what does that say about me? I've spent many, many years avoiding the answer to that question. And in my cowardice, I've made poor decisions, as a father, as a human. Those decisions hurt you. I'm sorry.

Bee threatened to disown me if I didn't read every word of your plan and give it proper consideration. Made me write out pro and con columns about adopting your ideas. And every time, it came down to me being the one who wanted to fix things and no longer being the one with the best answers.

One thing I learned in Paris: Life's too short to pretend I'm right all the time. And as much as I hope I still have a lot of years left in me to try to be a good example for you, it's time for me to admit you have things to teach me too.

I pushed you away because of this once before. Made you choose between me and Auden and your dreams and potential. I shouldn't have.
And no way can I do it again.

Whether you're happiest in Montreal or Vermont, know I'm so proud of you. Not just because of your success. I mean, you've done some impressive stuff since college, son, but more important to me is how you were willing to drop it when your mom and I really needed you.

We'll always owe you.

And if you and I can find a "new normal," like your mother and I were able to do, know I'm willing to put in the work.

Love,

Dad

There's a postscript. It's in blue ink instead of black and lacks the formal precision and steady hand of the previous lines.

P.S. If you want it all, it's yours. I believe in you.

The paper flutters in my grip. I put it down, fisting my shaking hands on my desk.

Proud.

Believe in you.

Love.

Hope spreads in my chest. Thank God my door is closed because my eyes dampen.

I take my glasses off and swipe at the moisture with the back of my hand.

He means it. He didn't have to send this. How the hell he did, I'm still not sure—must have sent it in a larger envelope and addressed it care of the office. One of the receptionists probably opened it by accident and gave it to Paul to drop off.

I shake my head. It doesn't matter. He got this to me, in his normal low-tech style, and he apologized. Did more than apologize.

It's all yours—what's all mine? His appreciation? His pride?

Or is he talking about the business?

Curiosity builds in my chest, soothing my tears.

Is that what I want? A week ago, I might have said yes. Then Auden shut me down, stealing any avenue of it working, even if I were willing to leave OfficeMart. So long as he's unwilling to take relationship chances, it doesn't matter where we live. We'd end up unhappy and resentful. Me, frustrated he was constantly holding back; him, angry I was always asking him to give more than he was able.

I yank my cell out of my suit pocket and dial Dad's office.

Hopefully he answers and not Auden. With all the feelings swirling around my core, I'm liable to make an ass of myself.

"Carter?" Dad answers.

"Dad."

"You got my letter?"

"I did."

"What do you think?" he asks cautiously.

"I… I don't know. I wasn't expecting it." And it's worth being honest about. "I haven't felt worthy in a very long time." My voice cracks.

His does too. "I'm sorry, son. Everything about you is worthy."

"Thank you for noticing the career I've built." He's driven my need for success more than I've let myself admit, and his acknowledgment is like letting off a pressure valve.

"It's beyond time I did." He clears his throat. "But your job title doesn't make you special, Carter. I'd be proud of you if you were cleaning floors at that company of yours."

"Cleaning floors is an important job, Dad."

"I know it is. And I know you did it a few times while you were pitching in for me. Auden pointed out how much you worked. I underestimated what I asked of you, and yet you put your mom and me first…"

"Love matters, Dad. Especially when you've been together for forty years. Our *family* matters."

"I agree. And I can't handle the thought of you not feeling a full part of it because of me and my stubborn choices."

Pausing, I gather the courage to receive the answer I'm not sure I want to hear. "What did you mean by 'it's all yours?'"

"Imprescott."

Breath whooshes from my lungs. "*Mine*, mine?"

"Yes. If you want it. I'd retire."

If he'd said this a decade ago, I'd have raised my hands in victory, jolted to my feet like a medal winner on a podium. But the satisfaction is slow, an exultant tingling in my limbs, as if I'm warming up after being out in the cold in shorts and a T-shirt.

Getting to put my business plan in place, grow something from the ground up—

No. That's only part of what matters.

"I don't know if I could run the shop now. Without Auden..."

There's the fucking lump in my throat again.

My computer dings, the alert for my upcoming meeting flashing on the screen. Two seconds later, one of the admin assistants pings me, letting me know the person is here.

"I have a meeting, Dad. I'll call you and talk to you more this evening, okay? Or maybe come for a night this weekend and have dinner with you and Mom."

"We'd love that."

We hang up.

Shit, I'm going to have red eyes for my meeting. The person pitching to me is either going to think I was taking advantage of Canada's lax cannabis laws this morning, or they're going to figure out I just had a twenty-plus-year dam of emotions break on me.

I scramble in my desk for the Visine I keep there for the handful of days a month I wear my contacts. After squirting in more than the recommended dose of drops, I wipe away the excess, put my glasses back on, and square my shoulders.

Opening my door, I lean out into the hall, calling for my executive assistant. "As soon as my eleven thirty gets here, send them—"

A hulking figure appears far across the open workspace.

I lose my balance and catch myself on the doorframe.

Auden, in a suit?

Nah, can't be him.

I blink a few times, watching Paul point my ex, my present, my everything-but-my-future, in my direction.

Auden's trimmed his beard and styled his hair within an inch of its life, and his three-piece suit would put Tom Hardy's best to shame. He turns a corner, and my mouth hangs open. It's a kilt, not pants. Fuuuuuck.

He strides toward me, the confidence in his step innate and smooth, like he looks when he's using the presses. He stops in front of me, a foot or two from where I'm needing the jamb to hold me upright to a pathetic degree.

"Hi, darling," he says, the R as thick and rolled as I've ever heard it come off his tongue. He twists his hands, losing a bit of the poise he carried with him down the hall. "Nice suit."

"You too," I croak.

Anne-Emmanuelle is standing a few yards away in my executive assistant's cubicle. "You have an office, you know."

"Right. Jesus. Auden, come in." I groan. "Except I have a meeting in"—I check my watch—"one minute."

He brushes a hand down the side of my face. "I am your meeting."

My mouth gapes. "What do you mean?"

"I mean, I called and talked to people until I worked my way into getting a meeting with you."

My mouth is still wide open. "My schedule said this meeting is about a new product line."

"Exactly," he says, holding up a black leather portfolio I hadn't noticed him carrying.

"Mon Dieu, Carter. As-tu perdu tes billes? Il est ici avec une proposition de produit." Anne-Emmanuelle rolls her eyes.

I've lost more than my marbles. I've lost my heart. And it makes zero sense that Auden is here to pitch me a new product, as my 2IC so kindly pointed out.

"I don't understand," I say, turning and waving him into my office. Once he lumbers past me, I shut the door and lock it. I sit on the edge of my desk, legs outstretched, arms crossed.

I have to keep this conversation about the job. If I bring up anything to do with him shutting me down, I'm going to fall apart.

You're already falling apart.

He pulls over a chair from my small conferencing area and sets it in front of me. He sits, bracing his elbows on his knees.

After my dad's letter, and the conversation— Wait.

"You brought the letter."

"I did." He bows his head.

Oh no. He's not pulling out the penitent-ex routine on me. "What is this about?"

When he lifts his head, his eyes are damp, a wild, piercing green. "Me loving you. Me being wrong."

"What the fuck, Auden? You come to my workplace, the place you clearly stated I belonged, and make a meeting with me to tell me what, that you were wrong to love me? Didn't you get enough shots in when you rejected every one of my attempts to compromise?"

"No, Christ..." He lurches to his feet. It puts him a foot above me, but the raw vulnerability on his face makes it clear he's not trying for the upper hand. He starts pacing. "I was wrong to say everything I said last week. Not to be willing to trust you'll keep loving me. I should have. I'm sure as hell never going to stop loving *you*, so I don't know why it was so hard to believe you would do the same."

"Never going to stop... What?" The words bounce around in my head, too quick to make sense of.

"Loving you, Carter. I will never stop."

His arms hang at his sides, jacket fitted perfectly to his shoulders and biceps. And that kilt, made from suiting material and showing off the socks hugging his thick calves. He's so fucking beautiful. His palms face forward, almost in supplication. And him being so damn dressed up to tell me he loves me...

I don't want to hope.

(With this man, I always will.)

I rake a hand through my hair. "And you came to tell me this *here*? In custom formalwear?"

"No, I came here—in my only formalwear—to pitch you a line of stationery."

"And to never stop loving me," I murmur.

"Correct. I will love you until the day I die." He flexes his hands. "*And* I want to pitch you a line of stationery. Mass-produced, high-quality. Part of your house-brand line."

It doesn't matter how many times I blink at him, nothing he's saying is making sense.

"How do you know that's what I need?" I say.

"The love or the paper?"

He's standing there like three-piece attire was invented solely so he could wear it. Fingers teasing his ruler-straight part into a mess. Somehow talking about commitment and business, and my heart's tumbling in my chest because if I'm misunderstanding things, I don't think I'll ever recover.

"Both," I say.

He walks between my legs, tips my face up with a finger. "I know you're not going to be able to work with your da."

He kisses the corner of my mouth. I feel the brush all the way in my belly.

"And I know we're not going to be happy if you're having to split your time between here and Burlington," he continues.

"I think we could—"

"Shh," he says. "Let me finish." His broad palm cups my cheek. "I can't have you only half your days. I need all of them. Which means me coming to you. Selling you my designs for your house line. Applying for an ongoing position in your specialty products department. We work well together. It doesn't have to be in Vermont."

He drops his hand from my face and waits.

I want him to touch me forever. When he's with me, I'm whole, and when he's not, it's like parts of me are missing. Like setting up the press wrong and only having half the type meet the page. A half a print.

A half a life.

And as much as I love his big frame being all sexy in crisp-cut wool, I want him in plaid and jeans. I want him working with antique machines, coming home smelling like oil-based ink and old paper.

I risk touching him, stroking his newly trimmed beard. It's smooth under my fingertips. And the soft yearning on his face weakens my knees. "You're telling me you want to move here?"

"Aye."

"No."

28

AUDEN

"No?"

The dull echo is the only thing I can get out over the implosion in my chest. It's crashing through me, floor by floor like a building under demolition. I'm choking on the dust of my hopes.

"You can't work here. It won't make you happy." Carter shakes his head and adjusts his glasses. They frame eyes spilling with emotion. "You need... I need—"

His throat bobs and he reaches for me.

Backing away a step, I try to bolster myself for the inevitable shift from numb to having every nerve in my skin exposed to the air, to Carter's rejection. I stare at the floor so I don't have to look at my heart living outside my body, leaning against a polished, expansive desk.

I knew this was a possibility.

It's not a done deal, not yet.

I have to believe this. I'm not the infinitely leavable human I've, for far too long, believed myself to be.

I lift my chin, take in Carter, who's gripping the edge of his desk. His brown gaze is soft, locked on me as if he's waiting for me to catch up. "I didn't come here to hear no. I love you," I say. "And eight days ago—"

"You were counting?" He's amused, almost victorious over this.

"Yes, I was fucking counting. You said you loved me. I know I've been slow to come around, but now that I'm here, I'm not giving up."

He whispers something that sounds like *fucking finally*, but it's so quiet I can't be sure. Straightening, he reaches for me again. And I let him take me this time. Those hands I love caress my upper arms, pulling me within a foot of him. He smells like pricey soap and fabric softener. Like he's *mine.*

I give myself over to his gaze, slowly drowning in the deep brown happiness there. What he's saying and how he's looking at me are not exactly aligning. "Don't you want me here?"

He pulls me closer, one hand sifting into the hair at my nape, the other settling at the base of my spine. His cheek presses to mine. A puff of breath tickles my ear. "Here? In my arms? Yeah. But in this office building, working in a cubicle, and with your name in generic corporate type on a business card? No. You're not made for the Soulless Big Paper life."

There's a titch of humor there.

"Huh?"

"Trademark, Francis John Prescott," he says, a smile in his tone. His fingers drift farther up the back of my head, strong and reassuring, even as confusion settles low in my stomach. He kisses my cheek.

The heat of his lips sparks clarity. "I don't know what else I can bring with me. I don't want to start up a new shop in a new country. And living off your generosity while I try to find something that isn't OfficeMart—I can't ask that of you."

"I say this with every part of me—what's mine is yours. But you need to keep creating. And why would you do that here when you already do it so well elsewhere?"

"Because you're here."

Letting go of me, he reaches behind him and holds up the small box of Imprescott business cards I made for him. He tosses them into the small bin beside his desk.

The metallic *thunk* rings through me, the dismissal of my labor and our memories.

"Ouch."

The corner of his mouth rises, making a dimple pop. "They're wonderful, but I need them to say *coproprietor*."

My knees shake. If he means it…

I stumble back and my arse lands on the edge of the chair. He grins at me with that gorgeous, bewitching face of his. I want to take a mental snapshot of that face and then spend the rest of my life trying to press it into paper, using ink and shadow to capture the multitudes of beauty in every angle.

"Are you—?" I shake my head. "You're not going to work with your dad, are you?"

"No."

"Why *co*proprietor?"

He glances around the room for a second, then kneels on the floor in front of me and braces his hands on my bare knees. "You think I can run Imprescott without you?"

"You obviously could."

"What would be the point?" He's balanced on knees and toes, not sitting on his ankles, so his face isn't that much lower than mine. He cups my cheeks. "My dad's willing to retire for us, baby. And I want to take him up on the offer but only if you're willing to risk being the boss. *One of* the bosses."

"I'm not a Prescott."

"Yeah, you are. I always felt you were more of one than I am. And now I'm wondering, maybe I just needed to see that in you to be able to find it within myself. You're family, Auden. You're my person. And I want you to be my business partner too."

I let him guide my head down, slanting my mouth over his in an awkward, perfect kiss. The heat of it trickles down, settling at my groin and making me half-hard.

Christ.

Focus.

I rest my forehead against his and croak, "I was willing to toss my life aside and move here. You think I won't risk a sure thing like being your business partner?"

"And what about being my person?"

"I've always been that."

"Fuck," he breathes, a reverent prayer of thanks. His hands sneak to my knees, slide up my thighs, under the material of my kilt.

"We can't," I say. "Not in your office."

"Definitely in my office," he says.

"We have bollocks luck with getting interrupted."

"I locked the door. And I've been wanting to get my hands under your pleats since the last time you wore one of these."

I will never complain again about my cousin asking me to shell out a week's pay for this getup.

I run a thumb on Carter's lower lip. "I wasn't keeping track of my wardrobe."

His smile is satisfied, dirty. "When we kissed on the street, and then when you drove me home. I was too up in my head to insist I get to take you inside and flip the fabric up and devour you then. But if you're going to strut in here wearing this, insisting you love me, I'm going to enjoy it. I should christen the place at least once before I quit."

"You're quitting," I muse, spreading my legs a little wider.

"Happily." His hands creep up, hooking his thumbs in the leg holes of my underwear and delving under to brush the tender skin between my balls and rim.

I hiss in pleasure.

"Thought real Scots didn't wear underwear under a kilt," he says.

"They do in a place of business."

"Such a shame."

He circles a thumb, and I curse low.

"I can't be quiet enough," I say. "I'll get you fired before you get the chance to quit. I... Give me your keys. I'll go wait at your flat until you're finished for the day. I'll keep the suit on, I promise. Even the vest."

"It's not the vest I find fascinating." He grins, pressing my sensitive flesh with one thumb and sneaking farther with the other to rub the base of my cock. "And you'll *be* fucking quiet, and I'll kiss and suck you until you come, and you'll love it."

Biting my lip, I let out a near-silent moan. "I love *you*."

"Damn right, you do." With a quick flip and tug, he has my kilt up, my underwear down, and my dick on display. And as he takes my swollen tip between his lips, he lets out a strangled, vibrating groan.

Pleasure jolts through me, and my hips lift. "Shh."

His eyes glint, as if to say *it's on*.

They also promise to take care of me. All of me—my desires, my insecurities, my needs. The ugly and weak parts, the ones I like to put on display and the ones I've always kept for me alone. Even when we were together before. I'll share them with him now though.

His mouth licks and caresses, the tender passion making my world spin. I grit my teeth and squeeze the arms of the chair as a silent outlet. It's a heady feeling, knowing Carter Prescott intends to direct all his incandescent intensity toward me and everything I love in life.

One thumb teases my hole. He fists my erection, long strokes of palm and lips and warm, wet suction. The edges of my vision sparkle.

"You're teasing me." My voice is barely above a murmur, but it sounds like a cannon in my arousal-sharpened ears.

He lifts his lips from my shaft, twists his tongue around the tip, eyes wicked. "You're teasable."

The words sing along my skin, prickling, pulling my balls tight.

He sucks me again, and the look in his eyes alone is enough to push me to the precipice.

"I'm—" I tug his hair, a piss-poor warning I'm coming. I dissolve into bliss. Limp and loved and hopefully not a thing of legends around the OfficeMart executive suite for that time the VP of merchandising blew his boyfriend in the middle of a midday meeting and got escorted out of the building with a cardboard box.

I know Carter's going to follow through on his resignation, and I know it's in part because of me. I don't want it to be because of our sex life.

Crouching back on his heels, he puts my underwear and kilt to rights and smiles at me. He reaches for my hands to pull me up.

I grip his warm palms but shake my head. "Can't move."

He lowers his head, bending awkwardly to kiss my knuckles. "Goddamn, I always feel ready to take on the world after I make you come."

Still swimming in a pool of endorphins and what can only be the love you feel when you trust a person with your whole heart, I send him a wobbly smile. "Anytime you need to boost your confidence, my dick is here for you."

He laughs and tugs my hands again.

I sway to my feet, then grip his shoulders for stability. I bury my face in the crook of his neck, against the soft collar of his suit jacket. "Think I'll just lean here for a while."

"Stick a sign there that says it's yours." He plays with the hair at the back of my head. When he kisses the curve of my ear, it's with smiling lips.

"Oh, so now you want me to start making signs? You're going to work me so hard we'll never get an hour off."

He lifts my chin with a finger and stares at me with a sternness that makes me want to call him sir and start apologizing for being naughty. "If we're going to take over the letterpress world, it's not going to be at the expense of this. Of going home together at night and taking holidays together and sleeping in on weekends—

unless we decide to be parents, then sleep's out the window, but I think I'd be okay with that—"

I clutch at his tie and cover his mouth with mine, stealing whatever words were supposed to come next. "Yes, please. The sleeping in, the holidays, the kids… And home. Definitely that part. If you're there, it'll always be home for me."

EPILOGUE

THREE MONTHS LATER

CARTER

I'm already late when I arrive in my parents' driveway, parking at the back of the long row of cars lining one side of the gravel shoulder.

It's okay. Auden's not annoyed.

He's excited, in fact. I texted to warn him I got held up signing paperwork for my real estate agent in Montreal. I jog toward the house, enjoying getting to wear a short-sleeved button-up shirt on what's turned into an unseasonably warm, April weekend afternoon.

"Carter!" My dad waves me over to the front porch. "Can I grab you for a minute?"

Sighing, I text Auden again to let him know I'm here but held up by my dad. I trudge up the steps. "What can I do for you?"

"Well, your mom and I have decided we want to travel some more. And the upkeep of the house—it's more work than we want during retirement."

He's been calling himself retired for a month or so now and is finally no longer sounding like he's choking on the word. Once

Auden and I committed to being in Burlington, Dad needed some time to ease himself out, as much as he was willing to hand over the passwords and keys. Which worked for me, as I ended up living between cities while I transitioned my team and Anne-Emmanuelle and put my condo on the market.

As of today, said condo is no longer mine, and Auden's rental is officially *ours*. I can't wait to tell him.

My dad's buzzing with eagerness though. I'm not going to slough him off to rush to talk to my boyfriend.

"You looking to hire someone to do some maintenance for you?" I ask.

He shakes his head and sweeps a hand to the side. "Buy this place from us."

It's the verbal equivalent of a record scratch.

Me, own the house?

I step back, and my ass hits the railing. It creaks under my weight. Needs new nails.

Something that would be my responsibility if my name was on the title.

The nails, my parents' precious fruit trees, the close-to-forty years of family memories…

Except it wouldn't be only me. It would be Auden too, which requires a long and complicated conversation somewhere more private than a home-for-good celebration.

Glancing at the spots of peeling paint on the siding, I scrub a hand over my face. "Let me think about it, okay? Talk to Auden."

The bright hope in Dad's eyes tells me he missed the caution in my tone. He walks around the house to the backyard with me, chattering about his and Mom's travel plans.

The space between the house and the small, unoccupied barn is a kaleidoscope of cheerful decorations and people. My yard, potentially…

I shake my head.

I can contemplate Dad and Mom's offer later, after the party. My family has put a hell of a lot of work into the ambiance and food and filling the space with guests. Relatives and Auden's work friends—quickly becoming my friends—along with a few of my high school and university buddies who I've finally had time to reacquaint with over the past month. The smiles, waves, and shouted hellos are overwhelming, to be honest. These people are here to celebrate me being around in ways that have nothing to do with work, and I'm not used to that yet.

My gaze immediately goes to the burly, flannel-clad man by the drinks table. I mean, how can I not look? It still steals my breath to watch his strong hands, capable and sexy as he taps a pony keg of Shipley cider. So fucking handsome. Beard trimmed but hair a little long, falling over his forehead in an adorable curl my fingers itch to push to the side. He grins at my aunts, at ease, eyes bottle green in the afternoon sun.

His contentment is partly because of me.

I can be sure of that. He's reminded me of it more than once.

Also, I feel the same. I'm sure my own grin is large and sloppy and overflowing with the heady emotions of being in love with Auden.

I smile at my sister and Auden's boss as I skirt the outside of the gathering, aiming for my boyfriend, my person.

Once I'm a few yards away from him, he finally notices me. His gaze lights up.

"Darling, you snuck in," he says, pulling me close with his muscular arms and kissing the life out of me.

My breath is hitching by the time he releases me. "Sorry I'm late."

"It's done though?" he says happily.

"Su casa es mi casa." Maybe not for long. "I sure hope you want me in your apartment, because I don't have a backup anymore."

"Our apartment," he chides, pulling a bottle of sparkling wine out from an ice-filled cooler and popping the cork. He pours glasses for him and me, as well as Bee and Gracie.

They all toast me.

"No longer a homeowner and all the richer for it," Gracie says, smiling softly.

"Which has nothing to do with your bank account," Bee adds.

It's an unnecessary clarification, but I don't mind the confirmation of what I've got in my life now. The arm wrapped tightly around my back. The crowd of people who are gathered here, welcoming me back to Vermont.

I want to make a home with Auden more than I've ever wanted to do anything in my life. And up until ten minutes ago, his-now-ours apartment a few blocks off the mall seemed the perfect place for us. We fit comfortably there. It's so damn close to work, and it's homey and bright.

This place has its charms too though. More space, a yard of our own. All the memories of which we'd become the keepers, the guardians.

Will Auden want to take that on?

Sighing, I pull my attention back to the party. Bee and Gracie's fingers are all over the backyard. The miles-long string of cloth pennants they sewed by hand for their wedding (it gets dragged out at every outdoor family affair) hangs between the fruit trees, the back porch, and the barn, creating a hexagonal frame of sorts.

I point at the sign hanging off the food table. It screams FINALLY in large, tempera-painted letters. "Your doing?" I ask Bee.

She cackles in response. "Everyone else was leaning far too much toward being nice to you. Someone had to point out your glacial path to getting your head out of your ass."

"As long as you brought dessert, I'll forgive you." I'm hoping for pie, but she has a masterful touch with anything flour- and sugar-related.

Her eyes glint. "You'll see."

My stomach growls. "I'll see... now?"

She shakes her head.

"Your parents have been cooking all day," Auden says. "The kitchen smells like a dream."

I flash to a future memory of Auden at the worn counter, skillfully preparing his family's traditional Sunday roast-and-York-shires meal while I bumble around him, trying to peel carrots and potatoes without shearing a layer off my pointer finger.

Fuck, I like that memory. I want to be intimately involved in creating it. Turning it into a monthly habit, a time where we estab-lish something together and share it with family.

My relatives whom we already love, friends whom we choose and absorb into our circle. Kids when we decide it's time to be parents.

I link my fingers through Auden's. "Take pity on my empty stomach. So much subject removal. I'm starving."

"More like you got busy and forgot to eat."

"Might have."

He tugs me in the direction of the food table, where I'm nearly taken out at the knees by my niece.

"Hi, sweetheart." I ruffle Cypress's curls and hand her the biggest intact potato chip from the bowl. "Don't tell your mom."

"Her mom saw," Jill interjects, toting Odin on her hip. She winks and holds out a flat palm. "Where's mine? I busted my butt on half this food."

I kiss her cheek and pass her a couple of chips. "Thank you. You did good."

Piled high, the table's clearly a combination of Mom, Dad, and Jill's work, as well as a few mismatched plates I assume were brought by some of our friends. My sister starts telling me about kindergarten shenanigans while Auden mother-hens me, adding extra mini sausage rolls and prosciutto-wrapped asparagus to the pieces I've taken for myself.

"Thank you, baby," I murmur to him and pop a mushroom puff between his lips.

Jill rolls her eyes. "Still haven't gotten a room, I take it."

My dad sidles up, cup of cider in hand. He takes a purposeful sip, staring at Auden and me over the rim. "Hopefully they'll have lots of rooms soon."

My heart jumps into my throat, and I send Dad a warning look.

Auden cocks a brow at me. I nibble on a sausage roll, trying to look casual.

"Speech time, son," Dad says, squeezing my shoulder. He grabs a fork off the food table and, after frowning at his plastic cup, clinks the utensil against my champagne glass. "Carter has something to say!"

"I do?" I madly chew the savory pastry and glance around at the crowd. My sister, who's shamelessly co-opted Auden and me for babysitting duty every second weekend. (We're only too happy to help the kids destroy her house with pillow forts and homemade Play-Doh that sticks to the pot.) Harrison, who puts up with me nerding out over merchandising and store layouts every time I grab a coffee from V and V. Olivia, who works her ass off on afternoons and weekends, letting Auden and I sleep in and laze about on Saturdays. I swallow both my mouthful and the lump of emotion making it hard to breathe.

I'm surrounded by love. Once I moved away, I stopped letting myself open up to people like this. Fuck, that led to a deficient existence.

"I mean, of course I have something to say! Nothing long. Just —" I take Auden's hand. "Thank you. For coming today and for being in my life. *Our* life."

Auden squeezes back, and we accept the applause and whistles of approval filling the yard.

"And soon," Dad adds in a loud voice, "this house will be part of their life!"

I'm not sure how the crowd reacts—the buzzing in my ears is too loud. All I can focus on is Auden's shock.

He glances at my grinning father, at me, at the ground. His Adam's apple bobs. When he looks up, his eyes are wet. "Owning it, you mean?"

"You bet!" Dad crows.

I reach for Auden, but he slips out of my grasp. "It's not what you—"

"I think I forgot something in the kitchen." He strides off.

AUDEN

The screen door bangs shut, and Carter rushes into the kitchen, not bothering to remove his shoes.

I'm no more prepared to talk to him than I was when I left him a minute ago, pale and protesting, outside. I brace myself against the counter and try to breathe in some logic. My thoughts are a jumble.

This house. *Buying* this house.

I mean... Carter's money is his money. And having success-fully sold his condo, he has a whole lot more of it. He'll likely always have a fatter bank account than I will, which is fine.

His secrecy is *not* fine. The first slide back into him making big decisions that affect both of us without at least talking to me about it. We've never discussed buying this place from his parents or the lifestyle owning a worn-around-the-edges farmhouse would entail.

He comes to my side, tentatively leaning a hip against the counter and rubbing my shoulder with a hand.

"How long have you been planning this?" I ask.

His breath catches. "I'm not *planning* anything."

Glancing at him from the corner of my eye, I inhale, long and deep. I can trust him. He's shown me I can, time and time again since January. Leaving his job. Communicating during the times he felt pulled between being in Montreal and adjusting into his dad's previous role. Following through on day-to-day plans and really committing to building a life here. The number of people enjoying themselves out on the lawn are proof he's done it.

I loosen my grip on the counter, stand a little straighter, and turn my face to meet his gaze. "Okay, so what's your dad on about then?"

"Getting ahead of himself." Carter takes advantage of my more upright position and ducks under one of my arms, claiming the role of filling in the me/Formica sandwich. He palms my cheeks, fingers spread wide. "I haven't agreed to anything."

"But you have talked to him about it."

"Today! He ambushed me when I arrived in the driveway. And I had to hear him out, but Jesus, I would never make a decision like that without you." A shadow flits in his eyes. "Not like I used to. You believe me, right? That I'm working at being a different man? A better partner?"

"Yeah, I do." I lean in, kissing him softly. His hands slide from my beard, one to the back of my neck, one down my chest. He hooks a finger into a belt loop, holds my front against his. Only clothes separate us, making me hot and bothered and tempted to desert the folks in the yard.

I let my lips trail across his clean-shaven jaw. "We both have habits we need to break. Just because we decided we want to be together doesn't mean the work's done. Or that it'll always be easy or that we'll always react correctly. I'm sorry I reacted before giving you the chance to explain."

"No worries," he says. "I'm sorry my dad brought it up before I could."

"He thinks you're buying the house?"

He shakes his head. "He *wants* me to. He and Mom want to travel and don't want to worry about the upkeep anymore. I obviously told him I'd have to talk to you."

"It's your childhood home, Carter. It's about so much more than me," I say in a low voice.

"It's very much about whether you'd be interested in living *in* my childhood home. I never planned on owning this place. Do I love it? Certainly. Do I need it? Not if you don't."

I study his curious expression. The commitment in his gaze, the tenderness there. He's not pushing.

"I haven't had a place like this—not physically or figuratively—since Mum and I moved away from the croft," I say.

"I know. And if it's not what you envisioned for our future, I'm not looking to force it."

I take his hands in mine. "I love the idea of sharing a house. And to get one already established with love and time, with the messiness of life—how could I say no?"

"Very easily. What you described is a lot to take on. And if it's too much, I understand."

"It's not too much," I whisper. "Add in a dog and some chickens and it would be perfect."

He laughs. "Me? My family? This farmhouse? Nothing about it is perfect."

"Which is what makes it exactly so."

THE
END

ACKNOWLEDGMENTS

Signing on to write this book was one of those jump-on-the-tread-mill-at-high-speed moments of life for me and I would have ended up on my ass with some serious belt-burn were it not for the expertise, time, and support of many wonderful people.

To Sarina—thank you, not only for welcoming me and my characters into your world but for saying "You're welcome to stick to a brewery, but what about artisan stationery?" Thank you to Jane, Jenn, Natasha and everyone with Heart Eyes Press for your hours and wisdom. To the World of True North authors, thank you for making the world seem that much more real and for being so generous with your knowledge, humour, and brilliant stories. Thanks to Annabeth, Garrett, and Eden for sharing your characters.

I can't send enough hugs and praise to Sara Lunsford for being a truly thoughtful and skilled editor. Thanks also to Annie S. at Victory Editing for finding my errors and hundreds of unnecessary commas. To Elaine Spencer—your "go for it" nudge was invaluable and your unflagging support was and is a blessing. And to my Crit Coven who were there for the initial brainstorms in Ashley's driveway—I couldn't have done this without you.

My writing wife, Dee J Holmes, has always been my rock in

this business and her pushes and insight on Turnabout were, as always, exactly what the story needed. Gotta admit—sending this one into the world was a fair bit terrifying. The advice and care of those who read it first (Melanie, Bee, Tiana, and Stacy) made it a whole lot easier. Somewhere out in the digital ether is a graveyard full of *that*s busy ruing the day Stacy and I became crit partners.

To my love, my partner, Rob—life is more beautiful with you in it and I couldn't have made this book exist without you. (#TeamCommaForLife) All my love to my best Mouse and best Bear, and to all my family, who have provided so much support. To Shellee—you're the best soulmate (BFF edition) and cheer-leader a gal could ask for. And Erin and Carla and all my other friends who have patiently listened to me talk about fictional people like they actually exist—thank you.

And saving the most important for last, thank you to the readers and reviewers. I hope Turnabout tickles your stationery geek fancies and that Carter and Auden bring you joy.

Printed in Great Britain
by Amazon